SUFFER THE CHILDREN

A Welsh detective tackles a kidnapping and a tricky cold case

CHERYL REES-PRICE

THE BOOK FOLKS

Published by The Book Folks

London, 2020

ISBN 978-1-913516-57-4

www.thebookfolks.com

Suffer The Children is the third title in a series of standalone murder mysteries set in the heart of Wales. Details about the other books can be found at the end of this one.

Prologue

My dearest family,

Before I begin, I want you to know that I love you with every fibre in my body. You're my whole life, but it's a life I have stolen. I know that I don't deserve to have your love and trust. I can't change what I've done or even begin to excuse my actions but at the very least I owe you some sort of explanation, and the truth, before it's too late and your lives are ripped apart in the most unimaginable way. Soon you won't be able to bear to hear my name spoken let alone my words.

It's difficult to know where to start. I'm not the person you think I am. You've been living with a stranger. Imagine the worst thing that you could do, and it wouldn't come close. I took an innocent life and destroyed a family. It wasn't some dreadful accident. My actions were avoidable and deliberate. When I look back it seems like some horrible nightmare, another person, another life. I guess I was another person — no, that's not true. I am that person. I've just stolen another life, and lived a lie for so long it became my reality. I cannot ask for your forgiveness, but I hope that the people whose lives I destroyed may one day have some peace with the truth.

Every day I expect a knock on the door. In my imagination, it is always two men dressed in suits with a look of contempt on their faces as they say, "we know what you did". My blood turns to ice at the thought. The guilt and anxiety eats me away from the inside, twists my stomach and claws at my skin. I smile and continue with my life, and all the while you don't notice that you are living with a monster.

Chapter One

Natalie didn't want to move away from the warmth of Ryan's body, but her legs were cramping from lying on the edge of the sofa. Her knees stuck out over the edge and the only thing hiding their nakedness from the other occupants of the room was a thin blanket which barely covered their bodies. Natalie's eyes stung, and pain shot through her temples as she looked around the room. Her eyes rested on Claire who was curled up like a cat in the armchair, a coat covering her body and dirty feet sticking out from underneath. On the other armchair Dan laid with his legs stretched out, head back, and mouth open, emitting snores. Her eyes travelled down to the floor where Jamie lay in a heap, his coat used as a pillow.

Natalie groaned as she slowly straightened her legs and swung them off the sofa. As she sat up, her head screamed in protest. Next to her Ryan stirred and pulled at the blanket. She stood up and scrabbled around for her clothes which she found heaped with her dirty trainers.

I'll drop Ella off at nursery, chuck this lot out and go back to bed, she thought as she pulled on her underwear. Her jeans felt damp and cold as she pulled them over her legs, and she noticed mud caked into the fabric but couldn't be bothered to go upstairs to fetch a fresh pair. Instead she pulled on her T-shirt and jumper and stepped over Jamie before padding barefoot towards the kitchen. She pushed open the kitchen door and two dogs jumped at her legs, their claws scraping at her as they furiously wagged their tails.

'Get down,' she commanded. She sidestepped a puddle of dog pee and opened the back door.

'Out!' The dogs scuttled outside, and she shut the door before the three mewling cats had a chance to enter. 'You can wait.'

She glared at the cats before flicking the switch on the kettle and digging around in the pile of used dishes in the sink for a mug. She pulled one out and tipped the remains of dirty dish water into the sink before rinsing it under the tap. As the water fell on her hands she noticed the mud caked under her fingernails. An image of digging in the dirt with her bare hands flashed across her mind; she let it retreat into the fog of her hangover and piled coffee granules into the mug. She filled the mug from the kettle, not bothering to wait for it to come to the boil. The bitter liquid took away the stale taste in her mouth. As she headed towards the sitting room to find her tobacco, she noticed the front door was open.

'No wonder it's fucking freezing in here.' She closed the door and secured the handle with her free hand.

Ryan groaned as she pushed aside the empty cans and mugs on the table. She found her tobacco, plucked a paper from the packet, added a filter, and started to roll.

'Make us a coffee,' Ryan said as he sat up on the sofa and ran his hands over his face.

'Make it yourself,' Natalie replied as she licked the edge of the paper. 'I've gotta get Ella to nursery.'

She popped the cigarette in her mouth, lit up and drew in a lungful of smoke. Her head buzzed from the nicotine rush.

'What time is it?' Claire unfurled in the armchair.

'Dunno.' Natalie picked up her mobile phone from the table and hit the screen. 'Fuck, it's nearly eleven. It's too late to take Ella to nursery now.'

'Should've set your alarm, dozy bitch,' Ryan said.

'Yeah, well she's usually screaming the place down by eight. How was I supposed to know she'd sleep in,' Natalie said. She took a drag of the roll-up, the thought of looking after Ella all day set a dark cloud over her mood. 'Maybe I could take her in for the afternoon, I'll say I had an appointment this morning.' The thought cheered her as she headed upstairs.

The door to Ella's room was open, and as Natalie approached, she could see that the cot bars had been pulled down. She was sure she'd put the bar up when she'd put her to bed.

'Ella?' Natalie approached the empty cot. Little bugger has learned to pull down the bar and climb out, she thought.

'Ella!' Natalie got down on her hands and knees and searched under the cot. Huffing she got to her feet and searched the bedroom, then the bathroom, and into her own room.

'Ella, where are you? Come on, we have to go to nursery.' Anxiety prickled at her skin as she ran downstairs into the sitting room. 'She's gone, Ella's not here.'

'Huh.' Ryan sat on the sofa wearing only his jeans, ash from his cigarette falling on his bare chest.

'She's not in her cot. She's not upstairs.' Panic raised Natalie's voice.

'I'll go and look.' Claire rose from the chair and headed out of the room.

'Well, don't just fucking sit there,' Natalie shrieked at Ryan.

Dan and Jamie stared at her with bleary eyes, not appearing to comprehend the seriousness of the situation.

'The front door was open. Shit, she could've gone outside.'

Natalie hurried to the door, pulled it open and stepped outside. She ignored the cold wet stone on her bare feet as she ran through the open gate and onto the pavement. Her heart thudded in her chest as she looked in both directions.

'Ella!' she screamed as she ran along the pavement, her eyes darting into the front gardens of the neighbouring houses.

She rounded the bend and looked up the road that led out of the estate and onto the main road. Someone would've seen her and brought her home if she'd come this way, she thought. She turned and ran back towards the house but stopped short as she passed the alleyway than ran between two houses and led into the woods that backed on to the estate. Images of Ella wandering lost among the trees and heading for the river flashed across her mind. A cold fear coiled around her chest, she sucked in the air but there didn't seem to be any oxygen. Her vision blurred, and her head spun, she could feel the darkness threatening to take over. She forced down the panic and took off down the gravel path, the small stones stabbed her feet, but the pain helped her to keep a grip on reality.

She entered the woods and looked around. The trees were bare from the winter but still dense enough in parts to block out some of the light. Narrow pathways led off in various directions, cut away by years of children's play and ramblers. She ran deeper into the woods calling out, but all was silent. I need help, she thought. She turned and ran back to the house. Her next-door neighbour, George, was stood at his gate.

'Everything alright, love?'

'No.' Natalie bent double as pain tore through her side. 'Ella is missing,' she said.

'I'm sure she can't be far. Do you want me to help?'

Natalie shook her head and went back into her house. She could hear the others calling out as they searched the house.

'She's not here,' Ryan called out as he appeared at the top of the stairs. 'I've checked all the wardrobes and cupboards.'

'I'm calling the police.'

Natalie felt in her pocket for her phone, nausea constricted her stomach and she felt bile rise in her throat.

'No, wait.' Ryan thudded down the stairs. 'Don't call the cops yet. Your sister has probably got her.'

'What? Why would Nia take Ella without telling me?'

'Because she's a spiteful bitch. Yeah, I bet she came around this morning, saw that you'd been having a good time and was jealous, so she took Ella to freak you out.'

'I don't know, she's not that much of a bitch.' Whilst the thought of her sister taking Ella angered her, it also gave her a spark of hope.

'Yeah, she is.' Claire joined them. 'She's always calling you a crap mother.'

'Stuck-up cow,' Ryan said. 'Look, you know I can't be here if the police come. Call your sister while I get my shit together and if she hasn't got her then call the cops when I'm outta here.'

Natalie dialled Nia's number and waited; it went to voicemail. She left a message trying to keep her voice from quivering. Ryan had grabbed a holdall and was chucking things into it.

'You lot better go.' Natalie turned to Claire, Jamie, and Dan who were standing in the sitting room looking awkward.

'Okay, gives us a call when she turns up.' Jamie grabbed his tobacco from the table and followed Dan out the front door.

'I'll clear some of this stuff,' Claire said and started gathering the empty cans. 'What do you want me to do with this?' She held up an old cracked teapot.

'I dunno, chuck it in the kitchen somewhere. Just leave the rest.'

'Okay.' Claire shuffled to the kitchen.

Natalie felt a sudden urge to pee. She ran upstairs to the bathroom and shut the door. Her hands shook as she tried to undo her jeans. She could hear Ryan in the bedroom next door rummaging around.

'I'll call you later,' Claire shouted but Natalie didn't bother to respond. She was washing her hands when the phone trilled.

'What do you mean, "have I got Ella"?' Nia demanded.

Natalie felt her hope evaporate and an icy chill ran down her spine. 'She's not here.'

'She must be, have you looked everywhere? She's probably hiding.'

'She's not hiding!' Natalie shrieked.

'Okay, calm down. Look, children don't just disappear. Check everywhere again. If you can't find her then call the police. I'll be there as soon as I can.'

Natalie wanted to tell Nia about the open door but was afraid of her sister's reaction. Tears spilt from her eyes. 'Okay.' She sniffed and hung up. Wiping away the tears with the back of her hand, she stepped out of the bathroom.

'Well?' Ryan stood at the top of the stairs, the holdall clutched in his hands.

'She hasn't got her.'

'Right, well I'm outta here. Text me to let me know what's going on.'

He headed down the stairs, wriggled his feet into a pair of trainers and left without a goodbye.

Natalie sank to the floor. The house felt unnaturally silent and she felt alone and abandoned. With trembling hands, she dialled the police.

Chapter Two

There was a cheerful atmosphere in the Bryn Mawr police station. DI Winter Meadows was handing out cream cakes from a large white cardboard box as DC Edris set down a tray of tea and coffee.

'What's with the cakes?' DS Blackwell grunted as he plucked a juicy doughnut from the box.

'Well we couldn't let Valentine's first official day as part of the team go unmarked,' Meadows said with a smile.

'No one brought in cakes on my first day, I just got on with it.' Blackwell huffed and bit into the doughnut; a dollop of jam oozed out over his fingers.

'I doubt it was a happy occasion for anyone,' Edris said.

'Fuck off, golden boy,' Blackwell snarled and sauntered back to his desk.

Meadows groaned inwardly. He thought after their last case together, where Blackwell had showed a softer side to his nature, things would be different. But Blackwell was back to his old self, barking and snarling at everyone.

'I hope he's not going to be like this all the time,' Val whispered.

Meadows gave her an apologetic smile. DC Reena Valentine was the newest member of the team. She had worked with them on their last case and had just been moved from uniform. She was a pretty dark-haired girl with a cheerful disposition that Meadows hoped wouldn't be extinguished by Blackwell's moody demeanour.

'He's just a big grumpy teddy bear,' DS Rowena Paskin said and smiled as she plucked a chocolate éclair out of the box.

Meadows glanced across at Blackwell. *More like a bulldog.* He fought the urge to laugh.

'Well, welcome to the team, Valentine. I'm sure you and Blackwell are going to get along fine.' Meadows looked at Blackwell.

Someone has to work with him.

'Yeah, as long as you remember who is boss, I'm happy to let you learn from my experience,' Blackwell said.

'I'm sure we're going to have a wonderful time,' Valentine said with a wink.

Blackwell snorted and turned his attention to his computer.

'Any problems let me know,' Edris said.

The door opened and Sergeant Dyfan Folland entered the room. The expression on his face brought silence to the office and the cheery atmosphere evaporated.

'A child has gone missing from her home on the Coopers Wood estate. Eighteen-month-old Ella Beynon.'

Folland approached Meadows and handed him the details.

'Her mother Natalie called it in half hour ago. Hanes is over there. I've sent DS Brianna Lloyd, she's the best FLO we have. I've also sent as many uniforms as I can spare to start house to house. I thought it best until we know what we're dealing with.'

It was the kind of case that every officer dreaded. Meadows felt the adrenalin kick his brain into action, and scenarios began running through his head. The atmosphere in the room was tense as his team looked at him for instructions.

Meadows grabbed his jacket.

'Okay, Edris with me, let's go and see the mother. Valentine, can you get maps of the area printed and contact search and rescue, put them on standby. Blackwell, check to see if any known paedophiles have moved into the area.'

'On it,' Blackwell said.

Meadows noticed the look of horror on Valentine's face.

'It's just a precaution. Hopefully the little one has just wandered off or there's an absent father who has taken custody issues into his own hands. Paskin, see what you can find out about the family. I'll brief you all as soon as I know more. You better call Lester,' he called over his shoulder as he hurried out of the office with Edris at his side.

'I haven't worked a missing child case before,' Edris said as soon as they got into the car.

'I have, in London. It didn't end well. It's not something I'd like to experience again.' Meadows felt a pain catch at the back of his throat. The memory of not being able to save the child brought back the guilt and hopelessness of the case. 'It never leaves you. Let's hope we can get this little one home safe.'

He turned the car out of the station.

'Missing from her home, Folland said. Doesn't sound like a kidnapping,' Edris said. 'Probably just hiding in the house.'

'That would be the best outcome, but no doubt Hanes has already checked.'

They drove through the centre of Bryn Mawr where shoppers, wrapped up against the cold, dotted the pavement.

'I don't know why anyone would want to shop here,' Edris said as he looked out of the window.

'I suppose it fills the time if you're retired or want to get out of the house with a little one.'

'To look at charity shops and bargain stores. It's all crap.'

'Not to everyone. There are many that can't afford new things.'

'Yeah, I suppose,' Edris said.

The houses dwindled as they left the outskirts of Bryn Mawr and fields spread out on either side of the road before the road darkened with overhanging trees. They passed by an old stone church before the road rose steeply and they took the turning to Coopers Wood estate.

The estate was a labyrinth of roads lined with grey brick paired houses. A few of them were surrounded by scaffolding where the council was updating the properties. Some of the houses were well kept with trimmed lawns to the front while others were overgrown with weeds. Meadows drove towards the bottom of the road that backed onto Coopers Woods.

'Home to druggies, scroungers, and a few ex-cons,' Edris said as he looked around. 'Plenty of undesirables here.'

'That's what I like about you – compassion and understanding,' Meadows said with a laugh. 'I think you'll find there are some long-term elderly residents as well as recovering addicts, and young families trying to make a go of things.'

'You're too soft,' Edris said.

'Just because people are hard up, it doesn't make them criminals.' Meadows pulled up behind a police car.

'Half the estate is full of dealers,' Edris said.

Meadows got out of the car and glanced around at some of the unkept houses.

'You could be right. Come on, let's see what we've got.'

A fine drizzle of rain dusted his coat as he walked through the gate and passed an old rusting fridge. He could see police officers knocking at doors a little further up the road. PC Matt Hanes opened the door of Natalie Beynon's house as they approached.

'Alright, Hanes.' Edris nodded at the young policeman.

'The mother is in the kitchen with Brianna.' Hanes stood aside for them to enter.

Meadows stepped over the threshold and his nostrils were assaulted by a stale odour of dog pee, dirty nappies, and cigarette smoke. He imagined Edris wrinkling his nose in disgust behind him and resisted the urge to smile.

'Thanks, Hanes. We'll take it from here. Perhaps you could join in with the house to house.'

'Yeah, no problem.' Hanes smiled and left the house, softly closing the door.

The smell became stronger now the door was shut and as Meadows made his way towards the kitchen, he noticed the walls were streaked with dirt, and the door frame to the kitchen looked like it had been clawed by an animal.

In the kitchen Brianna, the family liaison officer, stood at the sink which was overflowing with used dishes. She appeared to be struggling to find space to empty the sink. Every available space on the worktops was covered in clutter. A mixture of dirty plates, empty packets, and ashtrays. The cooker was grimy with built up food encrusted into the hob and a pile of dirty clothes were heaped in front of the washing machine. Meadows stepped over a piece of wet newspaper not wanting to think about what was underneath. He could feel his shoes sticking to the tiles which were caked with grime.

A woman stood hunched against the counter. Meadows judged her to be mid to late thirties, but she could be younger, it was difficult for him to tell. She wore baggy jeans and an oversized jumper. The clothes looked like they had been worn for several days and were too big for her skeletal frame. She looked at Meadows with sunken eyes as she sucked on a roll-up. Her skin was pale, almost grey, and reddish blond hair lay flat on her head.

'Natalie, this is DI Meadows and DS Edris.' Brianna indicated the two men, then turned back to the task of cleaning mugs.

'Have you found her?' Natalie's voice was barely a whisper.

'No, I'm afraid there's no news yet. We need to ask you a few questions,' Meadows said.

'But I already told the other copper everything I know.' Natalie sniffed and wiped her nose with the back of her hand. 'Why isn't anyone out looking for her?'

'There are officers out looking and talking to your neighbours to see if they've seen anything, but it would really help if you could give us as much information as you can.'

Meadows gave an encouraging smile. He saw Natalie glance at Edris and even in this grim situation he caught a look of interest.

The eye candy never fails to get noticed. He gave Edris a look to indicate that he should use his charm.

'Come on, Natalie, why don't we go into the sitting room and have a chat. You look like you need to sit down. Perhaps Brianna can bring you a cup of tea,' Edris said.

'Coffee. I don't have any milk and I can't drink black tea.'

'Okay, love, go and sit down. I'll bring you a coffee.' Brianna smiled.

A pungent smell of dirty nappies lingered in the air as Meadows followed Natalie and Edris into the sitting room. A bin stood in the corner, its contents spilling over the floor. Ash covered the coffee table which was a jumble of wrappers, letters, and various objects. Meadows scanned the room. There was a large flat screen TV on a stand next to a pile of toys. The carpet was dirty and stained, the walls bare. No pictures of the child.

Natalie slumped down in the armchair, while Edris perched on the edge of the sofa and took out his notebook. Meadows sat on the other armchair which smelled of stale milk.

'I understand Ella is eighteen months old,' Meadows said.

Natalie nodded.

'Do you mind me asking how old you are?'

'Twenty-six.'

Meadows tried not to let the surprise show on his face. Maybe she'd had a rough time.

'Does Ella have any medical conditions that we should be aware of?'

'No, not really. She had a chest infection, but the doctor gave her antibiotics so she's okay now.'

'That's good. Can you talk me through what happened this morning?'

Natalie took a tin from the table, opened the lid and plucked a cigarette paper from the packet.

'I went to get Ella up for nursery and she wasn't in her cot.'

She sprinkled tobacco along the paper, added a filter, and began to roll.

Meadows noticed the tremor in her hands and the dirt gathered under her fingernails.

'You called the station at eleven thirty. Does Ella often sleep that late?'

'No, I slept in.' Natalie fidgeted in her seat.

'There you go, sweetie.' Brianna walked into the room and handed a mug to Natalie. 'Can I get you two anything?' She turned to Meadows.

'No, thank you.'

'I'm good, thanks,' Edris said.

Brianna left the room and Natalie put the mug on the table before lighting the cigarette.

'Was there anyone else in the house this morning?' Meadows continued.

'My friend Claire and her boyfriend Dan. They stayed over last night but they didn't take her, they helped me look for her.' Natalie's legs jiggled as she spoke.

'Could we have their surnames?' Edris asked.

'Claire Phillips, I think. I don't know Dan's name.'

'Okay, we're going to need an address for them.'

'They live in a flat above the dog grooming place in Bryn Mawr.'

'What about Ella's father?' Meadows asked.

'What about him?' Natalie scowled.

'Are you still together?'

'No, he's an arsehole. He left before Ella was born.'

'So, he doesn't have any contact with Ella?'

'Yeah, he has her every weekend. Picks her up after nursery on a Friday and brings her back on Sunday afternoon.'

'His name?' Edris asked.

'Dylan Lewis.'

'Did Dylan have Ella this weekend?' Meadows asked.

'Yeah.'

'And did he bring her back at the usual time yesterday?'

'Yeah.'

'Have you spoken to Dylan today?'

'No, why would I?'

'To let him know that Ella is missing.'

'Oh. Yeah I didn't think of that.'

'Can you give us Dylan's phone number and address?' Edris asked.

'Yeah but he will be in work. DVLA, so he won't answer.'

Meadows turned to Edris. 'Better give Blackwell a call, ask him to check out the father.'

As Edris left the room to make the call, Natalie's eyes followed. Then she turned to face Meadows.

'Do you think that Dylan has Ella?'

'Is there any reason why Dylan would take Ella?' Meadows leaned forward in the chair.

Natalie shrugged and dragged on the cigarette which was burned down to the edge of her yellowing fingers.

'Dylan having Ella on the weekends, is that a private arrangement?'

'I don't know what you mean.'

'Are the visits arranged by a family court or did you come to an agreement with Dylan?'

'We agreed. I work Tuesday to Saturday, so he has to take her some time. It's only fair.'

'And where do you work?'

'At the packing factory, Coopers Hill.'

'So, things between you and Dylan are amicable?'

Natalie looked blank.

'You and Dylan are friends?'

'Not really.'

'But he was happy with the arrangement?'

Natalie shrugged.

Edris came back into the room, nodded at Meadows, and resumed his position on the sofa.

'What time did Dylan bring Ella back yesterday?' Meadows asked.

'Same time as usual, five. He never keeps her any longer, can't wait to hand her back.'

'Did he come into the house?'

'No. I go outside when he comes.'

'Does Dylan have a key?'

'No, why would I let him have a key?' Natalie frowned.

The front door crashed open and a woman entered the room. She was smartly dressed in black trousers and a red coat. She rushed over to Natalie.

'Have you found her?'

'No.' Natalie's lip quivered, and tears flooded her eyes.

'And you are?' Edris asked.

'Nia Taylor, I'm Natalie's sister.' She sat down on the edge of the armchair and put her arm around Natalie's shoulder. 'I'm sure she can't be far.'

'They think Dylan has taken her?' Natalie said.

Nia frowned. 'Why would Dylan take Ella?'

'We've no reason to believe that Dylan has taken Ella, but we have to rule out the possibility,' Meadows said.

'Well, I don't think he'd pull a stunt like this,' Nia replied.

'You wouldn't,' Natalie snapped. 'You don't know what he's like.'

Nia looked like she was about to retort but changed her mind.

'An officer is on his way to talk to Dylan, in the meantime we have to explore other possibilities.'

'Like what?' Natalie's eyes widened.

'Do you keep the doors locked at night?'

'Yeah of course, there's some dodgy people on the estate. But...' Natalie looked down at her hands. 'The door was open this morning.'

'You mean unlocked?'

'No, it was open.'

'What!' Nia stood up. 'Why the hell was the door open? She could've walked out into the road.'

'I didn't leave the door open.' Natalie covered her face and sobbed.

'It's okay, Natalie,' Meadows said. 'Can Ella unlock the door?'

'No, I don't think so.' Natalie sniffed.

'Could she open the door if it was unlocked?' Edris asked.

'I don't know, she hasn't gone out the door before.'

'But it's possible?' Meadows added.

'I guess, she can reach the handle.'

'Oh God.' Nia's hand flew to her mouth. 'She could be anywhere.'

Meadows looked at the two sisters. They had the same hair colouring and were roughly the same height but that's as far as the similarity went. Nia sat with her legs crossed at her ankle, resting a manicured hand on her leg. Natalie sat with her shoulders hunched and nibbled on her thumb nail.

'Natalie, can you talk me through what happened last night?'

'Nothing happened.' Natalie folded her arms across her chest.

'What time did you put Ella to bed?'

'About half six.'

'And did she settle straight away?'

'Yeah, I put her in her cot, gave her a dummy, turned out the light and shut the door.'

'Were your friends here at that time?'

'No, they came about seven.'

'And other than Claire and Dan did you have any other visitors?'

'No.'

Meadows caught the look that Nia shot Natalie.

'Oh yeah, Jamie was here, I forgot.' Natalie squirmed in her seat.

'Jamie?' Edris asked.

'Dan's friend,' Natalie said.

'Do you know his surname and address?'

'Nah.'

'Not to worry, I'm sure we can find out.' Edris scribbled in his notebook.

'I called in around ten,' Nia said. 'I had some clean washing to drop off.'

Odd time to be calling around with washing. And why is she doing her sister's laundry? Meadows looked at Natalie.

'Oh yeah, she did. I forgot that as well,' Natalie said.

'More like you were too occupied.'

Meadows observed the growing tension between the sisters.

'She means I was having a drink with my friends,' Natalie said. 'It's my night off.'

'You don't have a night off when you have children,' Nia snapped.

'Did you see Ella when you called around?' Meadows asked.

'Yes, I looked in on her while I put the washing in her room. She was sleeping peacefully.'

'Anyone else call around?' Meadows turned his attention to Natalie.

'No.'

'Did you go outside at all during the night?'

'No. I don't think so.'

'Okay so what time did you lock the front door?'

'After Claire and Dan came.'

'So, you let Nia in?'

'No. I have my own key,' Nia said.

'I see, so did you lock the door when you left, or did Natalie see you out?'

'I locked up.'

'Where are your keys, Natalie?'

'Hanging on the hook by the door.'

Edris got up and left the room, then poked his head around the door jangling keys.

'Are these the front door keys?'

'Yeah.'

'And yours?' Meadows asked Nia.

Nia opened her bag and took out a bunch of keys.

'Here, they're with me.'

'Anyone else have a set of keys?' Edris asked.

There was a slight hesitation before Natalie answered.

'No, just my mother.'

Meadows noticed the look Nia cast her sister but didn't push the question. He would talk to Nia later and find out what Natalie wasn't telling him.

'We'll have to check that your mother still has her set of keys,' Edris said.

'What time did you go to bed last night?' Meadows asked.

'About twelve.' Natalie reached for the tobacco tin.

'Did you check on Ella?'

20

'No, I didn't want to disturb her.' Natalie huffed. 'Look, can you just get on with finding her?'

'We just need to look at Ella's room, then we'll leave it there for now.' Meadows stood.

Nia stood up.

'Just Natalie please,' Meadows said.

Natalie got out of the chair, lit another roll-up and led the way upstairs. They entered a small room and Meadows looked down at the cot. The top blanket had been pulled down, there was no under sheet on the mattress which was grubby and stained. The rest of the room was a mess apart from a basket of neatly folded child's clothes that had been placed on top of a chest of drawers. The bedroom window was closed.

'The cot bar was up when I left her last night,' Natalie said.

'Can Ella pull it down?'

Natalie shrugged. 'She's been trying to climb over the top. I was going to get her a little bed.' Natalie's lip quivered.

Meadows wanted to reach out and give her a reassuring touch on the shoulder. 'We'll do everything we can to find her,' he said but he didn't want to make any promises.

'What was Ella wearing last night?'

'Her princess pyjamas, they have her name on the front.'

'Is anything missing from the room?'

Natalie stepped further in and looked around; her eyes rested on the cot. 'Buba is missing.'

'Buba?'

'It's Ella's pink rabbit. It's her favourite toy, she takes it everywhere.'

'Okay, Natalie, thank you. I understand how difficult this has been for you.'

They walked down the stairs and into the sitting room.

'We'll be talking to Dylan, and a search of the area is already underway. Brianna will stay with you and keep you informed of our progress.'

'She doesn't have to stay,' Natalie said.

'It's better that she does,' Edris said.

'I can stay until three, I have to get the kids from school after that,' Nia said. 'Come on, Nat. We'll clean this place up. You'll feel better if you do something.'

Meadows doubted anything could make Natalie feel better.

'It would be better if you didn't clean up just yet. I'm going to send over a forensic team. It's just a precaution. We are also going to need an up-to-date photo of Ella.'

Natalie looked around the room. 'Erm, I don't think I have one. There's plenty on my phone.'

'Can you show me?' Edris asked.

Natalie unlocked her phone and handed it to Edris. Edris located the pictures and sent copies to the station before handing back the phone.

'Do you have any other family that need to be informed?' Meadows asked.

'Just our mother, and sister Leanne. She lives on the Isle of Man. I can call them,' Nia offered.

'Good, we may need to come back to ask some more questions. In the meantime, if you have any questions or concerns, Brianna is here to help you. We'll see ourselves out.'

Outside Meadows sucked in the fresh air. The next-door neighbour was stood at the gate, a Yorkshire terrier yapping next to him.

I bet he sees all the comings and goings on this estate, Meadows thought. He smiled as he walked past, then climbed into the car, his mind buzzing.

'What do you think?' He turned to Edris who was clipping on his seat belt.

'Skanky ho,' Edris said with a grin.

'A what?'

'A Skank… oh, never mind. The place was stinking, I need a shower. I could've caught salmonella or syphilis from that sofa.' Edris grimaced.

'You can't catch either from a sofa.' Meadows chuckled. 'Anyway, just because she lacks domestic skills doesn't mean she deserves to have her child go missing.'

'I guess not, but it's all a bit odd, don't you think?'

'Yes, very odd. If the door was locked, then someone must have used a key. There was no sign of a break in. Even then it would be risky, if Ella woke up and started to cry then it would have alerted Natalie. Most mothers sleep lightly.'

'Most mothers, yes, but that one looked out of it. She was definitely hungover, you could smell the alcohol and she looks like a user.'

'I think you could be right. So, she and the others could've slept through it. Maybe whoever took Ella knew they were drinking and likely to be out of it. But where's the motive?'

'Seems most likely it's the father,' Edris said.

'Let's hope so. The alternative is that the door was never locked, and Ella got up to a houseful of sleeping adults and walked out sometime this morning.'

'Yeah but how far could an eighteen-month-old get on her own?'

'I don't know, someone could have picked her up, or she could have wandered into the woods.'

Meadows looked out of the windscreen as he started the engine. The dense wood was over the tops of the houses.

'We're going to need a lot more than a few uniforms to search the area if that's the case. Then there's the possibility that Natalie is involved.'

'Do you think? She seemed genuinely upset,' Edris said.

'She could be faking it. She wouldn't be the first mother to snap. It doesn't look like she is coping that well. In any case, time is against us. News will spread on social media and if someone has Ella they will be rattled. If she's in the woods I dread to think what could happen to her.'

He let the thought hang in the air as he drove towards the station, the responsibility of finding the child already crushing down on him.

Chapter Three

The station was a hive of activity when Meadows and Edris walked in. Folland came out from behind his desk and walked towards them.

'I've cancelled all leave and called in everyone who's on rest days. So far there's been no sightings. I still have a couple of boys out in the woods. Lester has just come in, he's upstairs waiting for you. Let's get this kiddie back before dark.'

Meadows didn't want to dampen Folland's enthusiasm.

'Great, thanks Folland.'

'I've put Dylan Lewis in an interview room,' Blackwell said as he joined the group. He turned to Folland. 'Can you get someone to give him a cuppa?'

'If I must. I suppose it's beneath you to make one yourself.'

'Too right,' Blackwell said.

'Get anything from him?' Meadows asked.

'He seemed genuinely shocked at the news. I gave him a pretty good grilling. Says he was in all evening after dropping the kid off and was in work by eight this morning.'

Meadows imagined Dylan Lewis being dragged from his desk and faced with Blackwell, he instantly felt sorry for the guy, especially as he could well be innocent.

Still, at least Blackwell gets the job done.

'Any reason to think he's involved?'

'No, I figure if he'd snatched the kid he'd be well away by now.'

'I think you could be right, but we won't rule him out just yet. I'll talk to him again after the briefing. Come on, we better get upstairs. I don't want to keep Lester waiting any longer than necessary.'

Paskin was pinning the photograph of Ella to the incident board. DCI Lester stood talking to Valentine, his back erect, hands neatly to his side. A few uniform officers were stood together silently, among them PC Matt Hanes.

Funny how everyone stands a little straighter, and they pick their words carefully when the DCI is around. Meadows smiled to himself.

'I'll let you get on with the briefing,' Lester said.

'Thank you, sir.' Meadows approached the incident board and everyone pulled up a chair. Blackwell took front position, seated next to Valentine and Edris.

'Ella Beynon.'

Meadows pointed to the photograph of the smiling child. She had strawberry blond hair which coiled at her shoulders. A picture of innocence that Meadows knew would pull at the heart of every officer in the room.

'Eighteen months old, missing from her home in Coopers Wood estate sometime last night or early this morning.' He gave an account of the information they had gathered from Natalie then paused to let the information sink in as he wrote the names on the board.

'Natalie is a single parent and, on the face of it, doesn't seem to be coping with a young child, work, and keeping a home. Judging by her appearance she is, or was at some time, a user. She certainly appeared to be hungover when we talked to her. Blackwell has already spoken to Ella's father, Dylan Lewis; he has an alibi for last night and this morning which needs checking out. He's downstairs and we'll talk to him again later. For now, we have to assume that he hasn't taken her. There were three other people in the house last night. Claire Phillips, her boyfriend Dan and another friend – Jamie. We don't have the surnames, but we have an address for Claire and Dan.

'At the moment, we are looking at three possibilities. One – someone known to the family, who had access to the house, took Ella at some time during the night. Two – the door was left unlocked and Ella left the house on her own. Or three – someone in the house is responsible for Ella's disappearance.'

'Are you ruling out the possibility that some nonce watched the house and took an opportunity to take the child?' Blackwell asked.

'I'm not ruling out anything at this stage. If someone did take Ella from her cot, either stranger or known, they would've been taking quite a risk. There were four adults in the house, any one of them could've awoken, especially if Ella had started to cry. Did you check if there are any registered offenders in the area?'

'Yeah, I have a list from a thirty-mile radius. I'll check them all out.' Blackwell cracked his knuckles.

Meadows imagined Blackwell throttling the information out of anyone with a record.

'We'll leave that to uniform for now, if there's any reason to suspect that one of them is involved then you can bring them in.'

He nodded to the officers sat at the back. Blackwell grunted and leaned back in his chair.

'If Natalie or one of the others in the house is responsible for Ella's disappearance, that would mean getting out of the house, taking Ella somewhere, dropping her off and then walking back in again without being noticed,' Paskin said.

'Maybe while the others were asleep,' Valentine said.

'I suppose, but where's the motive?' Paskin shrugged.

'There's more than one reason why someone would take a child,' Meadows said.

I'm not going to spell it out, the thought makes me feel sick.

He saw Blackwell's lips curl in distaste.

'I think we can rule out kidnapping for money, it's obvious that Natalie has no money. There's always the possibility that something happened during the night and they were all in on it, but I get the impression that Natalie is genuine.'

Blackwell scoffed.

'Something to add?' Meadows challenged.

'No.' Blackwell scratched the side of his head and crossed his legs.

'Okay, as most of you know, Coopers Wood estate backs onto a vast area of woodland.' He pointed to the maps that had been pinned to the board. 'If Ella wandered into the woods, she could've gone in any direction.'

'It's also an ideal place to dump a body,' Matt Hanes added from the back. All heads swivelled towards him and colour rose in his cheeks. 'I'm only saying what everyone is thinking. There's no sighting of Ella reported so far – if she had wandered out on the road, someone would have seen her.'

'Sadly, he does have a point,' Meadows said. 'Valentine, how did you get on with search and rescue?'

'They're on standby,' she said. 'They can get the initial search team to us within an hour, and more resources if needed.'

'Good, I don't want to take any risks. If Ella is in the woods then time is against us. It's cold, we haven't got much daylight left and there's also the river.' He noticed Lester nod his approval from the back. 'Call them in, Valentine. Blackwell, I would like you to head up the search. The community will want to get involved so I expect a lot of volunteers.

'There's the possibility that if someone did put Ella in the woods then they'll turn up to keep an eye on the search. Blackwell will be in a good position to keep an eye on who turns up for the search. There's also the coordination and keeping some order. There's a danger that the public could go trampling over a crime scene, but I don't think we will be able to keep them away. Besides, we need all the help we can get. It's a vast area to search. Meanwhile, I'll continue looking into the family background. I don't think we have the whole picture from Natalie.'

Blackwell got up from his chair. 'I'll head over to the woods now, unless you need me to stay for the rest of the briefing.'

'No, it would be good if you can be there to co-ordinate with search and rescue from the start. You know the area, so you can direct them, but bear in mind search and rescue know their job.'

Blackwell nodded and left.

Was that a hint of a smile on his face?

Meadows watched Blackwell leave and turned his attention back to the group.

'Search team are on their way.' Valentine slid back into her seat.

Meadows nodded. 'We need to interview Claire, Dan and Jamie, check their story against Natalie's. Edris and I will do that after we have spoken to Dylan. I want all of Dylan Lewis' family checked out. Ask to look around the property. Most will agree if they've got nothing to hide. If they refuse, get a warrant.'

'I'll get on to that,' Hanes said.

'Good. Valentine, Paskin, I want the neighbours interviewed. See if anyone has been seen hanging about on the estate or asking questions. Ask them what they think of Natalie and find out what kind of visitors she has at her house. Check if there's been any complaints made. Look at her social media. I want to know who Natalie talks to. If she's taking drugs then she's likely to be in contact with some known dealers.'

'There are plenty on the estate,' Edris said.

'Have you anything to add, sir?' Meadows looked at Lester. He felt a keen sense of urgency, the adrenalin was tensing his muscles and he wanted to end the briefing.

Lester came to stand in front of the group. 'I think it would be prudent to activate the child rescue alert, given the age and the vulnerability of the child. We need the support of the public and as many people as possible out looking for Ella. Trafficking is on the increase and we need to ensure that the child is not moved out of the country, if it's not already too late. There are those who would pay a lot of money for a child.' Lester's expression was grim as he turned to Meadows. 'I will make arrangements for a press conference and appeal. I'm happy to handle the media. I'll pull in all the resources I can from other stations. Keep me updated.'

'Will do.'

Meadows left the team to their tasks and headed to the interview room with Edris. Dylan Lewis was pacing around the room when they entered. A cup of tea stood untouched on the table.

'Sorry to have kept you waiting, Mr Lewis,' Meadows said and quickly made the introductions.

'I should be out there looking for my daughter, not shut up in here,' Dylan ranted.

'Please take a seat, Mr Lewis, Dylan. I'm sorry but we need to ask you a few more questions. I can assure you that we're doing everything we can to find your daughter. We have officers searching the woods behind the house. If she's wandered in there, we will find her, but we also have to look at other possibilities.'

Meadows pulled up a chair and sat at the table. Edris followed. Dylan stared at the two of them then reluctantly took a seat. Meadows surveyed the young man that sat before them. He was dressed smartly in a pair of taupe chinos with an open neck shirt and blazer.

He's not what I imagined Natalie's ex-boyfriend to look like. He's clearly distressed about his daughter's disappearance. Or is he just a good actor?

'I understand from Natalie that you had Ella on Friday evening until Sunday afternoon, and that you took her home at about five yesterday.'

'Yes, I told that other detective all this,' Dylan said.

'Did you go back to Natalie's house after that?'

'No, I went home.'

'Can anyone corroborate this?' Edris asked.

'Yeah, I live with my parents, I have since Natalie chucked me out. I'm trying to save up a deposit to get my own place.'

'Did you talk to Natalie yesterday?'

'Not much, I handed over Ella as usual. She only really talks to me if she wants more money or if she needs me to take Ella for an extra night.'

'You have a key to Natalie's house?' Edris asked.

'No, is that what she said? She's lying. I gave her back the keys the day I left, and I haven't set foot in the house since. Look, I have nothing to do with this. I've been talking to a solicitor to see if I can get custody of Ella. He thinks I have a good case. Why would I mess it up? Please, I just want to find my daughter.'

Dylan put his head into his hands. He appeared to be struggling to keep his emotions in check.

'Why would you want to take custody of Ella?' Edris asked.

'Because Natalie can barely look after herself, let alone Ella. She never wanted her, and she hardly bothers to spend any time with her. If she was a decent mother then Ella wouldn't be missing.'

'What do you mean by that?' Meadows asked.

'She works all hours, and when she's not working she's more interested in having a good time than looking after Ella.'

'A lot of mothers work, it's not easy being a single parent,' Meadows said.

'I do my bit, more than she does anyway, and I give her money. She works the two-till-ten shifts. She dumps Ella in nursery first thing in the morning and she doesn't get home until Ella's in bed asleep. I have her all weekend. Does that sound like a good mother to you?' Dylan clenched his fists.

'Sounds like you have good reason to want to take Ella,' Edris said.

'I told you, I haven't got her. I don't know where she is. You should be asking Ryan, if that bastard has done anything to her I'll rip off his dick and make him eat it.' He banged his fist on the table.

'Ryan?' Meadows ignored the outburst.

'Ryan Phillips, Natalie's boyfriend.' Dylan's lips curled.

Do I detect a hint of jealousy? Maybe he doesn't like the idea of Natalie having a boyfriend. Someone playing daddy to his little girl, but there was no mention of a boyfriend. Surely Natalie would have said something. He's also assuming someone has taken Ella and that she hasn't wandered off.

Meadows looked hard at Dylan, he was a nice-looking guy, in a geeky sort of way. Not the type he imagined to be with Natalie. He sat rigid in the chair, his foot tapping against the floor.

'Natalie didn't mention a boyfriend,' Meadows said.

'She wouldn't, would she? She's not supposed to see him.'

'And why is that?'

'There was a raid on the house. Drugs were found, and Ryan was arrested. You should know all this if you were doing your job properly. Look, you can check with my parents. I didn't leave the house last night. Search the place, but when you're wasting your time with me Ella could be…' Dylan's voice broke.

Meadows gave Dylan a moment to compose himself, he glanced across at Edris who shrugged his shoulders.

Dylan certainly had enough reason to take Ella, but then again, that would blow his chance of getting custody. Even Blackwell didn't think Dylan was involved. Meadows felt disappointed. He had hoped that this was going to be a simple family matter.

'We will certainly talk to Ryan. Is there anyone else you can think of who would take Ella?'

'No.' Dylan shook his head.

'Are you sure about that?'

'Yes.' Dylan scowled. 'I'd tell you if there was. Can I go now?'

'Just a couple more questions. When you and Natalie were together did she ever take drugs?'

Dylan shrugged his shoulders.

Meadows noticed Dylan's discomfort, but he could feel his patience slipping.

'I'm not interested in what you got up to in your spare time, I'm trying to find your daughter, so I need to know everything you can tell me about the time you and Natalie were together.'

'Okay, look, we smoked a bit of weed and took the occasional line. Like I said, Natalie likes to have a good time. She was pissed off when she got pregnant, even threatened to have an abortion. I thought we could make a go of things and make a fresh start. I quit all that shit. I wanted to be a good father.'

'And Natalie?'

'She still liked a smoke, we argued about it.'

'And the other drugs.'

'She said she had stopped, but I could never be sure. Is that it?'

33

'Yes, for now. I would like you to give a DNA sample and fingerprints before you leave, for elimination purposes.'

'Fine.' Dylan stood. 'I've nothing to hide.'

'In the meantime, I would ask you to stay away from Natalie.'

'You can't stop me looking for my daughter.'

'No, but we would prefer that you didn't interfere with the search and we may need to speak to you again. It would be better for you to stay at home. Soon as we have any news, we'll contact you.'

Meadows stood.

'You have my mobile number if you need to contact me.'

Dylan walked out.

'I think he's telling the truth,' Meadows said. 'Although I think he knows something.'

'What, like who's taken Ella?'

'I don't know, we need to keep an eye on him and check out all his family and friends.'

'I was hoping for a better outcome.' Edris sighed.

'So was I. Well, if he was in the house SOCO will pick it up. There's always something left behind, even if it's just a hair.'

The office was quiet when they walked in, only Valentine and Paskin were left.

'Got anything, Valentine?' Meadows asked.

'Yes, there was a raid on the house six months ago, one arrest.'

'Ryan Phillips?'

'Yes, case is still on going. Drugs were found in the house, enough cannabis for intent to supply, some cocaine. Both Natalie and Ryan claimed they'd had a party at the house, so it could've come from anyone. Social services were informed. Ryan has previous, did six months for possession two years ago. He was also arrested for GBH on his last girlfriend, the case didn't get to court as the girlfriend wouldn't testify.'

'Probably frightened of him and what would happen if he didn't get sentenced,' Edris said.

'Sadly, it's often the case,' Meadows agreed. 'Not the sort of guy you would want around your child. Better give Martin Hughes at social services a call, ask him to find all the information on Natalie he can, tell him we'll be with him in an hour. We'll call on Natalie's friend Claire first.' He turned his attention to Paskin. 'Anything on social media?'

'Natalie is very active on Facebook, lots of pictures of Ella, looks like the model mother. She's already put out a post about Ella going missing. You got the usual responses. "Sorry to hear the news", "anything I can do", "I'm here for you, hun." That sort of thing. She talks a lot to Claire who appears to be Ryan's sister.'

'That's interesting, she'd be likely to cover for her brother. Check out the other friends, and Dylan. I want to know who they hang around with.'

'Do you think it's one of the parents?'

'I don't know what to think. If Natalie has something to do with Ella's disappearance then Claire, Dan, and Jamie would have to be in on it,' Meadows said.

'I can't see that a stranger has gone into the house,' Paskin said, 'but if that's the case we have a serious predator on our hands. Valentine and I will talk to the neighbours and check out the list of family and friends.'

'Great, keep me updated. Our best hope is that she wandered off of her own accord, then there's a good chance we will find her.'

But I have a bad feeling that's not the case.

Chapter Four

Meadows drove the short distance to the flat that Claire shared with Dan, all the while turning over the information and possibilities in his mind. The clock on the dashboard reminded him that precious time was slipping by.

'Let's hope they're in,' Meadows said as he parked the car.

Edris unclipped his belt. 'Probably hungover after the party they had last night.'

The flat was above a dog grooming parlour. Meadows located the side door and led the way up a flight of steps. He knocked loudly on the door as Edris stood looking around the dimly lit hall where a stack of rubbish bags filled up the corner.

'You think they'd take them outside, the place probably has rats.' Edris grimaced.

'I'm beginning to think you have a dirt phobia,' Meadows said and laughed as he hammered on the door again.

'Alright, I'm coming,' a voice called from behind the door.

'Sounds like we woke them up,' Edris whispered.

The door opened to reveal a woman in dark grey joggers and a T-shirt stretched over a hanging belly. Her brown hair lay limply on her shoulders. A sickly smell of cannabis drifted past her.

'Claire Phillips?' Meadows asked.

'Yeah.'

'DI Meadows and DC Edris.' He showed his ID. 'Can we come in?'

'Well, um, it's not a good time. Perhaps you should come back later.' She started to close the door.

Meadows stuck his foot out and the door came to a halt. 'I'm not here for your weed. A child is missing. I suggest you go back inside and put out what you are smoking. I'll be thirty seconds behind you.'

Claire scowled but turned, shuffled down the passage and disappeared into one of the rooms.

Meadows heard the words "cops" and "shit" as he counted to ten in his head.

'That's enough time,' Edris said.

Meadows stepped over the threshold and swiftly entered the small sitting room. Two men were stood next to a sofa looking shifty, while Claire covered an ashtray with a coaster. The air was thick with smoke and Edris coughed next to him.

'You better open a window before Edris here gets stoned,' Meadows said.

'You've no right to come in here,' the taller of the two men said. He was wiry with a protruding Adam's apple.

'I think you'll find that we do. We can always do this at the station. I suggest you sit down before I change my mind and arrest you all for possession.'

'Alright man,' the other man said. 'Jamie, open the bloody window.'

'So, I take it you're Dan,' Meadows said as he sat in the armchair.

'Yeah.' Dan sat down on the sofa and was joined by Claire and Jamie. The three of them squeezed together.

'We need to talk to you about last night. I understand the three of you spent the night in Natalie's house.'

'Yeah,' Claire said. 'We were just saying we should go and offer to help look for Ella.' Jamie and Dan nodded in agreement.

'I'm happy to hear you want to help.' Meadows smiled. 'So, you won't mind Edris looking around. We have to check everyone who is associated with Natalie.'

'Go ahead,' Dan said.

'Thank you.' Edris left the room.

'Do you live here as well?' Meadows asked Jamie.

'No, just couch surfing at the moment, until I get a place of my own.'

'What time did you all arrive at Natalie's last night?'

'About seven,' Claire said.

'Did you see Ella?'

'No, she was in bed,' Claire said.

'What did you do all evening?'

'Had a few cans and just hung out,' Dan said.

'Do you often go around to Natalie's?' Meadows looked at each in turn.

'Yeah, it's easier if we go there, Nat doesn't have to get a babysitter.' Claire shuffled forward and picked up a bottle of coke from the table and took a swig.

'Did Ella wake up at all during the evening or night?'

'Didn't hear her.' Claire wiped her mouth and put the bottle back on the table.

Meadows looked at Jamie and Dan.

'No,' they said in unison.

'Did any of you leave the house at any time during the evening or night?'

'No, we didn't go anywhere,' Dan said.

'What about Natalie?'

'No. She didn't go out.'

Edris came back into the room, and took a seat.

'What time did you all go to sleep?' Meadows looked from one to the other.

'Dunno, late I think,' Claire said.

'Okay, who went to bed first?'

'Me I think,' Jamie said. 'I crashed out on the floor. I was wasted.'

'Natalie fell asleep on the sofa with—'

'Me,' Dan cut across Claire.

'Was there someone else there?' Meadows leaned forward.

'No, just the four of us.' Claire shifted in her seat.

'What about Ryan?' Edris asked.

'Ryan?' Claire looked at Edris.

'Your brother,' Meadows said.

'No. Ryan weren't there.' Claire shook her head.

She wasn't likely to tell him even if he was. Meadows sat back in the chair.

'Anyone else call around during the evening?'

'Just Nia.' Claire sneered. 'She didn't talk to us, only stayed a few minutes.'

'Were you the last one awake?' Meadows looked at Claire.

'Dunno, we all sort of went to sleep at the same time.'

'But all of you were downstairs?'

'Yeah.'

'What happened this morning?'

'Nat got up and made coffee, then went to get Ella up for nursery. She was a bit pissed off that she had overslept. Next thing she's running down the stairs screaming that Ella had gone.'

'What did you do?'

'We all helped to look for her, Nat ran outside saying the door was open,' Dan said.

'We looked all over the house and out in the garden,' Claire added. 'Nat came back in a hell of a state. I offered to stay and help but she wanted us to go.'

'Don't you think that's odd? You'd think she'd want some support.'

'I guess she wasn't thinking straight,' Claire said.

'Okay.' Meadows stood. 'It sounds like you all had a fair amount to drink last night.'

'You could say that,' Dan said with a grin.

'And smoked a fair bit.'

The three of them remained silent.

'Bit late for playing innocent,' Meadows said.

'Yeah okay, we had a few joints,' Jamie said.

'Well, if anything comes back to you when your heads have cleared, call the station. As I said before, I'm only interested in finding Ella.'

'Right dozy lot,' Edris said as they left the building.

'I don't think they could mastermind a kidnapping or a cover-up between them.' Meadows unlocked the car. 'It sounds like Ella was alone upstairs all night, if she was still there by the time they went to sleep. They were all probably too stoned to notice if a clown came in and did a striptease. Let's hope we can gain some insight from Martin.'

* * *

Martin Hughes was waiting at the reception area of the social services offices when Meadows and Edris arrived.

'I've got the case files. I've only had a chance to skim through them,' Martin said as he led them into his office. 'It's not one of my cases although I've been present at some of the meetings regarding the welfare of Ella Beynon.'

'Thank you for seeing us so quickly.'

Meadows took a seat and watched Martin spread the notes out on the desk. He looked tired and stressed.

'No problem. I just hope you find her.' He rubbed his hand over ginger stubble as his eyes scanned the documents.

Edris sat silently with his pen poised.

'We were called in initially when Ella was three months old and Natalie took up with Ryan Phillips,' Martin began.

'He's known to us,' Edris said.

40

'I would be surprised if he wasn't.' Martin smiled. 'It was difficult to get to see Natalie and Ella at first. Every time someone called around they were told she was at work by the neighbours. We wrote to her requesting a meeting, in the meantime a visit was made to the nursery that Ella attended during the week from 9 a.m. until 5 p.m. when Natalie was at work.'

'Long day for a little one,' Edris commented.

'Yes,' Martin agreed. 'But it's sometimes necessary if the mother is to keep on working. Not only single mothers, as in Natalie's case. Some families can't afford for one parent to stay home to look after the child. In Natalie's case, she had government help with childcare as well as tax credits. Despite this, she appeared to be well behind with the nursery fees. There were no concerns raised at the nursery regarding Ella's welfare. She appeared to be clean and thriving. Eventually my colleague managed to meet with Natalie and Ella. Again, there were no major concerns. Ella was up to date with her vaccinations and boosters. The house was a little untidy.'

I'd call it a little more than untidy, thought Meadows.

'Ella looked healthy, but some concerns were raised over Natalie's appearance. My colleague noted she looked pale and drawn. Dark circles around her eyes, cracked lips and underweight. Natalie said she had been working hard and recently had a bout of flu.'

'According to Dylan Lewis, Natalie works the two till ten shifts. Who looks after Ella after five?' Meadows asked.

'Well, Natalie's mother for a while,' Martin said.

'And who made the complaint?'

'Dylan. We thought maybe it was a case of a bad break up and Dylan didn't want Natalie to have a boyfriend. Although he seemed genuine in his concern for Ella. An assessment was made and a further two visits, the case worker was satisfied that Ella was not at risk.'

'Did the caseworker discuss Ryan, do you know?' Meadows asked.

Martin flicked through the pages. 'There is a note to say that Natalie denied that Ryan was living with her and they were only friends.'

'Was that it?'

'Yes, until six months later, we were notified that Ella had visited casualty on two separate occasions. Once with a knock to the head, which is common when children start to crawl and lift themselves up onto furniture. The second time she visited casualty was for a fracture to her left arm, not so common. Natalie claims that she fell off the bed when she was trying to change her nappy.'

'Were either Ryan or Natalie suspected of deliberately harming Ella?' Meadows asked.

'Obviously we investigated. Again, there were no signs of neglect or abuse. Natalie admitted that Ryan was her boyfriend but again denied that he was living there. She was adamant he hadn't been in the house when Ella fractured her arm. We had no evidence to the contrary.'

'Did anyone speak to Ryan?'

'No, we spoke to Natalie's mother and asked her if she had any concerns regarding her granddaughter's wellbeing.' Martin looked down at the notes. 'She said her only concern was that she didn't like her daughter associating with Ryan, she described him and his friends as a bad lot. The case worker was satisfied that Ella was not at risk, particularly as she would be seen in nursery every day and also by her grandmother and Dylan.'

'I take it Dylan was angry about Ella's injuries.'

'Yes, he is reported to have turned up here at the office ranting.'

'Can't say I blame him,' Meadows said.

'No, and unfortunately things are difficult for fathers in this situation. Anyway, further visits were made and then there was the drugs raid. Obviously with drugs being found in the house, Ella was put on the at-risk register. I was involved in the meeting to discuss the care plan. Natalie claimed that there had been a party at the house while Ella was in Dylan's care and that she hadn't known that drugs had been brought into the house. She said that she had split with Ryan.

'An agreement was made that Ryan was not to visit the house or have any contact with Ella. Subsequent visits were made, and Natalie seemed to be keeping to the agreement. The house, if not tidy, was in a reasonable condition – food in the cupboards and Ella seemed to be well and happy. No complaints from the nursery. We offered support to Natalie, parenting classes and money management. She attended a few but said she found it difficult while she was working. On the whole, she seemed to be coping well.'

'So, what went wrong? When we visited today the house was filthy, even the cot mattress was stained. It didn't get that way overnight,' Meadows said. He could still recall the smell that permeated the air in Natalie's house.

'It was disgusting.' Edris wrinkled his nose.

'Natalie's mother became unwell. Pulmonary embolism, she was in hospital for quite some time. Then she caught pneumonia, and as a consequence she couldn't look after Ella. Another complaint was made that Ella was being looked after by hosts of different people including Ryan. The house was reported to be filthy and concerns were raised that Natalie was taking drugs.'

'I take it that Dylan was the one to raise the concerns.'

He must have been pretty desperate at this stage. Desperate enough to take matters into his own hands? But where would he hide Ella?

Martin was talking again, and Meadows forced his attention back to the conversation.

'No, it was her sisters. Nia and Leanne. They called on separate occasions. Firstly, Nia who said she was concerned for both her niece and her sister's welfare. She claimed Natalie wasn't looking after Ella or herself. Leanne had been over on a visit for Christmas and was upset when she went to see her niece.'

'They must have had serious concerns to have made a complaint against their own sister?' Edris said.

'Yes, the main one being that Ryan was living at the house. Both sisters suggested that Ella would be better off living with her father. Again, it proved difficult to see Natalie. When a visit was arranged, she denied that Ryan was living in the house. The house was reported to be dirty and cold. Natalie claimed that she had been finding it difficult to work and to keep the house without her mother's help. She said she'd had to take on extra shifts to pay the bills. As for childcare, she said it was mainly her friend Claire that would take care of Ella in the evenings. Natalie agreed to look into getting a qualified child minder.'

'Surely after the complaints were received from family members there would've been cause to remove Ella from Natalie's care,' Meadows said.

'Not necessarily. Just because Natalie wasn't bringing up Ella the way her family thought she should doesn't make her a neglectful parent. We had no solid evidence that Ryan was living at the house. Yes, there were some concerns, but it was agreed that Natalie would need some more support.'

'So, basically no action was taken?' Edris said.

'We already have more children in care than the system can cope with. There's a short supply of foster carers. When we can work with families to help them improve their situation it is best for the child. In Natalie's case, there are no concerns of abuse or neglect. The family still keeps an eye on the situation.'

Martin ran his hand through what was left of his hair.

'I appreciate that your job can be difficult,' Meadows said. 'Do you think that Natalie is capable of harming Ella?'

'Like I said, I'm not Natalie's caseworker, but as there were no signs of abuse, I don't think Ella is at risk from her mother.'

'But now she's missing,' Edris said.

'Yes, and I pray that we didn't miss anything on the visits that could have prevented this. She wouldn't be the first mother to snap.'

'I'm sure you've done your best.' Meadows smiled.

But sometimes that isn't good enough. He's obviously thinking the worst.

Chapter Five

'Where now?' Edris asked as he fastened his seat belt.

'I think we should have a chat with Natalie again, see what she has to say about Ryan. Dylan seems certain that she's still seeing him.'

'Yeah and he sounds like a nasty piece of work. Maybe we should just get him in for questioning.'

'Not yet, he has a record and probably knows his way around the law. I want to have good reason to bring him in, evidence that he was there last night. That way we can keep hold of him and push hard to get his place searched. If we rattle him now, he'll have a chance to cover his tracks. That's if he is involved.'

Meadows pulled onto the main road.

'Do you think that Natalie would keep her mouth shut if she thought he had something to do with Ella's disappearance?'

'Who knows.' Meadows sighed. 'She could be afraid of him.'

'Or afraid that social services would take Ella if they found out he was hanging around the house.'

'You wouldn't think it would matter, she should be more concerned with finding her daughter.'

'Unless she wanted rid of her. Maybe the kid was cramping her lifestyle.' Edris rubbed at his stomach. 'I'm bloody starving.'

'You're always hungry,' Meadows said. 'There's not much chance of getting food any time soon. This case is a mess, too many variables. I just hope I'm not wasting time and resources searching the woods. I just want to make sure we cover every angle.'

The woods are a good place to hide a body. Meadows felt his stomach harden as Hanes's words came back to him.

As they pulled up outside Natalie's house they saw Paskin walking down the next-door neighbour's path.

'Anything of interest?' Meadows asked as he climbed out of the car.

'No one home here, I'll try again later. I had better luck on the other side. Hayley Rees lives there with her two-year-old son. She says she was woken last night about twelve by what she describes as a party in the garden. She looked out of her bedroom window and saw a group in the garden, it was too dark to make out faces, only the light from their cigarettes. She says they were messing around, laughing. She thought it a little odd as it was raining.'

'Interesting. So, the back door was likely to be open and they wouldn't have heard Ella if she woke up crying,' Meadows said. 'Anything else?'

'No, she said she doesn't see a lot of Natalie. Used to see Natalie's mother but not in a while. A lot of people come and go but she couldn't give me any names. Valentine has a list of family and friends of Dylan's, we'll check them out next. Oh yes, nothing at Dylan's parents. They were happy to let us look around. They seem genuinely upset that their granddaughter is missing. There's been a huge response on Facebook, so I guess Blackwell will have his hands full,' Paskin said with a grin.

'I'm sure he can handle it. I'll go and see him after we've finished here.'

'Catch you later.' Edris winked.

The sound of a car pulling up made them turn around. PC Matt Hanes jumped out of the car and hurried towards them.

'We found this about half a mile into the woods.' He held up a clear plastic bag with a toy rabbit inside. 'Blackwell wants the mother to identify it. Still no sign of the kid.'

Meadows took the toy and held it up to inspect it. It was faded pink with patches of worn fur.

'I'll take it in and check, but it looks like it could be Ella's.'

'I'll get back to the search,' Hanes said and headed back to the car.

'Looks like she might have wandered into the woods,' Edris said.

'Or someone could have carried her in.' Meadows knocked on Natalie's door. He looked at the rabbit. 'I'm not sure if this is good or bad news.'

Brianna opened the door and ushered them inside.

'She's curled up asleep on the sofa, probably the best thing for her. I doubt she'll get much opportunity to rest. SOCO have been.'

'Is Nia here?'

'No, she left about half hour ago to pick up her children. She said she would be back later.'

'Any other visitors or phone calls?'

'Just her other sister, Leanne, wanting to know if there was any news. Natalie seems to spend a lot of time on the phone, texting or tweeting.'

'Okay, thanks.'

Meadows walked into the sitting room. An effort had been made to tidy up. The coffee table was clear apart from a tobacco tin and a half-drunk cup of coffee. The mud that had been on the carpet earlier had been hoovered but did little to improve the appearance.

The mud must have come from the garden, they must have been very drunk to take the party outside in the rain.

Natalie stirred on the sofa, she opened her eyes and looked at Meadows. It seemed to take a few moments for the situation to return to her mind.

'I suppose there is no news?'

'No, not yet I'm sorry, but there is something I need you to look at.' Meadows handed Natalie the rabbit.

Natalie pulled herself up to a sitting position keeping her legs tucked under the blanket, she looked at the toy and her eyes filled with tears.

'It's Ella's, where did you find it?'

Meadows nodded to Edris to indicate that he should let Blackwell know. Edris took out his phone and left the room.

'In the woods.'

'Oh God, she's going to be frightened and cold.' Natalie clutched the toy to her chest. 'I should be out there looking.'

Brianna came into the room and perched next to Natalie.

'There's a search team covering the woods,' Brianna informed her, 'and lots of people have turned up to help. If she's in the woods, they will find her. They know what they're doing. You can be more help here, giving as much information as you can, and you'll want to be close when they find her, no good if you're traipsing around the woods.'

'We still can't be certain that someone didn't take her, they may have used the woods to get away and there is less chance of being seen,' Meadows said. He didn't like to point out the alternative. 'Meanwhile, I'm afraid we need to ask you a few more questions.'

Meadows sat down in the armchair. Edris walked back into the room, he looked at the other vacant armchair seemingly reluctant to sit but eventually perched on the edge.

'We need to ask you about Ryan Phillips,' Meadows said.

'Ryan?'

'Yes, your boyfriend,' Edris said.

'I told you, I don't have a boyfriend.' Natalie swung her legs off the sofa and reached for her tobacco tin. 'I split with Ryan ages ago.'

'That's not what we've heard,' Meadows said.

'Yeah, well, people are always making up crap to cause trouble.' Natalie scowled as she rolled a cigarette.

'Was Ryan here last night?' Meadows leaned forward in the chair.

'No, why would he be?' She lit the cigarette.

Meadows noticed the flush that spread up her neck.

She's lying.

'Look Natalie, if you are afraid of Ryan—'

'I'm not afraid.' Natalie laughed.

'We know what he did to his last girlfriend,' Edris said.

'She just made that up cause she wanted him back.' Natalie glared at Edris. 'People say shit about him because they don't want us to be together.'

'What do they say?' Meadows asked.

Natalie shrugged her shoulders.

'This has nothing to do with Ryan.'

'Do you talk to him? Text him?'

'Yeah, we're friends. No one can stop us being friends, can they?'

'Look, Natalie, I need you to be honest with me. If Ryan was here last night you need to tell us.'

'I told you he wasn't.' Natalie's nostrils flared. 'I wish everyone would get off my case.'

'Okay, so you and Ryan are just friends. Do you argue sometimes?'

'I suppose.'

'Have you argued with him recently?'

'No.'

'When was the last time you saw him?'

'Dunno, 'bout a week ago.' Natalie took a drag of the cigarette and let out a plume of smoke.

'How did Ryan get along with Ella when you were together?' Edris asked.

'He was good with her, looked after her when I went to work sometimes.'

'And he was okay with that? Did he ever get angry, perhaps when she woke up at night?' Meadows asked.

'What are you getting at?' Natalie's legs jiggled as she pulled hard on the butt of the cigarette.

'We have to ask these questions and look at everyone who has had contact with Ella.'

'Ryan wouldn't hurt Ella, he hasn't got her.'

Meadows felt a sudden urge to shake her, she didn't seem to want to help, and it made him all the more suspicious of her motives.

'We are going to run an appeal on the early evening news. We would like you and Dylan to read a short statement.'

'What? No!' Natalie looked horrified.

'Please, Natalie, it's important. If someone has taken Ella, we need to appeal to them to hand her back safely.'

'You think someone has taken her, don't you? No, she must have got out of the house and is lost.'

'If she has wandered off then we will find her, we have search and rescue out looking for her, but we have to consider the possibility that she was taken some time during the night. It's more likely to be someone known to you. Do you understand? That's why it's important you tell us everything no matter how insignificant it seems. Has anyone shown a recent interest in Ella?'

'Your friends won't mind us asking questions,' Edris coaxed. 'They'll want to help you find Ella.'

'Yeah.'

'Good,' Meadows said. 'We've talked to Dan, Claire, and Jamie, so was there anyone else other than Nia that called at the house last night?'

'No.' Natalie looked down and picked at her nails.

'Anyone you can think of that would want to cause you distress?'

Natalie shook her head.

'Last night you said you didn't leave the house. Are you sure about that?'

'Yeah.'

'Yet you were seen with your friends out in the garden around midnight.'

Natalie reddened. 'Yeah, we did go out to the garden, I thought you meant leave the house, you know go out somewhere like the pub.'

'Why did you go out into the garden? It was raining.'

'For a smoke.'

'But you usually smoke in the house or were you smoking something other than tobacco?'

'No! We went out because... because it was getting smoky inside with all of us smoking.'

'But your friends like a smoke, they admitted to having a few joints last night.'

'Yeah, so, it doesn't mean that I joined in with them.'

'I see, so the back door was open, and Ella was alone in the house,' Edris said.

Natalie's head snapped towards Edris.

'Are you saying it's my fault Ella's missing? I was out in the fucking garden, it's not like I was out clubbing and left her alone.'

'No one is saying it is your fault,' Meadows said, 'but the sooner we know what happened here last night the better chance we have of finding Ella. How long were you and your friends outside?'

'I don't know.'

Great, she could have been missing any time after Nia saw her at ten. 'Anyone go in the house on their own for a while, Claire or Jamie?'

'No, we were all outside together.'

'Anyone go out the front door, maybe to get something from the car?'

'Don't think so.'

'Right, we'll leave it there for now. Brianna will take you to the station for the appeal.'

Meadows stood. Worry creased Natalie's forehead.

'Don't worry, it will be fine. An officer will help you prepare a statement to read out.'

Edris closed his notebook and stood.

'Okay.' Natalie nodded.

'Good, we'll see you later. In the meantime, if you think of anything else let Brianna know.'

As they stepped outside the door Meadows noticed the next-door neighbour at his gate. A small dog attached to a lead walked at his heal.

'How is she holding up?' he called out.

'As well as can be expected.' Meadows joined the neighbour at the gate. 'May we have a word with you Mr...?'

'Call me George.'

'Perhaps it would be better if we went inside,' Meadows suggested.

George hesitated for a moment.

'Erm... well, I... okay.' He led them down the path and into the house. 'Take a seat,' George said as he unclipped the dog.

Meadows sat and looked around. It was sparsely furnished, tidy but in need of a good dusting. A bachelor or widower maybe.

A large widescreen television was fixed to the wall and below it a shelving unit held rows of DVDs, some jutted out as though marked out as favourites. Meadows tilted his head.

Is that boobs?

'What can I do for you?' George asked, drawing Meadows' attention from the DVDs.

53

Edris was still standing, his eyes scanning the room and into the kitchen beyond.

'Do you live alone?' Meadows asked.

'Yes.' George looked nervously at Edris. 'I divorced a long time ago.'

'Have you lived here long?' Edris inquired as he plonked himself down on the sofa.

George looked relieved. 'About thirty years.' He sat down in the armchair.

Meadows judged George to be in his mid-sixties. He had short grey hair that was thinning on top, and a stocky build, but not too heavy to be classed as overweight.

'How well do you know Natalie?'

'Well, we have a chat now and again, don't see that much of her. I let the dogs in and out during the day. When she's at work.'

'You've got a key?' Meadows asked.

Natalie didn't mention that. How many more have keys?

'Yeah, only for the back door.'

'Can you show me?' Edris asked.

George stood and moved to the mantle where he picked up a single key on a chain.

'Here, where I always keep it.'

The dog started fussing around his legs. He returned to the chair and patted his lap. The dog jumped up, licked George's face and settled down.

'Do you mind if I have a look around?' Edris stood.

'Why?' George's brow furrowed.

'We have to check everyone. As you have a key, I'm sure you understand.' Meadows smiled. 'It's just a quick check of the rooms, he won't rummage through your drawers.'

'Yeah, okay I suppose, but I would never take that little girl. Sweet little thing.'

Meadows nodded to Edris who stood and made his way upstairs.

'Thank you. Do you have any children of your own?'

'A daughter. She's grown up now, lives in London.'

'Do you visit?'

'No, I tried a few times, but London is not for me. She comes down to see me when she has time off work.'

'That's nice,' Meadows said. 'I imagine given that your house adjoins Natalie's you must hear a fair amount.'

'I don't stand with my ear to the wall,' George replied.

'No, but you would hear an argument, Ella crying, or a party?'

'There's been a few of those.' George nodded.

'Parties?'

'Yes, she has friends around most Sunday nights.'

'Like last night?'

'Yeah.'

'Do you know the friends that she had around last night?'

'Not by name.'

'Was there a lot of noise? Shouting?'

'No more than usual. They were out the garden for a while.'

'Did you hear Ella crying?' Meadows sat forward.

'No, I sometimes hear her but not last night.'

'How long were they out the garden?'

'I don't know, I went to bed. I sleep in the front bedroom.'

'Did you hear anything after that?'

'I don't sleep very well and get woken up easily. A car pulled up outside about two, I looked out the window and saw Natalie getting into her car. There was another car parked behind but there wasn't anyone in it.'

Meadows felt a flutter of excitement, this was the first bit of information that could give them an idea of Ella's whereabouts. Edris had returned to the room and stood listening intently.

'Are you sure it was Natalie?'

'Yeah, she was wearing that pink coat she always wears.'

'Was there anyone else in the car with her?'

'There could've been, it was dark.'

'Was Natalie carrying anything?'

George shrugged his shoulders. 'I don't think so, she just got in the car and drove off.'

'And what about the other car, did you recognise it?'

'No, but then I don't really take that much notice of the cars that come and go. It's just that it was there when I looked out; it could've been there all evening for all I know. It was a hatchback, can't tell you much more.'

'Did you happen to hear what time Natalie came back?'

'I heard the car about half hour later, or maybe forty-five minutes. I'm not sure, I didn't look at the time. I looked out and saw Natalie's car was back and the other car was pulling away.'

'Did you see the driver?'

'No, only saw the back of it.'

'Okay, thank you, George.' Meadows stood. 'Anything else you remember, please let us know.'

* * *

'I reckon we should go inside and confront her,' Edris said as they sat in the car.

'No, not yet. I want to see how she handles the appeal. It's strange that all of them conveniently forgot to mention they had been out in the garden. Did something happen out there?'

'They could all be in on it,' Edris said. 'Thought if they kept the story simple they would get away with it. Half an hour would be enough time to drive to the woods and—'

'Yeah, I get the picture, but all of them?'

'There could've been an accident and they panicked.'

Meadows ran his hand over his chin. It would explain why they'd all scarpered before the police arrived, but surely one of them would crack, and why wait until eleven to report the child missing?

'Give Brianna a call, ask her to see if Natalie has a pink coat, I'll look at the car.'

Meadows climbed out of the car and walked over to Natalie's Fiesta. It was in the same state as the house had been earlier that day. Empty packets, crumbs, and fizzy drink cans littered the floor. The ashtray was crammed full and the seats were stained. A child seat, dirty and battered, was strapped in behind the passenger seat. Meadows knelt and looked at the wheels. There was mud ingrained in the tread. An image of Natalie driving into the woods with a lifeless Ella entered his mind, his stomach tightened, and he chased away the thought. The mud could be from anywhere.

He returned to his own car where Edris sat waiting.

'No pink coat hanging up, but Brianna will check what coat Natalie puts on when they leave for the appeal,' Edris said. 'George could be lying about seeing Natalie go out in the car – could be trying to cover himself. He's got a key and he was really nervous when we went in.'

'I think that has more to do with his porn collection,' Meadows said with a smile. 'I caught a glimpse of some of his DVD covers.'

'Yeah, well that just shows he's a pervert.' Edris pulled on his seatbelt as Meadows started the engine.

'Never watched any yourself?'

'Well I…' Edris reddened.

'From where I was sitting it looked harmless, but like you say he does have a key. Get Valentine to do a background check. At the moment, I am more interested in where Natalie went in the early hours of the morning. We better let Blackwell know the latest development, he may have to extend the search area.'

Chapter Six

Meadows drove past the footpath entrance to the woods where an officer stood looking bored. The next turning off the estate led to a single track into the wood. It was only wide enough for one vehicle, but a rough grass verge gave room to pass. They were waved on by two PCs who were monitoring the incoming vehicles. Up ahead a large search and rescue van was parked with several other cars lining the verge.

'How far does this track run?' Meadows asked as he pulled up.

'All the way through, as far as I know.'

Great, that's a vast amount of area to cover if Natalie did drive in here with Ella.

He got out of the car and drew in a lungful of air.

'Blackwell looks like he's in his element issuing orders,' Edris said.

Meadows followed Edris' gaze. Blackwell was stood in front of his car, surrounded by a group of people who appeared to be listening intently as he pointed in various directions.

'Looks like he's doing a good job.'

'Hello, Tristan.'

Meadows turned and saw a pretty young woman approaching Edris. She had waist length wavy dark hair and soft chocolate eyes. It took him a moment to recognise her as the lady that ran the cake shop where he had bought the cakes that morning.

'Hi, Marina,' Edris said.

Not another one of his conquests.

'Hello again.' Marina smiled at Meadows. 'I heard a little girl was missing and that you were searching the woods. I thought I'd get a few friends together and bring hot drinks and food for the search party. It's cold and it will be dark soon.'

'That's very thoughtful of you,' Edris said.

'It's probably best to ask Sergeant Blackwell.' Meadows pointed him out. 'He's in charge of the search but I expect he will be grateful for a hot drink and something to eat. We've just got to have a quick word with him first.'

'Okay, I'll do that, thank you,' Marina said.

Edris winked. 'See you around.'

'Don't tell me she's one of your ex-girlfriends or on the hit list,' Meadows said as they walked towards Blackwell.

'Okay I won't,' Edris said, 'anyway I'm still seeing Harry and not about to cheat on her.'

'Glad to hear it.'

'At least I have some fun outside of work.'

'What's that supposed to mean?'

'Well, it's about time you made a move on Daisy.'

Just her name made Meadows skin tingle. 'I told you, I don't think she's interested.'

'Bollocks, she is waiting for you to ask her out. She's not going to make the first move. At this rate, you'll end up like George. Alone with a porn collection.' Edris laughed.

'Cheeky sod. I did dance with her at the Christmas party.'

'Three months ago.'

'Well I haven't had a chance to see her. It's not like we are knee deep in bodies.'

'How bloody romantic,' Edris said. 'You don't need a dead body for an excuse to see her and there are telephones, you know.'

Meadows didn't respond. They had come within Blackwell's earshot. He'd seen them approach and broken away from the group beckoning one of the men to join him.

'How's it going?' Meadows asked.

'Slow progress.' Blackwell huffed. 'We've split the woods down into areas we think she would most likely be, given the direction she came from, her age, and how far she could have walked. It doesn't help that we don't know exactly how long she's been missing. We found the toy off the footpath about half a mile in and we're concentrating the search in that area. This is Craig. He's head of Search and Rescue.'

He indicated the man stood next to him.

'I would've expected to have found her by now or at least picked up some sign that she is in the woods,' Craig said. 'Although some areas are quite dense and it's possible that she could've fallen or is exhausted. She could well be lying among the bracken or even have fallen into brambles. We're almost out of light, it will make the search harder.'

'We've formed groups who are working in lines off the path leading in, they're due back shortly. Another team are on their way with the dogs, they should be able to pick up her scent,' Blackwell said.

'If she has wandered in here what are her chances of surviving?' Meadows asked.

'Not good,' Craig said. 'It depends how long she's been out here. She'd be in her night clothes which are probably soaked by now. I don't rate her chances of spending another night exposed to the cold and damp.'

'If she's in here,' Blackwell said.

'We can't take any chances,' Meadows said. 'There's another possibility. Natalie's neighbour said he saw her drive off in the car at around two this morning. She was gone about thirty to forty-five minutes.'

'Enough time to drive in here and hide the child.' Blackwell's face darkened.

'Exactly,' Edris said.

'But how did the toy get to the footpath?' Meadows asked.

'Someone could've carried her in and arranged to meet the car,' Blackwell suggested.

'Or they could've thrown the toy to confuse us,' Edris said.

'Or she simply wandered into the woods, someone has found her and taken her home.' Meadows sighed.

'Why would they do that?' Edris asked.

'Who knows? There is all sorts of reasons why people take children. There was that case in the Eighties where a woman who couldn't have children of her own took a little boy from his pram that had been left outside the post office.'

'Yeah and there's also perverts and whack jobs,' Blackwell said. 'I guess we better extend the search. Plenty of locals offering help and I expect more to turn up. They can search the immediate area, I'll let the pros search further afield.'

'I think that's wise,' Meadows agreed.

'Lester is sending a news crew, he wants an interview and some shots of the woods,' Blackwell said.

'I'll let you handle that.' Meadows smiled. 'I'm sure you can keep the media under control.'

'Damn right,' Blackwell said.

'We're going to interview the sister again. Natalie was known to social services and seems she had a boyfriend with a dubious past.'

'Oh, this just gets better,' Blackwell said. 'God knows what's happened to that poor little mite.'

'I'm not giving up hope and we still have to keep an eye on the father,' Meadows said.

'He's out with the search party. Seems on the level.'

'Okay, I'll let you get back to the search. I'll send someone to relieve you later.'

'I'm not going anywhere,' Blackwell snapped. 'I'm staying until we have combed every inch of this place.' He turned and sauntered off towards the group.

Chapter Seven

Meadows drove in and out of villages as they headed up the valley. Darkness was creeping into the sky with the mountain tops barely visible. They came to Bryn Coed village square where a blue painted pub sat opposite a church.

'There's a chippy there.' Edris pointed.

'I'll stop on the way back if you're that hungry,' Meadows said as he took a left turn. He drove over the old railway crossing then followed the road that ran alongside the river.

'Right, we better see what Nia has to say. I guess she didn't want to talk in front of her sister.'

Meadows parked the car outside Nia's detached.

'Nice place,' Edris said.

'Yes, looks like she's had better luck than her sister.'

Meadows looked out the window. The house was set back from the pavement, with a car port to one side. A paved area held pots with budding spring bulbs.

They made their way to the front door and rang the bell. Chimes could be heard echoing through the house on the other side. The door was opened a fraction and the head of a little girl peered around. Meadows thought her to be about ten years old. She had the same strawberry blond hair as her mother.

'Hello.' Meadows smiled. 'Is your mother at home?'

The girl nodded and opened the door. Nia was walking down the hallway with a mobile phone held to her ear.

'I have to go, I'll call you back.' She ended the call. 'You better come in.' She turned to the girl. 'Go and sit with your sister, Gracie.' Nia turned and led the way into the sitting room.

Meadows' eyes scanned the room. Gracie sat on the sofa with a younger sibling, both watching the television. The room was neat, decorated in pastel colours with a large family photo hanging over the mantle.

'Let's go into the kitchen,' Nia said. She led them in and closed the door. 'That was Leanne on the phone, I'm trying to dissuade her from coming over. She hasn't long been on a visit and she has her son to look after. There isn't much she could do if she was here.'

'Where was it you said she lived?' Edris asked.

'The Isle of Man.' Nia turned to the stove where two saucepans emitted steam into the extractor fan.

'How long has she lived there?' Meadows asked.

'About five years. Her husband is originally from the island.'

'How old is her son?'

'Elijah is two.' Nia gave a tight smile.

'I guess it must be difficult for her being so far away. She must be really worried about her sister and niece.' Meadows leaned against the counter.

'She is, but like I said there isn't anything she can do.' She adjusted the heat on the stove and turned to face Meadows. 'What can I do for you? I don't mean to be rude, but I'd like to feed the girls before I go to the station. I want to be there to support Nat when she does the appeal. I don't have a lot of time.'

Meadows noticed the dark circles beneath her eyes, visible now her makeup had worn off.

64

'We won't keep you long, but we do need to ask you a few questions. We can talk as you prepare food, just move us along if we are in your way.' Meadows smiled. 'When you called at Natalie's last night did you go into the sitting room?'

'Only briefly.'

'What were Natalie and her friends doing?'

'Getting drunk and stoned.' Nia sighed. 'It's what they usually do.'

'They were smoking cannabis?'

'Yeah, the place stank of the stuff.'

'Was Natalie smoking?'

Nia shrugged. 'I guess so, you don't need to smoke the stuff, you get stoned just sitting there.'

'Who was in the room?'

'Nat, Claire, Dan, Jamie…' Nia opened the oven and peered inside.

'Who else was there?' Meadows stepped back from the heat of the oven.

Nia straightened up. 'Ryan was there.'

'Why didn't you mention this earlier?' Edris asked.

'Because he's not supposed to be there. Nat would kick off if I said anything.'

The kitchen door opened, and a man walked in. He was dressed in a charcoal suit with a blue striped shirt and spotted tie. He looked from Nia to Meadows and Edris. 'Any news?'

'No,' Nia said. 'This is Detective Meadows and Detective Edris. They just came around to ask a few questions. This is my husband, Andy.'

Andy shook hands with the two men. 'Take a seat,' he said. 'Can I offer you a cup of tea?'

Nia shot her husband a look. 'They're not staying long. I need to get ready.'

Meadows pulled out a chair and sat. 'We appreciate that Nia is busy,' he said.

'Well I'm sure you could do with a cuppa. I'm having one.' Andy smiled.

'That would be great,' Edris said and joined Meadows at the table.

While Andy set about preparing the tea, Nia took a stack of plates from the cupboard and began placing them on the table.

'You were telling us about Ryan,' Meadows said breaking the silence.

'Yes, he was there last night. He's there most of the time but Nat will deny it if you ask her.'

'You don't approve of her relationship with Ryan?'

'He's a druggy, not fit to be around a child.'

'Is that why you contacted social services?' Edris asked.

'That's supposed to be confidential,' Nia snapped.

'Given the situation, social services were at liberty to tell us,' Meadows said.

'Well, I'd appreciate it if Nat didn't find out. If she stops me going around then who is going to keep an eye on Ella?' Nia bit her lip and turned away.

'She had no choice,' Andy said. 'Natalie wouldn't listen to her, she kept on seeing Ryan.'

'Do you think that Ryan is capable of hurting Ella?' Meadows asked.

Nia turned and looked at Meadows.

'You know about her broken arm?'

'Yes, Natalie said she had fallen off the bed.'

'That's her story,' Nia said.

'That one lies so much you can't believe her radio,' Andy said.

'You think that Ryan was responsible and Natalie protected him?' Meadows asked.

'You don't know what she's like, she's selfish,' Nia said.

'But do you really think she would put Ryan before her own daughter?'

Nia shrugged her shoulders. 'I don't know but there were other injuries. Bruises on her legs and arms. I think Ryan has some sort of hold on Nat. Probably drugs.'

'Have you seen Natalie take drugs?' Edris asked.

'No but you've seen the state of her, she looks more like forty. She's lost so much weight and I swear she's out of it most of the time. She looks like one of those junkies you see on TV.'

She's got a point. Classic look of a user.

'She does manage to hold down a job.'

'Maybe she takes something to get her through the day,' Nia said.

'Have you asked her?'

'Yes, but she denies it of course. I even asked around, see if I could find out if someone was supplying her with drugs.'

'What did you find out?'

'Nothing really, people won't talk to you unless you're one of them.'

Andy placed two mugs on the table. Meadows took a sip of tea. It tasted wonderful, the last cup he'd drunk had been at the station. It seemed like days ago.

'Social services reported that Natalie seemed to be coping. There were no major concerns regarding Ella's welfare.'

Nia laughed. 'Well, they would think everything is okay. They made appointments to see her. Gave her a chance to get Ryan out of the way, clean up, and put on a show of mother of the year.'

'But you didn't make a complaint to social services until three months ago. Ryan has been around a lot longer. Why wait?'

'My mother got sick. Before that she was over there every day, cleaning, taking care of Ella, and making sure there was food in the fridge. She covered up for Nat. I've tried but I have my own family, as well as Mum to look after. I also work. I can't be there every day to watch her. I even tried helping her to sort out that bloody garden so Ella could have somewhere to play. I paid for new slabs, I thought she'd take an interest in a new patio, but she wouldn't even come out to help me and Andy pick up the old ones.'

Meadows took another glug of tea. 'Do you think that Natalie would hurt Ella? You obviously think that she's an unfit mother.'

'No, I can't see that she would hurt her, but look what happened last night. She left the front door open. I think she needs help. She works all hours. I think it's more to get out of looking after Ella than the money. She doesn't have anything to show for it. She's always skint and asking Mum for money. Maybe if Ryan was off the scene, she would get her act together.'

'Are you saying that before Ryan came on the scene she was doing alright?'

'That one was never alright,' Andy said.

'She's always liked to enjoy herself and be centre of attention. I don't know, if she had stayed with Dylan then maybe she would've settled down.' Nia turned to the stove and switched off the heat.

'Have you ever seen Ryan be violent towards Natalie or Ella?'

'No, but I've been there when he's looking after Ella, stoned and…'

'And?'

'Nothing, he just gives me the creeps.'

'So, you would be happier if Ella had been removed from Natalie's care?' Meadows asked.

'If I'm honest, yes. She'd be better off with Dylan.' Nia carried the saucepan to the sink and drained the potatoes.

'Do you support Dylan's application for custody?'

'Yes. Nat could still see her, maybe it would give her an incentive to clean up her act. At least Ella would've been safe with her father.'

Another thought struck Meadows. 'Does Natalie know about Dylan's intention to apply for custody?'

'No, I don't think so.'

'But if she did, do you think she would try and hide Ella somewhere? Maybe she's frightened of losing her child.'

'She hasn't got the brains to pull off something like that,' Nia scoffed. 'Anyway, where would she hide her? I'm sure she doesn't know about the custody application otherwise she would've been out to cause trouble for Dylan.'

'What sort of trouble?' Edris asked.

'Lies. She'd make something up. She told my mother that Dylan wasn't paying child support and that's why she didn't have any money. Dylan showed me the attachment of earnings on his wage slip. I'm sure she'd think of something to stop Dylan getting custody, just to be spiteful.'

'Do you think that Dylan would take matters into his own hands?'

'No,' Andy said. 'He wouldn't put the family through that, especially Nia's mother, and what would he gain?'

'We're going to have to talk to your mother at some stage,' Edris said.

'I know, I've told her what's going on, but I'd prefer it if I was there when you visit her, just in case she gets upset.'

'That's fine.' Meadows drank down the last of his tea and stood. 'We'll leave you to get on but before we go, could you tell us where you both were last night and the early hours of this morning?'

'What? You can't seriously think I would take my own niece.' Nia's nostrils flared.

'They have to ask, love,' Andy said.

'I told you, I went over to Nat's around ten, dropped the washing off and came straight home. I had a cup of tea, read for half hour and went to bed.'

'It was about ten thirty when we went up,' Andy said. 'We got up at seven. I went to work.'

'I took the girls to school and went into work, you can check the house if you like. She's not here,' Nia said.

'Why don't I show you around,' Andy offered. 'You can check it off your list.'

'Thank you.' Meadows nodded to Edris who followed Andy out of the kitchen.

'Who's the oldest out of you girls?' Meadows asked.

'Me, then Leanne, Nat's the youngest.' Nia took a masher and began pounding the potatoes.

'Did you get along when you were growing up?'

'I guess. We argued like all sisters do but nothing major. Nat was always a handful but got away with things because she was the baby of the family. After Dad died her behaviour got worse.'

'What happened to your father?'

'He died in a car crash. Nat was thirteen. She wallowed in it. Started drinking, smoking, and hanging around older boys. She blamed it all on the grief, but we all lost our father.'

'Does Leanne get along with Natalie?'

'They're not especially close.'

'Leanne also contacted social services.'

'Yes, when she was over at Christmas time she went to visit Natalie and Ella. Natalie had those friends over and they were all drunk. Leanne was appalled with the state of the place, she was in tears when she got back here. She said Ella's cot blankets were dirty.'

'I'm going to have to talk to her.'

Nia stopped mashing and pulled a pen and paper from one of the drawers. She scribbled down a number and handed the paper to Meadows.

'I don't think she will be able to tell you much more than I have.'

'Well, thank you for your time,' Meadows said.

Andy returned with Edris and walked them to the front door.

'She's really worried,' he said. 'I know she comes across as being hard on Natalie, but she only wants what's best for her and Ella. It's been hard for her since her mum got ill and I guess she feels that she is responsible for the family.'

'I understand,' Meadows said, 'families can be difficult.'

* * *

'They seem like a nice family,' Edris said as they walked to the car.

'Yes, on the surface, but what lies beneath?'

'You think they have something to do with it?'

'There's obviously a lot of friction between the sisters and she sides with Dylan. Then there was the other car that George saw parked outside last night. Would Nia go to her sister if she was in trouble?'

'And cover for her?' Edris looked doubtful.

'No, I don't think she would keep quiet if Natalie had hurt Ella, especially if Ryan was involved. I'm just trying to think of all the scenarios. Nia would only be involved if she knew Ella was safe. She could've helped Dylan get Ella out of the house but I don't think that's the case.'

'Then that leaves us with Ryan,' Edris said.

'Yes, I think it's time we paid him a visit.'

Chapter Eight

'It's number two hundred and sixty-three.'

Meadows grabbed a handful of chips from Edris' packet.

'That one.' Edris pointed to the middle-terraced house with a sausage before taking a bite.

Meadows pulled over and stuffed a few more chips in his mouth.

'You should've got your own,' Edris said as he picked at the last morsels from the packet.

Meadows laughed. 'You're lucky I stopped for you to pick up lunch.'

'Call this lunch, it's past my dinner time.'

Meadows pointed to the old battered Renault parked in front of the house. 'Looks like he's in.'

'We should give it a once over, check out the tyres and wind him up a bit,' Edris said.

'You've been taking lessons from Blackwell,' Meadows teased.

'Nah, Blackwell would drag him to the station by his balls.'

The image floated in Meadows' mind and he chuckled.

'Yeah, I guess he would. Come on, let's go.'

The door was opened by an overweight woman in her fifties. She had brown straggly hair and a pale complexion.

'Mrs Jean Phillips?' Meadows showed his ID.

'Miss.' She peered at the badge.

Meadows smiled. 'We'd like a chat with Ryan.'

'He's not—'

'We see he's in.' Meadows cut her off and pointed to the car.

'You better come in.' Jean huffed. She waddled down the hallway. 'Ryan, cops want to talk to you,' she said as she entered the sitting room.

Meadows followed her in and saw Ryan sprawled on the sofa. He had the same shade of hair as his mother and sister, which curtained his hooded eyes.

He glared at Meadows. 'What do you want?'

'We've come to have a chat about Natalie.' Meadows plonked himself down in the armchair. 'I'm sure Edris would love a cup of tea, Miss Phillips.'

'Forget it,' Ryan snapped. 'You're not staying long enough.'

Edris shrugged and took a seat in the other armchair. Jean hovered nervously by the door.

'As you'll be aware Natalie's little girl is missing,' Meadows said.

'So? Nothing to do with me.' Ryan stretched his arms behind his head.

'You're Natalie's boyfriend so it has everything to do with you,' Edris said.

'Who says?'

'Come on, Ryan, let's not waste each other's time,' Meadows said.

'She's not my girlfriend. We knocked around for a while, just a bit of fun.'

'Until you were arrested for possession and intent to supply and told to stay away.'

'Not my drugs.' Ryan smirked. 'Case didn't even get to court. What does that tell you?'

That you're a slippery little sucker.

'When was the last time you saw Natalie?'

'Dunno, I see her around. Could be last week.'

'Funny that, because we have witnesses that saw you at her house last night.'

'Yeah, well, your witness is seeing things.'

'More than one person saw you. Lots of people live on that estate, you'd be surprised how many of them watch who comes and goes.'

Ryan swung his legs off the sofa as he sat up and reached for his tobacco pouch. 'Alright I went to get a tenner off my sister, fat cow owed me. I was only there for five minutes.'

Just keep spinning the web until you trap yourself.

Meadows sat back resuming a relaxed position.

'Where did you go when you left Natalie's?'

'Came back here.' Ryan sprinkled tobacco along a paper and worked it back and forth with yellow stained fingers. 'Tell him, Mum.'

'Yeah, he was in all night with me, watched a film together,' Jean said.

'And what film was that?' Edris asked.

'Some shit that was on the TV, what does it matter?' Ryan put the cigarette to his mouth and flicked the lighter. 'That it?'

'No, that's not it.' Meadows felt irritation crawl at his skin. 'How do you get on with Ella?'

'She's Nat's kid, not mine.' Ryan blew out a plume of smoke.

'Yes, but you look after her when Natalie is at work, why is that? Did she pay you or did you have some other reason?'

Ryan's jaw clenched. 'I bet her sister's been bumping her gums again. Yeah, she's probably getting a kick out of this. If she'd bothered to help out and look after the kid I wouldn't have to. I helped out now and again, big deal.'

'Can't be easy looking after a young child. I can't see that you have a lot of experience.'

'It's not that hard.'

Pretty easy if you're stoned and take no notice.

Meadows couldn't imagine how anyone could leave a child in his care. 'Did you ever lose your temper with Ella?'

'No.'

'We know you have anger issues, you put your last girlfriend in hospital.'

'Didn't lay a finger on her. She dropped the charges. Made the whole thing up,' Ryan said.

'So how did she get the injuries?' Edris asked.

'Fucked if I know. Probably got someone to give her a hiding so she could stitch me up.'

'Did Ella deliberately break her arm to stitch you up?' Meadows asked.

Ryan glared at Meadows. 'I never laid a finger on that kid.'

'He's a good boy,' Jean said. 'Ryan wouldn't hurt anyone. He's been in trouble a few times but that's boys for you.'

'I've answered all your questions, so you can leave now,' Ryan said.

'Okay.' Meadows stood. 'But I'd like to have a look around before I go?'

Ryan leapt off the sofa. 'Got a warrant?'

'Do I need one?' Meadows challenged. He stepped forward until he was towering over Ryan. 'I could arrest you and search the house, makes no difference to me.'

'You can't take me in, you have nothing on me.'

'I think you'll find that I can. You were at a house last night where a child went missing. You lied when questioned, and you've got a history of violence.'

'Fine, look around, you won't find nothing.'

'Thank you, I appreciate your cooperation.'

Meadows left the room and headed up the stairs with Ryan close at heel. The first room he entered was the bathroom. He noted the single towel hanging over the rail, bottles of shampoo lining the edge of the bathtub and a face cloth hanging on the sink. He closed the door and moved to the next room.

'My mother's bedroom,' Ryan said from behind. 'I don't think you'll find the kid stashed under the bed, but you're welcome to look.'

Meadows ignored him and scanned the room. Purple covers on the bed matched the curtains, the cream carpet was clean, the dressing table neat and ordered. He stepped back and closed the door.

'I guess this must be your room,' Meadows opened the last door. The bed was unmade, and clothes were strewn around the room. A games console and TV sat on top of a chest of drawers.

The carpet is freshly hoovered, and it smells too clean in here. Not even an ashtray. Can't imagine he would sit and play games without smoking.

'Seen enough,' Ryan said.

'You don't seem very concerned that Ella is missing.' Meadows turned to face him.

'Not my kid, is it?'

'But Natalie is your friend and you looked after Ella. You must've got to know her quite well.'

'I've been down the woods with my mates to help look for her, so I've done my bit, it's your job to find the kid. You should be looking, not wasting time hassling me.'

'I am looking, I'm looking at everyone who's connected to Ella and we will find her.' Meadows walked passed Ryan and walked down the stairs. He took a quick look in the kitchen before returning to the sitting room.

Ryan followed him in and plonked himself down on the sofa.

'That will be all for now but don't go anywhere. I expect we will need to talk to you again.' Meadows turned to leave.

'Whatever,' Ryan said. 'You can see yourselves out.'

76

'He's not living there.' Meadows turned to Edris as soon as they were outside. 'He's either shacked up with Natalie or he has another place.'

Chapter Nine

Natalie sat huddled on the sofa with a blanket draped around her shoulders. It was dark outside and Brianna had switched on the lights and drawn the curtains before returning to the kitchen where she could be heard rattling plates and cutlery. Natalie wished she would go away, she hated having this stranger in her house, it felt like Brianna was watching her every move. She longed to put on the TV just to fill the time. The day seemed endless, her stomach was hollow, and her chest hurt from chain smoking. She wanted something stronger but didn't dare skin up. Maybe Ryan had left some tabs around, he usually has a stash somewhere, she thought.

Natalie pulled herself up off the sofa, her body ached, and she felt a chill run down her back. She pulled the blanket tight around her shoulders and started to rummage in drawers and along the mantle. Nothing. She knelt and opened the drawer in the TV cabinet, she shoved unopened letters and random bits of plastic aside. Her hand touched one of Ella's dummies and she felt a stab of pain in her chest. She quickly shoved it aside and continued her search. In the corner of the drawer she found a small block of hash wrapped in cling film. She shoved it in her pocket and stood up.

'You okay?' Brianna placed a plate with a sandwich cut into four neat triangles on to the table and held out a mug to Natalie.

'I was just looking for another lighter, I think I'm almost out of gas.' Natalie took the mug and sat back on the sofa.

Brianna smiled. 'We'll need to leave in an hour. I made you something to eat.'

Natalie looked at the plate and felt her stomach turn. 'I'm not hungry.'

'Try to eat a little bit,' Brianna said. 'It will make you feel better and you're going to need your strength.'

Natalie picked up a sandwich and took a bite, it was tasteless. She chewed slowly, forcing herself to swallow as she watched Brianna settle in a chair. The other woman's long shining hair, and flawless face made Natalie feel ugly. Natalie took another bite. She didn't want this stranger in her house, watching and pretending to be nice.

'I can't eat anymore,' Natalie said and pushed the plate away.

'That's okay, maybe you can try again later. Why don't you have a shower or relax in the bath.'

Natalie felt anger spike her skin. 'You think I need a shower?'

'Not if you don't want to, but it might help you feel more relaxed. Going in front of the cameras can be a little daunting. You need to be focused. I'm going to be with you the whole time and Nia will be there. Even a quick freshen up may make you feel a little better.'

Natalie stood, picked up her tobacco tin and coffee and headed upstairs. She locked the bathroom door and rolled a joint as the bath ran. The room soon filled with steam, and although she still felt cold, she stripped, opened the window, then lowered herself into the hot water.

Lighting the joint, she inhaled deeply and let her head rest against the back of the bath. A few more puffs and she felt her muscles uncoil, her jaw slackened, and her stomach unclenched. The drip of the tap caused ripples in the water, Natalie watched them swirl and felt her eyelids droop. The warmth spread through her body and she let her hand trail in the water.

Snippets of memories from last night floated across her mind. Rain like silver thread, falling on her face, covering her body until it glittered. Her body felt alive, her mind free as she twirled around, hands held out and golden laughter running through her veins.

'Are you okay in there?'

Natalie snapped her eyes open as Brianna's voice brought her back to the present. 'Yeah, I'll be out in a minute.'

We were out in the garden last night, what else did we do? she thought. She let her head fall under the water trying to chase away the bad thoughts.

Brianna was in the kitchen when Natalie came down dressed in a clean pair of jeans and jumper. She had roughly dried her hair and run a brush through it. She looked around, hardly recognising the place. The dogs lay snoozing on the floor, a fresh bowl of water set on the mat.

'Your neighbour George kindly took them out for a walk. I've given them food and fed the cats but that's the last of it,' Brianna said. 'Perhaps you can make a list and I can pick up some groceries on the way back from the station.'

Natalie shrugged. 'I need some more baccy.' She opened a drawer and took out a bar of chocolate. She suddenly felt ravenous. 'Are those two detectives going to be at the appeal?' She bit into the chocolate bar.

'Meadows and Edris?'

Natalie nodded.

'Yes, I expect they will be there.'

Brianna was still talking but her voice drifted away as Natalie let her imagination run. An image of Edris peeling off his clothes excited her senses, she took another bite of chocolate to stop herself smiling. She continued the fantasy, he was lying on top of her, looking deep into her eyes. Edris' face was replaced by Jamie's and Dan stood naked looking on. The chocolate suddenly felt thick heavy in her mouth. She tried to swallow the chocolate, but it stuck in her throat.

'Are you okay?' Brianna stepped closer.

Natalie gulped the dregs of her coffee, forcing the chocolate down her throat. 'I can't eat this anymore.' She threw the rest of the bar down onto the counter as tears stung her eyes.

'It's okay.' Brianna put her hand on Natalie's shoulder. There came a knock on the front door. 'Looks like it's time to go. Have you got a coat?'

'Yeah.' Natalie looked around the hallway. It wasn't in its usual place. She had a quick look around the sitting room. 'Can't find it.'

'What does it look like?' Brianna joined in the search.

'It's bright pink, can't miss it.'

They looked around the house and upstairs. Feeling frustrated, Natalie grabbed a hooded jacket and pulled it on over her jumper before leaving the house.

* * *

The journey made her feel nauseous, she longed for it to end but at the same time dreaded arriving at the police station. She peered out of the window and tried to quell the panic. She didn't want any more questions. Didn't want to see Dylan with his snooty parents who always looked down on her. She twisted her hands together. They'll blame me and tell everyone that I'm a crap mother, she thought.

'Okay?' Brianna swivelled around in her seat as they entered the station car park.

Natalie shrugged and opened the door as soon as the car stopped.

'I want a smoke before I go in.'

'That's alright.' Brianna came to stand next to her.

'There's a lot of cars here.' Natalie drew on the cigarette and felt the smoke fill her lungs. She imagined a room full of people all staring at her.

'There's always a lot of cars here but some will belong to members of the press.'

'Let's just get this over with.' Natalie ground the cigarette into the floor.

She was led into a room where the first person she saw was Nia. Relief at a familiar face made her throw her arms around her sister. 'Thanks for coming.'

'I wouldn't leave you on your own,' Nia said. 'Are you sure you're up to doing this?'

'No, but I have to try.' Natalie slumped down on the chair. 'I just want to get this over with.'

The door opened and a suited man walked in. He was dark haired with serious grey eyes. He had an air of authority which made Natalie feel uncomfortable. She pulled her jacket tightly around her body and folded her arms across her chest.

'Hello, Natalie, I'm DCI Lester.' He pulled up a chair. 'We've set up a room for the press conference and I have a statement prepared for you.' He handed Natalie a sheet of paper. 'If you would like to take a look and see if there is anything you'd like to add.'

Natalie looked at the paper, the words seemed to dance around. She tried to concentrate, but the words wouldn't sink in, she handed it to Nia.

'What do you think?'

'I think it's okay.' Nia nodded as she read through the sheet and handed it back to Natalie.

'Good.' Lester smiled. 'Is there anything you'd like to ask before we go in?'

'Is there going to be a lot of people?' Natalie picked at her fingernail.

'There are quite a few, yes, but the more coverage we get–'

'Will I be on my own in there?'

'Of course not. Your sister can sit with you, Dylan will be there to read a statement, and I will answer any questions from the journalists.'

'I won't have to answer any questions, will I?' Natalie felt her stomach knot.

'Not if you don't want to.'

'I don't.'

'That's fine.' Lester stood. 'Shall we?'

'What, now?' The knot in her stomach tightened.

'It's best not to have too much time to think about it. It'll be over very quickly.'

They walked down a corridor and Natalie spotted Dylan talking to a policeman who patted him on the shoulder before turning away. She didn't see why he should get any attention. Irritation crawled at her skin.

Dylan turned and gave Natalie a weak smile.

Natalie turned her head away from him.

'You okay, Dylan?' Nia asked.

'Holding up. How are you doing, Nat?'

'How do you think?' Natalie snapped. She wished Ryan was there.

Lester stepped between the two of them. 'It would be good if you could sit next to each other, show a united front.'

'I've got no problem with that,' Dylan said.

'Fine,' Natalie said. She could hear a hubbub behind the door and already imagined hundreds of eyes upon her.

Lester opened the door and the room fell silent for a moment. Natalie kept her eyes down as she walked inside. Immediately there was a rush of chairs being scraped back followed by clicks and flashes from the cameras. Natalie took her seat between Nia and Dylan and laid the sheet of paper on the table. She noticed the microphones placed in front of each person. The noise in the room gradually died and Lester talked through the events of the day. He then announced that Natalie would read a short statement.

She became aware of the eyes boring into her, she looked at the paper and opened her mouth, but no words came out. Her mouth felt dry and her tongue too heavy. Nia took hold of her hand and squeezed. Natalie took a shaky breath and tried again.

'If… if you have Ella, you need to give her back. She will be missing her mummy.' He voice sounded unnatural. Natalie felt her heart strumming against her ribs, blood pounded through her head making the room look hazy. She remembered digging with her hands, laughter wrapped around her like a warm coat and something else. Music? No. Wailing.

'She needs her family.'

Dylan's voice broke through Natalie's thoughts and she took a gulp of air. Her hands were shaking, she looked across at Dylan who sat rigid staring into the camera as he spoke.

'She needs her mummy and daddy, we love her very much.' Dylan's voice broke.

'If you have seen Ella then please call the incident room.' Lester's words washed over Natalie, she felt Nia's arm around her shoulder, then there was a sudden rise in noise as journalists shouted questions and cameras flashed and clicked.

Natalie allowed herself to be led out of the room, a cup of tea was placed in her hands as she was guided to a seat.

'You did well,' Nia said.

'No, I didn't. I looked like an idiot.'

The door opened and Meadows and Edris walked in. 'How are you feeling, Natalie?' Meadows pulled out a chair.

'I'm alright.' She didn't want to tell them how she really felt.

'It's pretty tough doing an appeal but we got the message out, that's the important thing. Lots of volunteers have turned up to help search the woods and many more will be looking for her, but I must tell you that it is looking doubtful that she wandered into the woods alone. We would've found her by now.'

'Maybe someone found her and didn't know what to do, now they'll know where to bring her.' Natalie said. Her mind wandered. It wasn't wailing, it was crying she'd heard. Ella was crying. She tried to grasp the memory. Ryan had grabbed her hand and said, "Leave it, she'll shut up in a minute." She felt panic snake around her body.

'We've spoken to Ryan,' Meadows said. 'He told us he was with you last night, we just need you to confirm what time he left this morning.'

'Erm, about eleven.' She caught the smile on Edris' face. Oh shit, maybe he told them a different time, she thought.

'Why didn't you tell us that Ryan was with you last night? It would have saved us a lot of time,' Meadows asked.

'Because everyone is always interfering in my life, saying he can't stay over.'

'You mean like social services?' Edris said.

Natalie felt the heat rise up her neck. 'The drugs weren't his, it's not fair.'

'You said you didn't leave the house last night, but you were seen getting into your car and driving away at two this morning.'

Natalie looked away from Meadows' gaze. Yes, they were out the garden, but she didn't remember coming back inside. She didn't remember anything.

'Natalie?'

Natalie met Meadows' eyes, he was leaning towards her, his look questioning.

'No, I wouldn't drive the car, I'd been drinking.'

'You were seen, wearing your pink coat. You do have a pink coat?'

'Yes, but I can't find it.' Anxiety gnawed her stomach and pain stabbed at her temples. 'Maybe someone took it. Maybe Claire went out and used my coat.'

'But you said no one left the house.'

'Maybe I was asleep.' Natalie felt her throat constrict. 'I don't know.' She put her hands to her head and gripped her hair.

'Is this really necessary, I think she's been through enough today,' Nia said.

'We really need to know who left the house.' Meadows stood. 'I'll let Brianna take you home now, but I need you to think hard about what happened last night. We need to know everything.'

Natalie nodded her head.

Chapter Ten

I sat and watched the appeal with you, listening to your comments and tuts. I should've left the room, but I couldn't escape from it. Everyone was talking about it — it was on every station and would be in the papers. I stayed on the sofa. If I couldn't act normal with my family then what chance did I have?

The camera showed the house and I had to bite my tongue to stop myself from shouting. The house brought the memory back in vivid technicolour. The stairs that creak on the forth step. The nursery with a beautiful sleeping child. A child that will sleep forever. A child limp in my arms. I bit the inside of my cheek to chase away the memory.

The little girl's mother struggled to speak, couldn't say the words. I can feel her pain, I want to feel pain. The child's father sat rigid, struggling to hold back the emotions, the heartbreak, the fear, the not knowing. The news cuts to the woods. A detective is talking, he looked tough, not the sort to have any sympathy. I hope he is not the one to come. They showed local people that turned up to join in the search. It was then I saw him walking by, he stopped and looked into the camera. I had to dig my nails into the palm of my hand. He was looking straight at me, I know what he's thinking. "I know what you did."

Chapter Eleven

'That's everyone on the list checked out,' Edris said, then yawned and leaned back in his chair. 'All Dylan's relatives, friends, work colleagues, the lot. Nothing on the guy.'

'Valentine, did you find anything on the neighbour, George?'

Meadows turned to the incident board and looked at the list of suspects.

'Nothing, not even a parking ticket. Story checks out. He divorced in his late twenties, one daughter who lives in London. He worked down the pits until they closed and hasn't worked since. No sign of him on social media.'

'Probably doesn't know how to use a computer,' Edris said.

'What about Natalie's mother?' Meadows asked.

'Naturally she was upset and is still recovering. She let us look around and she still has the keys to Natalie's house. She voiced her concerns about Ryan but seemed to be under the impression that they were no longer together.'

'I expect Nia kept it from her not to cause any worry,' Meadows said.

'She's protective of Natalie. Says she works very hard and is doing a good job managing as a single parent. I didn't want to push her on Natalie's lifestyle.'

'Okay, thanks, Valentine.' Meadows smiled. 'It comes back to this lot.' Meadows pointed to the names on the board. 'Natalie, Claire, Ryan, Jamie and Dan. They were all there last night and have all lied. One or all of them knows what happened to Ella, I'm sure of it.'

Paskin walked into the office and plonked herself down on a chair.

'Has there been a good response to the appeal?' Meadows asked.

'Yeah, the phone hasn't stopped ringing. Just taking a break.' Paskin swivelled back and forth on her chair.

'Anything interesting?'

'Lots of sightings, usual stuff. I guess people think they're being helpful. They think they've seen some kid that looks like Ella in a supermarket or the park. One claims that Natalie was renting her cottage in Lancaster over the weekend, even had a child with her.'

'Lancaster?' Edris laughed. 'Well, unless she has a teleporter we can rule that one out.'

Meadows stood and grabbed his jacket.

'I'm going to head out to the woods, it's time Blackwell knocked off. I'm not sure how beneficial the search is in the dark. The rest of you can go home and get some rest, we'll start early in the morning.'

'I'll stay on the phones a bit longer,' Paskin said. 'See if anything comes up that's worth checking out.'

'I'm with you.' Valentine stood up.

'I'm not going home before Blackwell.' Edris grinned. 'I'll never hear the last of it.'

Meadows felt a swell of pride. They'll stay until they can't keep their eyes open and then some more. No one is willing to give up on Ella.

'Come on then.' He threw Edris the car keys. 'You can drive.'

Darkness fell around them as they left the main road and streetlights and turned onto the track that led into the woods. The headlights picked out the way ahead but on either side only the silhouettes of trees loomed, the branches like gnarled fingers grabbing at the rooftop.

'Spooky here in the dark,' Edris said.

As they drove further in, they came across a group of people walking towards them, torches lighting their way. Meadows looked out of the window noting the tired look and despondency on their faces.

'I guess they were expecting to be in the pub by now, celebrating their triumph of finding the little girl and exchanging stories.'

'Now they're wondering how safe their own children are as they sleep in their beds,' Edris said.

Up ahead a group of vehicles stood illuminated by an overhead light.

'Is that—?'

'My mother,' Meadows said as Edris parked the car on the verge. He could see Blackwell with a cup in his hand talking to his mother who stood behind a makeshift table with Marina.

Meadows climbed out of the car and grabbed his coat from the back seat. His mother had spotted him and was waving as Blackwell sauntered away.

'I bet your mum has some of her cakes.' Edris grinned. 'Just what I need.'

'Hello, Winny love.' Fern Meadows reached up and kissed her son on the cheek.

Meadows was glad Blackwell wasn't close enough to hear his mother's pet name.

'What are you doing here, Mum? You know the cold and damp makes your arthritis worse.'

'Oh, don't make a fuss. I wanted to do my bit to help. I can't traipse through the woods, but I can bake and make sure all those out looking get a hot drink and something to eat.'

'Your mum's been a great help,' Marina said as she pulled a large water flask from the van.

Meadows smiled. 'I'm sure the search teams appreciate it.'

'I was just having a nice chat with Stefan,' Fern Meadows said. 'Lovely boy.'

'Only you could manage to find something likable about Blackwell.' Edris laughed, picked up a slice a cake, and took a bite.

'Now, Tristan, that's not very nice of you,' Fern scolded. 'He just needs a bit of love.'

'We'd better get on. Don't stay too long, Mum.'

'You haven't had any cake,' Fern said.

'I'm not hungry.'

'Nonsense, I bet you skipped lunch. Here.' She placed a large piece of cake in Meadows' hand. 'He's another one who needs a good woman to look after him.' She turned to Marina and smiled.

Meadows groaned inwardly. He gave Marina what he hoped was an apologetic smile and kissed his mother.

'You can shut up,' Meadows said to Edris as they walked away.

'I didn't say anything,' Edris protested.

'No, but you thought it.' Meadows gobbled down the cake as they came to stand next to Blackwell.

'Saw you on the news,' Edris said. 'You'll be fighting off the women now.'

'Fuck off,' Blackwell barked.

'Hey, I was giving you a compliment.' Edris shrugged.

Blackwell ignored him and turned to Meadows. 'I've sent the locals home. It's too dark for them and they're more of a liability.'

'Perhaps you should call it a night,' Meadows suggested.

'Search and rescue are still out with the dogs. I'll wait until they come back. If it wasn't for the fact that we found the girl's toy I would've given up long ago. I don't think she's here though.'

Blackwell's radio crackled to life, he hit the receiver and held it to his ear.

'On our way. They've found something.' He opened the car boot and took out three torches. 'You're going to need these. Come on, get in, I'll drive.'

Meadows felt his stomach tighten as they sped along the track, the car swaying from side to side.

This doesn't sound good, if they had found her alive they would've said and called for an ambulance.

'They're about two miles in.' Blackwell's jaw was clenched, his eyes fixed ahead. 'That's almost three miles from the entrance of the estate. Too far for her to wander alone, I reckon.'

Up ahead Meadows caught a glimpse of light. As they drew nearer they could see it was a man stood on the verge with a torch. An Alsatian dog sat at his heel.

'It's Craig.' Blackwell stopped the car and they all climbed out.

'It's not too far in but watch your footing, there's a lot of exposed roots.' Craig turned away.

Meadows wanted to ask what exactly they had found but dreaded the answer. He knew that was the reason that Blackwell and Edris remained silent as they followed Craig through the trees.

'I left the others to finish uncovering the earth.' Craig stopped and turned to face them. 'We're not sure yet.' He looked grim.

They continued in silence. Meadows kept his torch trailed on the ground. It wasn't an easy route, branches snagged at his jacket and tree roots stubbed at his toes. They came to a small clearing and two men could be seen kneeling on the ground, gently brushing the earth.

'Anything, Tom?' Craig said.

'Just these.' Tom stood and held up an item of clothing.

Meadows stepped forward and shined his torch on the small pyjama top. It was covered in earth, but a crown and the name Ella were clearly visible.

'That's what she was dressed in when she went missing.'

He watched as the pyjama bottoms were pulled out together with a vest and nappy. Anger spiked his veins, he turned to Blackwell.

'Get forensics out here.'

Blackwell took out his phone and stepped away from the group but could be heard barking orders.

'It looks like it's only her clothing. To be honest, when we found them we thought the worst.' Craig looked down into the hole.

'I don't think we are looking for a missing child anymore,' Edris said.

'The dogs are cross-trained. They can pick up the scent of a living person or...' Craig sighed. 'If she is here we'll find her, no matter how well hidden.'

'Why take off her clothes and bury them?' Edris asked.

'Because we're probably dealing with some sick fuck,' Blackwell said as he re-joined the group. 'SOCO are on their way.'

'Let's get these things bagged up and we better move the vehicles. We need to seal off this part of the woods.' Meadows looked around the small clearing. 'Hopefully not too many people have trampled this way, we might be able to get some prints.'

SOCO arrived and soon the area was flooded with light and a tent was erected over the hole to preserve any evidence. The hours ticked by as Meadows stood and watched the forensic team pick through the earth and take photographs. Now and again the voice of one of the search team could be heard giving commands to the dogs. When this happened, Meadows held his breath expecting a shout that they had found the girl, but none came.

'I don't understand,' Edris said and yawned. 'The toy was found near the footpath off the estate which is over two miles away and now we have a pile of clothes and nothing else. Surely, they wouldn't have walked all this way to find a random spot. What's the point of dumping the clothes here?'

'It does seem like a trail of breadcrumbs,' Meadows said.

'Yeah but leading us to what?'

'We have to assume that whoever took Ella carried her into the woods from the estate, she dropped the toy along the way which means she would be awake. Then possibly they met up with someone in a car. We know that two cars were outside Natalie's house in the early hours. According to George, Natalie drove off, or someone wearing her coat. They put Ella in the car and drove further in, parked up and walked to this spot.' Meadows ran his hand over his chin, he could feel the stubble coming through. 'So, they stripped her, buried the clothes and… no, it doesn't make much sense.'

'Are we going to tell Natalie about the clothes?'

Meadows looked at his watch. 'No point at this hour, it can wait.'

Craig and his team returned with the dogs.

'They're not picking up anything, I'm sorry.'

'Call it off and start again at first light,' Meadows said. An image of the little girl flashed across his mind.

I'm not giving up on you sweetheart – not yet.

Chapter Twelve

Meadows drove towards home. Each village he passed through was still – no lights on in the houses, and no cars on the road. He reached Bryn Bach and turned down the farm track to his cottage. Inside was cold and smelled of fresh paint. Half the walls were still orange in the sitting room, the other half had the first coat of stardust. All the furniture had been piled up in the centre of the room and covered with a dust sheet.

I shouldn't have started the decorating. It will end up looking like this for the rest of the year, he thought.

He pulled off the dust sheet and moved the armchair to the corner, placed a table and lamp next to the chair then went to the kitchen and brewed a cup of camomile tea.

Back in the sitting room he retrieved his stash from its hiding place and sat in the armchair rolling a joint.

What am I missing? He lit the joint and inhaled. *A house full of drunk and stoned adults, two cars outside, clothes buried in the woods.*

He felt the knots loosen in his muscles with each pull on the joint.

Were we meant to think she was in the woods to pull our attention away from somewhere else? We've checked all the homes of the relatives and those in close contact with Ella.

His thoughts swirled around with no conclusion. He stubbed the joint and closed his eyes letting his head fall back against the chair but he couldn't sleep. Sighing he got up and made himself a snack before taking a shower and changing into fresh clothes. His eyes ached with fatigue, but he knew his mind would not let him rest, not with the image of the small dirt-stained pyjamas etched in his memory.

* * *

The upstairs office in the police station was silent when Meadows arrived. He made a strong cup of coffee and sat at his desk with a pile of statements from friends and neighbours and reports from social services, and Ryan's drug arrest. He read until his eyes stung but nothing stood out. He groaned as he stood up and stretched before walking to the incident board.

It all comes back to Natalie and her friends. Meadows ran his hands through his hair as he concentrated on coming up with a plausible scenario. *Nia came at ten and Ella was sleeping. Natalie and her friends were in the sitting room, drinking, smoking, and probably taking something else. What then? Ella wakes up crying for attention, someone goes up, probably Natalie, tries to settle her down but nothing works. Natalie is frustrated because she's missing out on the fun, so she takes Ella downstairs. Now there are five adults all drunk, stoned, and incapable of watching a small child. Maybe there was an accident.*

Meadows walked to his desk and picked up the drug raid report. MDMA was found as well as cocaine and cannabis.

What if Ella picked up one of the pills? She would likely start fitting. They panic, take her to the car intending to drive to hospital but it's too late. They take her into the woods and come up with the story that Ella wandered out of the house. But we would have found her by now, and why bury the clothes separately? Then there was the other car that was parked outside. No, this has to be something other than an accident – a planned disappearance?

'In early? Or haven't you been home?'

Meadows turned around and saw Blackwell plonk himself down at his desk.

'The latter. Just a quick shower and change. You?'

'Much the same. You look like shit.'

Meadows smiled. 'Likewise.'

'SOCO got some good prints from the site where we found the clothes. They eliminated ours and the search teams, which leaves a size ten trainer and a size five boot. Mike should be here in a mo.'

'They must have been working all night.'

'Yeah well, I told them we needed something to go on,' Blackwell said.

I bet Mike's not going to be a happy man having had Blackwell on his case all night. Meadows lips twitched.

The door swung open and a dishevelled looking man walked in.

'Haven't got much for you I'm afraid.'

'You look how I feel, Mike.' Meadows smiled. 'I'll be happy with anything you've got.'

'Print is a size ten, well-worn trainer. Nothing special, probably worn by half the valley.' Mike handed a photo to Meadows.

'We got a few partials as well but that's the best one. What's interesting is that the tread is weighted at the front.' He pointed to the photo.

'A limp maybe.' Blackwell left his desk and came to peer at the photograph.

'Or shoes too big,' Meadows suggested.

'Could be,' Mike said, 'but that's your job to work out.'

'And the other prints?'

'Looks like a ladies' block heeled boot, size five, worn on the tread. We'll check out the make.'

'So, it looks like two of them went in, one male one female,' Meadows said.

As they stood discussing the prints the rest of the team filtered in.

'How come you look so fresh, Valentine,' Edris asked.

'Practice.' Valentine winked. 'You don't want to know how many times I've been out and only had a few hours' sleep before pitching up for work.'

'Yeah well, you'll be feeling it by this afternoon,' Blackwell said.

'What about the clothes?' Meadows asked. 'Did you get anything from them?'

'We're testing for DNA. We expect to find the child's and the mother's, but maybe there will be something to work with. No visible blood stains.'

'Well that's something,' Meadows said.

'Do we think she's still alive?' Paskin asked.

Blackwell shook his head. 'It doesn't seem likely.'

'Let's not give up hope yet. There may be some other reason the clothes were removed and buried. There have been plenty of cases of illegal adoption. If someone is willing to pay enough money, they can get a child to order.' He looked around the team who all looked doubtful. 'Well, it's a better alternative and one we have to consider. I want all this lot brought in.' He pointed to the board.

'All of them?' Valentine asked. 'Including Dylan?'

'Yes, one of them knows what happened to Ella, if not all of them. She didn't walk out of that house on her own. If they don't cooperate, arrest them. Better organise a search warrant. I want a thorough search of every property. I want their clothing, shoes, computers, and phones.'

'You think Dylan would sell his own daughter?' Paskin asked.

'He doesn't want her brought up by Natalie and if he thought he wouldn't get custody then maybe he would rather see her with a loving family. According to Nia,

Natalie has no interest in her child and is struggling for money. That's enough motive. And these three' – he pointed to Dan, Jamie, and Claire – 'would sell their granny for a bag of weed. As for Ryan Phillips, he's a slippery character. I don't want to imagine what he's capable of.'

Meadows let out a breath, he could feel the tension binding his ribs and his head was throbbing from lack of sleep.

'Okay, let's get to it,' Blackwell said.

'Good. First up, I'm going to see Nia. I'm sure she was holding back on us yesterday. As soon as the warrants are signed pick them all up. Valentine, can you give Brianna a call, tell her to bring in Natalie. Paskin, Blackwell, I'll leave you to sort the warrants.'

'Yeah, I'll gladly drag the magistrate from his breakfast,' Blackwell said with a grin.

'That's what I'm counting on,' Meadows replied as he walked out the door.

'Bit early to be calling on Nia, isn't it?' Edris jogged down the stairs behind Meadows.

'She has children, so she'll be up.'

'Are you okay?'

'Yes, why?' Meadows turned to look at Edris.

'It's just, well, I don't think I've ever seen you so wound up. Even Blackwell didn't argue with you.'

'I just keep seeing that picture of Ella, all smiles and innocence. She's got her whole life ahead of her. She should be home, safe and loved. Not alone, afraid, or even dead. Someone knows what happened to her, a child doesn't just disappear,' Meadows said. 'While there is a chance she is still alive, no matter how small, we have to keep trying.'

He started the car and gripped the steering wheel.

'It doesn't look good though,' Edris said.

'No, it doesn't, but I just have this feeling that she's out there somewhere.'

They drove in silence to Nia's house. There were plenty of cars on the road as people started to make their way to work. Meadows noted the absence of a second car in the driveway as he parked.

'Looks like her husband has already left, maybe she will feel able to tell us more if she's alone.'

Nia opened the door and Meadows noticed that she visibly paled when she recognised their faces.

'We don't have any news,' Meadows quickly reassured her, 'but we do need to ask you a few more questions. I'm sorry it's so early.'

Nia put her hand to her chest. 'For a moment, I thought you'd come to tell me… I thought it was bad news.' She stepped back to allow them to enter. 'I'm just getting the girls ready for school,' she said as she led them into the kitchen.

The two girls were sat at the kitchen table wearing identical uniforms and eating from bowls of cereal.

'Morning ladies.' Edris took a seat at the table. 'That looks yummy, I only got Marmite on toast this morning.'

'I think Edris can keep them entertained for a few minutes,' Meadows said.

Nia nodded. 'I'm just going to have a little chat with the policeman, why don't you ask Detective Edris to help you with your spelling test?'

Meadows followed Nia into the sitting room and waited for her to close the door.

'Even though we haven't found Ella yet, we have found evidence that she was in the woods at some point.'

'Natalie said you found Buba,' Nia said.

'We found a lot more than that, but I can't really go into it now. I got the impression that you wanted to say more yesterday. I need you to tell me everything you know, no matter how insignificant it seems.'

'I've told you everything.' Nia folded her arms.

Maybe I misread the situation.

'Has Natalie ever talked about giving up custody to Dylan, or adoption?'

'Not to me, she wasn't happy when she got pregnant but then she seemed to enjoy the attention.'

'Why don't you like Ryan, is it more than the fact that he takes drugs?'

Nia bit her lip. 'It's more of a feeling really.'

'Go on.'

'Last summer we had a pool party for Grace. Natalie brought Ryan. I didn't like the way he looked at the girls in their swimsuits.'

'You think he has an unhealthy interest in young girls?'

'Like I said, it's just a feeling. He took a lot of photos. I didn't want to say anything in front of Andy. Well, you can imagine what his reaction would be.'

'We have a warrant to search his mother's house so if there is anything like that I'm sure we'll find it. I didn't see a lot of his possessions at his mother's house, do you think he's living with Natalie?'

'His mother's house?' Nia frowned. 'He has a flat in Ynys Melyn, it's the old grocers that was converted to flats. He has the upstairs one. You haven't checked it out?'

Ella could be there. Meadows felt a twinge of hope.

'Are you sure he's still there? We found no record of Ryan renting a flat.'

'You wouldn't, the flat is in Jamie's name, and he claims housing benefit but lives with Claire.'

Meadows felt a sudden rush of adrenalin and a need to move fast. He called Edris from the kitchen and hurried to the car. Meadows quickly filled in Edris.

'Call Paskin and ask her how they are getting on with the warrants. Get a car to meet us there.'

He pulled the car onto the main road as Edris made the call.

'Warrants signed,' Edris said. 'I can't believe we missed it, the kid could have been there all along.'

'We'll go straight in, knock down the door if we have to.'

Meadows gripped the steering wheel as he sped towards Ynys Melyn. A police car was already parked outside the flats as they pulled up.

'He's here.' Edris pointed to Ryan's car that was parked a few doors up on the opposite side of the road.

'Let's' go.' Meadows climbed out of the car and was met by PC Matt Hanes.

'We've got the paperwork,' Hanes said.

'Good.' Meadows pressed the buzzer for the flat, counted to ten then pressed again, this time keeping the buzzer pressed in. 'He's had enough time.' He turned to Hanes. 'Break it down.'

Hanes moved quickly to the car and returned with a burly officer. Meadows and Edris stood back as they hurled the battering ram at the door. The noise echoed through the street. With another two hits the door gave way.

'Police!' Hanes moved the door to the side and continued shouting out as he entered the hallway.

As Meadows stepped over the threshold he heard the top door open and footsteps on the stairs. He stepped in front of Hanes in time to see Ryan rushing towards them, eyes wild and brandishing an iron bar.

'Don't be stupid, Ryan,' Meadows shouted.

The words had no effect and Ryan launched himself at Meadows swinging the bar.

Meadows moved quickly but the bar caught him on the shoulder, he felt the impact and pain seared down his arm. He saw Ryan raise the bar again. This time Meadows grabbed his wrist and twisted as he knocked Ryan's feet from beneath him. The bar clattered to the floor as Ryan fell backwards. Hanes and his partner took over, turning Ryan and cuffing him as he screamed a string of obscenities.

'Get him out of here,' Meadows said.

'Bastards!' Ryan yelled as Hanes hauled him to his feet and dragged him from the house.

'You okay?' Edris asked.

'I'll live.' Meadows rubbed his shoulder as he headed upstairs.

'I'm impressed,' Edris said. 'You don't take no prisoners.'

Meadows laughed. 'I'm losing my touch, he got one hit in.'

'You should get it checked out.'

'No time, come on let's search this place.' Meadows hurried into the sitting room, his eyes darting around.

Nothing.

He moved to the bedroom.

'She's not here.' Edris followed him in.

Meadows' hope fizzled out as he scanned the room.

'I suppose it was hoping for too much.'

His eyes caught sight of a power cable leading out from the top of the wardrobe and disappearing into a hole in the ceiling.

'The attic.' Meadows rushed out of the room, his eyes fixed to the ceiling as he looked for the hatch. 'There.' He pointed upwards.

'There's a step ladder in the kitchen.'

Edris disappeared and came back with the ladder, positioning it under the hatch.

'I'll go up.'

Meadows climbed the ladder and lifted the hatch. Warm air and the whirring of fans greeted him as he pulled himself through the hole and upright. He had to keep his head stooped to stop it from hitting the rafters.

The whole area had been boarded and insulated. Heavy duty black plastic tents emitted a soft glow and took up most of the space. Meadows knew what to expect before he unzipped the first tent, he had seen it before. He pulled back the plastic and saw rows of cannabis plants below a light with a built-in fan circulating the air through carbon filters.

He breathed in the heady aroma.

'Anything?' Edris' voice drifted up.

'Looks like he's trying to start up a farm.' Meadows climbed back down the ladder where a group of officers stood.

'Search every inch of this place. I want his shoes and clothes bagged and the computer sent to the tech boys. There is a fair amount of plants up there, should be enough to get him sent down for a couple of years.' He turned to Edris. 'Come on, time to round up the others.'

Chapter Thirteen

'Lunch,' Edris called as he dumped a large plate of sandwiches on the desk and emptied his pockets of bars of chocolate.

Valentine followed with a tray of tea and coffee. 'I couldn't remember who takes sugar, so you can help yourselves,' she said.

'Bit early for lunch,' Meadows said. 'It's not long past breakfast.' He rubbed his shoulder which, last time he checked, was sporting a black, angry bruise.

'Breakfast was hours ago, and I didn't get any lunch yesterday.' Edris picked up a sandwich and took a large bite.

'That's the lot.' Blackwell sauntered into the room and grabbed a sandwich. 'Took me a while to track down, but I got the little buggers. Folland says Ryan is still kicking off in his cell, demanding a phone call and solicitor. He reckons he was off his face when Hanes brought him in.'

'I think he's probably right, we'll leave him to come down to earth before we talk to him. Has the duty solicitor been called?' Meadows asked.

'Yep, I've got a couple lined up and waiting. Dylan doesn't want one.'

'Neither does Natalie,' Paskin said. 'Brianna brought her in, and I did explain that this will be a formal interview.'

'Good, well you can guarantee the others will want one, they know the drill. Do we have anything yet from the stuff brought back from Ryan's?'

'Match on the footprint,' Blackwell said. 'File on my desk.'

'You have been a busy boy,' Edris said.

Blackwell gave him a scathing look.

'Someone has to be on the ball around here.'

'Well at least we have something on him, not a lot to go on, though. I take it Natalie's house is being searched?' Meadows asked.

'Forensics are there now. This time they will be checking all the rooms, see if there are any signs that Ella was injured,' Paskin said.

'Good, better make sure they search the garden, they were all out there at one point. I want to know what they were doing.'

'I'll get onto it.' Paskin picked up the phone.

Meadows took a bite of his sandwich and swilled it down with tea.

'The forensic search could take hours, we're just going to have to question them with what we've got. We don't have time to sit around. Maybe one of them will let something slip. Edris, you can take Dylan. Blackwell, you can have Jamie. Paskin, see what you can get out of Dan. Valentine, are you okay to interview Claire?'

Valentine's eyes lit up. 'I'm happy to give it a go.'

'Good, just keep going over their statements for inconsistences. They all lied about Ryan being there and someone left the house that night. I'll talk to Natalie. We'll leave Ryan until last. Let him stew for a while.'

'Can I have a word?' Brianna asked as she entered the office.

'Yeah, grab a seat.' Meadows smiled.

'It won't take a minute.' Brianna leaned against the desk. 'I was cleaning away some stuff this morning in the kitchen. There was an old teapot on the windowsill. I went to swill it out but there appeared to be the remnants of mushrooms.'

'Of the magic kind?' Meadows asked.

'I can't be certain, but yes, looks like it. I've bagged them and sent them for testing.'

'Good work. Right, you can add that to the list of questions. I want to know who brought the shrooms to the party, and if they all enjoyed the brew.' He turned to Brianna. 'Do you want to sit in on the interview with Natalie? I think it may be useful.'

'I'm happy to do that, I think she trusts me.'

'Good,' Meadows picked up a file and headed downstairs with Brianna.

* * *

Natalie was sat picking at her nails, a cup of untouched coffee on the table in front of her.

'Hi, Natalie.' Meadows took a seat and laid a file on the table before turning on the recording device and dealing with the formalities. Brianna sat next to Natalie.

'Natalie, you do understand that this is a formal interview?' Meadows asked.

Natalie nodded, and her eyes rested on the file.

'Brianna said that it was normal for you to interview everyone.'

'Yes, we're interviewing everyone that was at your house on Sunday night. I need to remind you that you are entitled to legal representation.'

Natalie shrugged. 'I don't need a solicitor.'

'Okay, but you can change your mind at any time during the interview and we can stop.'

Natalie nodded.

'You need to answer for the record.'

'Yes, I understand.'

'Firstly, I have to tell you that we found items of clothing that we believe belong to Ella.' Meadows took a photograph from the file and pushed it towards Natalie. 'Are these Ella's pyjamas?'

Natalie ran her fingers over the photo. 'Yes, they're Ella's. Where did you find them?'

'They were buried in the woods.'

Meadows watched Natalie's eyes widen. She wrapped her arms around her body and rocked in the chair.

'I don't understand. Why would her clothes be buried? Did someone take them off her?' Her bottom lip trembled. 'You've found her, haven't you?'

'No, we haven't found her.'

'But you think she's dead, that's why you've brought me here,' Natalie said.

Meadows watched Natalie's movements. Her whole body trembled, and her face was drained of colour. She continued to rock with her arms tight around her body, her shoulders hunched.

Either she's a good actress or she has nothing to do with Ella's disappearance, unless...

'Natalie, you were seen leaving the house at 2 a.m. You were wearing your pink coat and drove away in your car. You were gone for forty-five minutes. Where did you go?'

'I didn't go out. I'd been drinking so I wouldn't have driven anywhere.' She looked towards Brianna. 'I didn't go out.'

'What size shoes do you wear?'

'Five.'

'Do you own a pair of boots?'

'Yes.' Natalie looked confused. 'Why?'

'Do the boots have a block heel?'

'Yes.'

'We found footprints near where Ella's clothes were buried, a size five block heeled boot and a size ten trainer. Ryan is a size ten, isn't he?'

'I don't know.' Natalie shrank into the chair.

108

'Forensic officers are at your house and are also checking your car. They will be able to match the footprint to your boots, and any samples they take from the tread of the car will be matched against the soil in the woods. So, if you did drive out there then we're going to find out.'

'I didn't go into the woods, why won't you believe me?'

'You haven't been very honest with us from the start, Natalie. You lied about Ryan.'

'I told you why.'

'How do you account for your car being driven off by someone wearing your pink coat and matching your description?'

'I don't know.' Natalie sniffed and wiped her eyes with the back of her hand. 'Maybe someone put on my coat to look like me and drove the car.'

'Why would someone do that?'

'I don't know, maybe whoever took Ella wanted you to think it was me. I can't find my coat.'

Maybe because you buried it in the woods as well.

Meadows sat back in the chair and folded his hands.

'Okay, Natalie, let's look at that possibility. Do other people drive your car?'

'No. Well, Claire sometimes. She drops me off at work, so she has the car to pick Ella up from nursery when I'm working late.'

'Does Claire know where you keep the car keys, or does she have a set of her own?'

'She has her own keys.'

'So, Claire could have waited until you were all asleep, put on your coat and taken Ella from her cot?'

'Yes, but Claire wouldn't take Ella, she loves her.'

'What about Ryan?'

'Ryan wouldn't take my car, he has his own.'

'He could have gone with Claire, maybe it was his idea to take Ella.'

'No, he was sleeping on the sofa with me, I would have felt him get up and come back later.'

'Well that depends on how drunk you were. How much did you drink last night?'

Natalie shrugged. 'A few I guess, the boys brought around some cans.'

'And you had a few joints?'

'Some of us.'

'Come on, Natalie, we know you like to have a smoke and we know you were smoking last night.'

'Okay.' Natalie huffed. 'I shared a joint with the others, everyone does it.' She looked at Brianna.

'Who brought the shrooms to the party?'

Natalie opened her mouth, then shut it again.

'We found the teapot with the evidence so there's no use denying it. You had yourself a little brew.'

Natalie shot Brianna a scathing look. 'I'm not saying any more.'

Meadows leaned forward and pushed the photo of Ella's clothes further towards Natalie.

'Your child is missing. Do you want to help us find her or is this just a game? Did you take Ella into the woods? Did she have an accident? You panicked then had to make up a story about her being taken.'

'No, that's not what happened.'

'Then tell us what happened,' Brianna coaxed. 'All we want to do is find Ella.'

'I got up in the morning and she was gone, I'm telling you the truth.'

'What happened? You've told us you were drinking and smoking marijuana. You all went out the garden. What were you doing out there?'

'I don't know.'

'You don't know, or you won't tell us.'

'I can't remember.' Natalie put her head in her hands. 'I don't know what happened,' she sobbed. 'I can't remember anything.'

Meadows felt a coldness creep over his skin. *If she doesn't remember, anything could have happened to that little girl. I thought maybe she had a few blank moments but what if she can't remember the whole night?*

'You took the mushrooms?'

'Yes, I remember what I was doing before that. We were just having a good time. I've taken them before and nothing bad ever happened.'

'Do you remember anything?'

'No, just flashes. I was out the garden, I think. It was raining, silver thread landing on my skin, it felt good.'

'Your clothes were covered in mud and there was dirt under your fingernails,' Meadows said.

'Yes, I was digging.'

'In the woods?'

'No, in the garden.'

'With Ella?'

'No, Ella wasn't with me.'

'Are you sure?'

'Yes.'

'Who brought the mushrooms?'

Natalie shrugged. 'What does it matter?'

'Well someone might not want you to remember Sunday night.'

'I can't tell you.'

'Because you're afraid, or because you want to protect Ryan? Isn't your daughter more important?'

'Yes, she is, but we all took the mushrooms, we were all out of it. I can't remember what happened last night, but I do know that I would never hurt Ella.'

'Until you remember you can't be certain of that. You could have had a bad trip.'

'No.' Natalie shook her head.

'You could have driven into the woods with Ella.'

'Oh God.' Sobs wracked Natalie's body.

'Natalie, we're going to keep you here until we've finished the search of your house. In the meantime, I suggest you think hard about last night and it may also be wise to take some legal advice now.'

111

Meadows stood and ended the interview. He watched as Natalie was led to a waiting room.

Blackwell came out of the opposite interview room, his face thunderous.

'Get anything out of Jamie?' Meadows asked.

'No, he's sticking to his story. I pushed as hard as I could. Reckons he was out of it most of the night.'

'Natalie says pretty much the same. Can't remember what happened after they took the mushrooms.'

'You believe her?'

'Yes, I think she's telling the truth. But that doesn't mean she wasn't involved in Ella's disappearance.'

'Great, well as it stands we have nothing to charge them with, it's not like we have a body.'

'We have the clothes, a missing child, and footprints.' Meadows sighed. 'You're right it's not enough. Let's hope forensics turn up something.'

'Or we could just charge the lot with abduction. One of them is bound to crack.' Blackwell said. 'They can't all claim drug-induced amnesia.'

'No, but it could've been planned. Two of them could have pulled it off. Got Natalie off her face and taken the child.'

'What, and sell the kid or kill her for kicks?'

Meadows felt a sickness in the pit of his stomach. 'It would help if we knew who brought the mushrooms to the party. Natalie's not telling so I'm betting she's protecting Ryan. Come on, let's see if he has returned to earth. You can sit in and use your charm.'

'My pleasure,' Blackwell said grinning.

* * *

Ryan sat with a scowl upon his face and fingers drumming the table. The solicitor sat next to him scribbling notes on a writing pad.

Blackwell turned on the recording device, announced the time, date, and those present, before sitting down. He pulled his chair forward and glared at Ryan. 'Where's the girl?'

'I dunno, told you I was only there for ten minutes Sunday night. Didn't even see the kid. If I knew anything, I would happily tell you.' A smile played on his lips.

'You were at Natalie's house all night Sunday. You didn't leave until eleven yesterday morning. We have witnesses,' Meadows said.

'They're lying. I've answered your questions, you've no reason to keep me here.' He looked at the solicitor.

The solicitor cleared his throat. 'As I understand it, you haven't charged my client.'

'Your client will be charged with an assault on a police officer for a start.' Meadows resisted the urge to rub his shoulder.

'Self-defence, mate.' Ryan smirked. 'I thought someone was breaking into the flat.'

'My officers clearly identified themselves when they entered your property. There was sufficient light and you were facing me when you attacked me with an iron bar. Not what I'd call self-defence,' Meadows said.

'You nearly broke my back,' Ryan retorted.

'I used reasonable force to disarm you. So, you're not going to worm your way out of this one.'

'I assume you had a warrant,' the solicitor said.

'You assume correctly.' Meadows took a copy of the warrant from the file and handed it to the solicitor.

The solicitor scanned the document and furrowed his eyebrows.

'This is in connection to the missing child.'

'Yes,' Blackwell said. 'Now we're all on the same page let's get on with it. We have witnesses that place your client in the home of Natalie Beynon on the night her daughter Ella went missing. We also have a match from the trainers taken from your client's home to a print found where the child's clothes were buried in Coopers Wood.'

'That's bullshit.' Ryan's fist slammed into the table. 'You're trying to stitch me up.'

Blackwell took two photographs from the file, laid them side by side and shoved them towards Ryan. He pointed to the first photograph.

'This is the print taken from the woods, size ten, the same as you wear. This one' – Blackwell jabbed at the photo – 'is from your trainer. Exact match. We also took a sample of the earth from the tread of your trainer and surprise, it's a match to the soil found in Coopers Wood.'

Ryan's eyes narrowed as he stared at the photos, then his face relaxed and he sat back in the chair.

'Yeah, I was in the woods yesterday. I went with Claire and Jamie to help search for Ella. Loads of people saw us.'

How convenient, he probably went into the woods to cover his tracks and keep an eye on things. Slimy sucker was undoubtedly laughing behind our backs.

'The thing is, the search parties were nowhere near where we found the prints.'

'Yeah, well I may have wandered off for a bit, had a smoke, for medical reasons. Had to go away from the group as you lot can be a bit funny about the herbal.'

'Stop pissing us about,' Blackwell snapped. 'You took that little girl into Coopers Wood, stripped her and–'

'No! I'm not a fucking perv.'

'What were you doing with her then?' Blackwell's eyes glinted dangerously.

'Nothing, I didn't take her.' Ryan turned to the solicitor. 'Are you listening to this shit? Are you going to say something or what?'

'My client has given you an explanation as to why his footprint may have been in the woods. It looks like a fairly standard trainer to me. A lot of young men wear trainers and are a size ten, wouldn't you agree?'

'And what's the probability of an exact match? That, together with the fact that your client was in the house at the time the child went missing and lied when questioned, doesn't look good,' Meadows said.

'I didn't want to get Natalie into trouble, I think she has enough on her plate,' Ryan said.

Meadows could sense Blackwell's frustration. A vein throbbed in his forehead and his jaw was set.

He's going to lose his temper in a minute. Time to try a different angle.

'Quite a little factory you've got going in your attic. Must have cost a bit to set up.'

'So now we get to it, you use the kid as an excuse to have a shifty around my place. Don't think you're allowed to do that.' Ryan smirked.

'Finding the drugs was a bonus,' Blackwell said. 'You're not going to squirm your way out of this one. So, what was it, someone paid you off to snatch the kid?'

'You've got a sick mind,' Ryan snarled. 'Actually, it's not my place, I'm just house sitting for a mate. Drugs up the attic you say, I've never been up there.'

'I'm sure forensics will say differently.' Meadows smiled. 'Where did you get the money for the set up?'

Ryan shrugged. 'I don't know what you're talking about.'

'Sunday night you had a party, drinks, and drugs. No point in denying it, the others have coughed,' Blackwell said. 'Even your sister. They're more interested in saving their own arses than covering for you. I suppose you're not much of a threat if you're banged up. They were more than happy to tell us that you brought some mushrooms to the party.'

Ryan grinned. 'Don't think so. I may have brought some bacon and eggs for brekky but I'm not keen on mushrooms.'

'Cut the crap,' Blackwell barked. 'Shrooms, hallucinogenic drugs. You were all off your faces.'

'If you've nothing to hide then your story should match what the others have told us,' Meadows said. 'Just tell us what happened on Sunday night.'

'I told you I don't know what happened to the kid. Nat put her to bed, I didn't see her after that. I'm not saying any more, let me go or charge me.' Ryan sat back in the chair his knees bouncing up and down.

'What's the matter? Nicotine withdrawals kicking in or do you need a toke?' Blackwell leaned across the table. 'Talk us through Sunday night and we can get things moving, or I'm happy to stay here for as long as it takes.'

Ryan huffed. 'Got to Nat's about six, she put Ella to bed. We had a few drinks, smokes, and a brew, then I crashed on the sofa.'

'You were out the garden,' Meadows said. 'What were you doing out there?'

'Just messing around. We were pretty wasted.'

This is just wasting time.

Meadows stood up. 'Charge him with assault and cultivation of cannabis and put him back in the cell.'

'What! You can't do that.' Ryan leaped from his chair. 'You have nothing on me.'

'Sit down,' Blackwell said. 'You can tell your story to the magistrate. In the meantime, I suggest you think long and hard about what happened on Sunday night. A little girl is missing, and it doesn't look good for you.'

* * *

Meadows left the interview room and headed back upstairs where the rest of the team were gathered. 'Please tell me you have something?'

'All the same story,' Edris said. 'Few drinks, a brew, and passed out in the sitting room. Didn't see or hear the child.'

'No one is owning up to supplying the mushrooms,' Paskin said.

'Claire wears a size six shoe,' Valentine said. 'She admits to taking the mushrooms and only vaguely remembers being out the garden, sounds like they were all tripping.'

'He's back in his cell and kicking off,' Blackwell informed them as he walked in followed by Lester.

'Carry on,' Lester said and took a seat.

'We've got Natalie's clothing, shoes, boots, and laptop,' Valentine said. 'So far there hasn't been a match to the boots.'

Maybe she has another pair of boots and they have conveniently gone missing like her coat.

'Okay, I want her finances checked, see if she was in debt and if she's received any unusual payments. Check the search history and social media on her laptop, see if she's been complaining about being a single working mother and if she searched any adoption sites. That goes for Ryan too, the money for his cannabis venture must have come from somewhere. Nia also suggested that he may have an unhealthy interest in children. Get the tech guys to give his laptop a thorough search.'

'What about Claire, Jamie, and Dan?' Paskin asked. 'We don't have anything solid to link them to Ella's disappearance other than the fact they were at the house. No match on the shoeprints.'

'Doesn't mean they're not involved,' Blackwell said.

Meadows suddenly felt an overwhelming fatigue. He walked to the incident board and massaged the back of his neck.

'They can stay here until the search teams have finished then I guess we have to let them go. Brianna will be with Natalie so she can keep an eye on her, but unless she gets some sort of flashback, even Natalie doesn't know if she's involved in her daughter's disappearance.'

Lester stood and looked around the team.

'You've all done an impeccable job so far, but I think it's time you all went home and got some rest.'

117

'I think there may be a chance that she's still alive,' Meadows said. 'She's already been missing for over thirty hours, maybe as much as thirty-eight. Her chances are diminishing by the minute.'

'The search teams are still in the woods, we are following up leads on the appeal, and I've got a team in to sub you. You can't work to your full potential when you're all exhausted. How much sleep did you get last night?'

I didn't.

Meadows looked around at the team, Lester was right, they all looked exhausted. 'He's right, go on, all of you get home and get some rest.'

'That goes for you too,' Lester said.

The phone on Meadows' desk trilled. Edris who was the nearest leaned over and picked it up. The room grew silent as they listened to Edris' conversation and Meadows felt a cold creep over his skin. Edris replaced the phone and looked at Meadows.

'They've found a body.'

Chapter Fourteen

I had to go and look. I couldn't help myself. It's like those detective dramas you see on the TV where the police hang around the victim's funeral convinced that the murderer will turn up. It's true, there is an inexplicable desire to return to the place you ran from, a place you never wanted to see again. It would've been different if I had someone to confide in, someone to tell me that it would be madness to go there, and maybe I would've stayed away, but there is no one. This is my burden alone, my secret. So, I went. It took me a long time to decide where to park the car. I thought of going into the woods, no one would see me there. But I couldn't, it was still cordoned off with the search. I parked on the other side of the estate and walked. I pulled my hair back and didn't bother with make-up. I was certain no one would know me and I would blend in.

As I walked towards the house, I could see a police car and a van parked outside. One man came out of the house dressed in protective clothing, he opened the van and took out a box before returning to the house. I hurried along, hoping to get a glimpse inside before he shut the door, but he was too quick.

I slowed down as I passed the house, my heart was thudding in my chest making my ears ring. I forced myself to keep moving and as I walked past I glanced down the side path. I saw them silently combing the garden and my stomach twisted. I thought I was going to be sick and found my feet wouldn't move. I was sure one of them was going to spot me and come down the path, demand to know what I was doing there. Panic made my hands shake and there didn't seem to be enough oxygen in the air. The pavement moved beneath my feet and I reached out a hand to steady myself.

I don't know how long I stood there, it seemed like hours, but it must only have been a few moments. It took all my strength not to walk down the path and put an end to it, instead I forced my feet to move; small steps. The next-door neighbour was stood at her door, a small boy at her feet. I talked to her for a few minutes and explained that I just wanted to see if there was news on the missing child. She told me no, but that the mother had been taken away in a police car and that her boyfriend had been arrested. I felt nothing but pity for the child's mother and what she must be going through. I realised how foolish I'd been to come and turned to hurry back to the car.

I almost made it, but he was walking past my car. I kept my eyes down hoping he wouldn't recognise me, but of course he did, he called my name and a smile lit his face. He invited me back for a drink, I couldn't refuse, I could tell by his face that he knew he still had a hold on me. The house was just the same, same worn furniture, same smell. It brought back the feelings of shame that left my skin creeping. I knew what he wanted, and it was the only way to buy his silence, so I told him to put the dog outside and not bother with the tea.

His greedy hands groped my body as we walked up the stairs to the bedroom. I felt sick. Now that he had found me again, there would be no end. There was only one way out.

Chapter Fifteen

A small crowd had gathered outside Natalie's house and were craning their necks to see into the garden. On the opposite side of the road, neighbours gathered on their doorsteps.

'How come this lot are hanging around, we've only just got the call ourselves,' Edris said from the back seat.

'Probably one of the neighbours peeking over the fence.' Meadows switched off the engine.

'Move them along,' Lester said over his shoulder. 'We don't want this lot speculating and calling the papers. The place will be crawling with the press.'

They got out of the car. Meadows and Lester took the side path leading to the garden, leaving Edris to deal with the gossips. A tent had been erected over stony earth where the patio had been pulled up. Natalie's dogs could be heard barking from within the house and were joined by the yapping of the neighbour's dog on the other side of the fence.

Mike was stood outside the tent while the other forensic officers carefully combed the rest of the garden. 'Not what we were expecting to find,' Mike said. 'There's just enough room for the two of you to squeeze in.'

Meadows followed Mike into the tent and crouched by the makeshift grave.

'Good Lord,' Lester exclaimed.

Meadows peered at the tiny skeleton, perfectly formed, with remnants of material and plastic clinging to the bones.

'Daisy's on her way, although I doubt there's much she'll be able to tell you at this stage,' Mike said.

Meadows felt a tingle in his stomach at the mention of her name and instinctively rubbed his hand over his face.

I should've shaved. Oh, stop your nonsense, there are more important things to worry about.

'Did you pull up the slabs?' he asked.

'No, most of them were already up and the earth disturbed. Lots of shoeprints and it looks like the dogs have had a bit of a dig, but the skeleton wasn't exposed. We just took off a layer of earth to be thorough. Just as well, as no one would ever have known the poor mite was there.'

'Someone knew,' Meadows said.

'One missing child and another buried in the garden, the press will have a field day with this,' Lester said.

'Looks like this one has been here quite a while,' Mike said.

'So, what's your story, little one, and whose secret are you keeping?' Meadows stood up in time to see Edris poke his head in the tent.

'Daisy is here.' Edris gave Meadows a sly wink.

'I'll give you some room,' Mike said. He left the tent, followed by Lester.

Meadows stood a little straighter as Daisy Moore entered the tent. He gave her a smile which he hoped looked natural.

She peered into the grave, her eyes filled with pity. Meadows thought he saw a look of pain flit across her face before she appeared to compose herself and kneel on the ground.

'Are you okay?' Meadows asked.

'Yes of course,' Daisy snapped. She sighed and relaxed her shoulders. 'Sorry, it's just… well, when it's a child…'

'Yes,' Meadows agreed, although he was sure there was more to Daisy's unease. He watched as she carefully examined the skeleton. Her long black hair was twisted and pinned up to reveal an elegant neck.

'She's about three months old.'

'A little girl then?' Meadows crouched down besides Daisy.

'No, well I don't know, but I'm not going to refer to her as it.'

'Okay, that's fine.'

This was not the Daisy that Meadows was used to.

Is she angry with me or is it something else? I hope it's the latter.

'Is there anything you can tell me?'

'Not a lot I'm afraid. It's going to be difficult if not impossible to give you a cause of death, unless I find any obvious fractures. She's been in here a while. Could be twenty years or more. You'll need a forensic anthropologist; I'll make a few calls. Meanwhile I'll take a few soil samples and get her moved. Maybe what's left of the material can tell us something. If you look here.' She pointed to the pelvic area. 'Looks like the remains of a disposable nappy, I think they became popular in the seventies.'

'You think she could've been here that long?'

'It's possible. Like I said, I will need to run some tests, but I'll push them through as quickly as possible, get a DNA profile, and sex.'

'Thank you.'

Daisy nodded and turned her attention back to the skeleton. 'Right sweetie, let's make a start on getting you out.'

'I'll leave you to it.' Meadows stood and left the tent. Lester was talking to Edris who looked like he was struggling not to yawn.

'I think it's worth talking to the neighbour,' Meadows said. 'He's lived here for thirty years. He might be able to tell us who lived here and who laid the patio.'

'It can wait until the morning,' Lester said. 'There's nothing you can do for that little one tonight. Drop me back at the station and go get yourself some rest.'

As much as Meadows wanted to stay, he had to admit that he was struggling, his head hurt, shoulder throbbed, and his mood was low. He didn't feel like going home so he dropped off Lester and Edris then drove to his mother's house. The smell of herbs and freshly baked bread in the kitchen eased his headache as he sat and watched his mother prepare camomile tea, her long plaited hair swinging across her back as she padded barefoot across the tiles.

'You look shattered, love.' Fern placed a mug on the table. 'You drink this, it will help you sleep. I bet you've been filling your body with crap all day to stay awake.'

'Yeah, I've drunk a fair amount of coffee, I can't exactly send Edris to get a cup of herbal,' he said. 'I get enough stick about being a veggie as it is. Anyway, I enjoy a cup of coffee and black tea.'

'Closet hippy.' Fern laughed. 'You should just be yourself.'

'I am.' Meadows sipped his tea. 'I came over to see if you've got something for my shoulder. I got in the way of an iron bar.' He undid his shirt and pulled back the material to reveal the bruise.

'I'll get some arnica. I've got a jar made up somewhere.' She rummaged through the cupboards. 'Then I'll make you something to eat.'

'Don't trouble yourself, I'm not hungry.'

'Nonsense.' Fern took a jar from the cupboard and handed it to Meadows. 'Rub that in, it will take care of the bruising.'

'Thanks.'

'Rumour is you found the girl buried in the garden.'

124

Fern took a loaf of homemade bread from the barrel.

'Typical, I suppose I expected the gossips to reach that conclusion.' Meadows winced as he rubbed in the tincture.

'So, it wasn't the girl?' Fern asked as she sliced through the bread.

'No, we found a skeleton of a three-month-old child but—'

'Yes, just between you and me.' Fern smiled. 'Sounds like that house is cursed. Do you think there's a connection?'

'Don't see how there could be, looks like the poor mite has been there for twenty to thirty years. Maybe longer. You don't remember any babies going missing, do you?'

'We kept to ourselves in the commune, didn't even bother with the newspaper. I do have a vague memory of a child being snatched from a hospital, Cardiff I think, must have been twenty-five years ago.' She placed a plate of bread and cheese on the table. 'It might not be a missing child, you often hear of teenage girls who get in trouble, manage to hide it and give birth alone.'

'Yes, but they leave the baby somewhere, not keep it for three months and bury it in the garden.'

'No, I guess not, but people do strange things.' Fern grabbed a slice of bread. 'Did you run into Daisy?'

Meadows felt the heat rise in his neck. 'Yes, but you shouldn't listen to Edris.'

'Oh, I'm not. It's obvious you like the girl,' Fern said.

'Well even if that's the case I'm not sure she likes me, she was a little off today.'

'I expect she has a lot on her mind. Who wouldn't like you?! You know that girl from the cake shop, Marina, I think she might be single. Lovely girl.'

'Mum, stop trying to set me up, I'm fine as I am.'

'No, you're not, you need someone to love. Someone you can go home to and offload your troubles. Not that I mind your visits. I look forward to them. I just want to see you settled before I go.'

125

'You're not going anywhere for a while,' Meadows said.

Maybe she's not well and she wants to prepare me. The thought knotted his stomach.

'Are you feeling okay?'

'I'm fine. I take it you have no leads on the missing child.'

'No, it looks like the mother may be involved but was drugged up at the time so doesn't remember anything. I'm fairly certain the boyfriend had a hand in the child's disappearance, but we have no solid evidence. There are things that don't add up and I feel like someone is playing games with us.'

'I'm sure you will work it out, you always do.'

'I hope so and that someone doesn't dig up another skeleton twenty years from now.'

Chapter Sixteen

Meadows walked into the office feeling clear-headed and fresh after a night of rest. The crisp spring air still clung to his clothes and the early morning sun shone through the window, lifting his spirits. Lester was sat at his desk looking anything but refreshed.

He should take his own advice and get some rest, he must be feeling the pressure from the media to get a quick result. I wouldn't like to walk in his shoes.

Meadows smiled as he approached the desk. 'Morning, sir.'

'Morning.' Lester looked up from his paperwork. 'I'm afraid the night didn't bring any developments. The financial reports and computer analysis you requested are on your desk. Nothing more was found in the garden and the search of the woods proved fruitless. Search and rescue are now extending the search to surrounding fields and the mountain. I don't hold out much hope of bringing her home safely. It's been three nights if we go with the assumption that she was taken during Sunday night.'

'There's still the possibility that she was handed over to someone, then she could be anywhere in the country. Any more sightings reported?'

'No, the phone calls have tapered off. I'll have to make an announcement to the press regarding the remains that were found in the garden. I'm hoping that the attention on the house will keep the missing child in the forefront of the public's minds.'

'I agree, it will keep people talking. We need to move fast to identify the child; once the news breaks there could be some anxious parents out there hoping that they can finally have some answers. I'll make a start looking at missing babies over the last thirty or more years. There can't be that many but we're likely to get an influx of calls once the news spreads. On the other hand, someone with a long-buried secret is about to get rattled.'

'Well, I'll leave you to it,' Lester said picking up his jacket. 'Keep me updated.'

Meadows grabbed a mug of tea from the kitchen and carried it back to his desk. The first thing he noticed was a set of photographs showing the skeleton taken from different angles. He laid them to one side and started reading through the reports. As he sat absorbed in the contents, he became aware of voices drifting into the room as the team filtered in looking fresh faced and full of the usual banter.

'Great timing,' Meadows called out. 'I've just finished reading through the reports on Natalie's finances and Ryan's laptop.' He swung his chair around so he was facing the group. 'It seems that Natalie is heavily in debt. She has CCJs for non-payment of council tax and water rates which resulted in an attachment of earnings. This takes a chunk out of her wages, which given the hours she claims to work doesn't add up to very much. She is maxed out on credit cards, catalogues, and has payday loans that are spiralling out of control. There are no large payments, just cash withdrawals, twenty or thirty pounds at a time but taken out most days.'

'So, if someone was to offer her a large cash sum for an illegal adoption, looks like she might be tempted,' Paskin said.

'Yes, I guess that could be a motive,' Meadows agreed. 'But if it is a staged abduction it wasn't well thought out.'

'It's not like they have many brain cells between them,' Blackwell said.

'The buried clothes could've been put there to distract us I suppose,' Meadows added. 'There are also weekly receipts other than her wages that come from a company called Serenity. I haven't had time to check them on Companies House yet.'

'You don't need to,' Blackwell said. 'It's a knocking shop fronted as a massage parlour.'

'Regular visitor, are you?' Edris grinned.

'Ha, bloody ha.' Blackwell gave Edris a scathing look.

'Better check it out; want to go, Edris?' Meadows said.

'I think it would be better to send one of the girls.'

'Pussy.' Valentine laughed. 'I'll go. I've always wanted to have a look around one of those places. I'll bring you back a whip, Edris.'

'Thank you, Valentine. Make sure you take someone with you,' Meadows said. 'Okay, back to the reports. Forensics didn't find any indication that Ella sustained any form of injury in the house. There were various drugs found within easy reach of a child, so we can't rule out the possibility that she accidently took something, and Natalie panicked. All of this is just supposition. We only have the witness statement that places Natalie in her car the night Ella went missing, there's nothing to tie her to the clothes found in the woods. Our main suspect is Ryan given the match to the footprint found in the woods. Unfortunately, it is not sufficient evidence and no jury would convict him on the footprint and circumstantial evidence alone. He's due before the magistrates on assault and drug related charges this afternoon.'

Meadows continued, 'The technicians found some fairly hard-core pornography on his computer, and although he appears to like his eh... actresses young, they do appear to be of legal age. There were also several home movies, one filmed on Sunday night which involved Natalie, Dan, Claire and Jamie.'

'You mean an orgy?' Paskin asked.

'Yes. The film was checked for any visible or audible signs of Ella, but none were found,' Meadows said.

'Basically, we have fuck all,' Blackwell grumbled.

'We have to keep digging. Intelligence is looking into known paedophile rings. Ella's face is all over the newspapers, and posters are on every lamppost. If someone has her, they aren't going to be able to keep her hidden for long. There are now over a hundred officers involved in the search, plus search and rescue. Every outbuilding is being searched and uniform are extending house to house enquiries. If she's still in the area, we will find her.'

'If she's still alive,' Paskin said.

'Yes, but until there is no hope, we keep looking and putting pressure on Natalie and her friends. In the meantime, we have this little Miss or Mr who deserves our attention.'

He picked up the picture from his desk and walked over to the incident board and pinned it.

'We don't have a lot to go on. Daisy is working on a DNA profile and a timeframe of how long this little one has been in the ground, could be thirty years or more. This is a three-month-old child, so it's unlikely to be a young mother who is trying to hide the birth of her baby. This little one must be missed by someone, so start by looking for missing babies, work backwards to say forty years. Also, we need a list of all the previous residents of the house. I'm going to see Natalie this morning, so I will call on the neighbour, he's lived there a long time. He may have some useful information.'

'Surely you can't think the cases are connected,' Blackwell said.

'No, but then again' – Meadows ran his hand across his temple – 'it's quite a coincidence that it's the same house. What if the person that buried the child in the garden had suffered a breakdown? Maybe they couldn't cope or the child died and they panicked. Something triggers them all these years later, they get confused, think of Ella as their own child and take her.'

'That's a bit of a stretch,' Paskin said. 'We don't know how long the skeleton has been hidden in the garden. If it's forty years, then it would put the mother in her sixties.'

'But if it's twenty years the mother could be in her forties,' Edris said.

'That's assuming whoever buried the child was the parent,' Valentine said.

'That's why we need to look for missing babies. If someone took a baby twenty or thirty years ago and got away with it they may have tried again and taken Ella,' Meadows said.

Blackwell huffed. 'We should be putting all our effort into finding Ella.'

'We are doing everything that can be done to find Ella. Until search and rescue find something, or we have something solid on Ryan and Natalie, we have hit a dead end. I think that this is our best line of enquiry, it's all we've got.'

'There's always the chance that someone will come forward with new information, especially given the media attention on the house,' Paskin said.

'Yes, there's that too and if there is any chance there is a connection between the two cases, no matter how small, we have to look into it,' Meadows said. He turned to the board and pointed to the tiny skeleton. 'This one deserves to have an identity, a decent burial, and maybe a family can gain some peace.'

'Yeah alright,' Blackwell grumbled.

'Good.' Meadows grabbed his coat before heading out of the office with Edris.

* * *

'You should just send Blackwell out with the search party, get the miserable sod out of our way,' Edris said as they drove towards Natalie's house.

'He's just frustrated that we haven't found Ella, I can't blame him.' Meadows' attention was caught by the posters that were pinned to the lampposts, all showing a smiling Ella with the words 'missing' printed in bold letters. 'Someone knows where she is.'

'Well there will be plenty of people who will want to dish the dirt on Ryan if they think he has anything to do with Ella's disappearance. I get the impression he's not well liked.'

'Yes, and most of the valley will know that he's being questioned. He better hope, for his own safety, that the magistrate doesn't grant him bail. The last thing we need is a lynch mob taking matters into their own hands.'

'Yeah, well it would serve him right if he's done something to that little girl,' Edris said.

'That's a big "if". We don't have any proof. I'm not even sure myself anymore. Besides, I would rather see him convicted by a jury and made accountable for his actions.'

'And what does Ryan have to do with the skeleton in the garden?'

'I don't know, probably nothing.'

'It's gotta to be him. He was there, and we matched his footprint,' Edris said.

'Yes, remember what Mike said about the print being weighted at the front. Ryan doesn't appear to have a limp or any problems walking. All the footwear taken from the house was the same size, so the trainers weren't too big.'

'Maybe he was staggering, he was off his face,' Edris said.

'Or someone took his trainers to implicate him.'

'But who? Natalie? She's been trying to protect him the whole time.'

'Or is that just a cover?' Meadows stopped the car and sighed. 'I don't know, I'm not sure what to make of her. She seems genuine when she says that she doesn't remember what happened that night but doesn't appear to feel guilty. Most mothers would be frantic with worry and full of remorse if they'd got off their face and their child went missing.'

'Yeah well, there's something wrong with that one, wheel is spinning but the hamster's dead, I reckon.' Edris grinned.

'You have such a way with words.' Meadows laughed. 'Come on, let's see what George can tell us about his past neighbours.'

There was no answer at George's house. Meadows stepped back and looked at the upstairs windows.

'Curtains are open so he must be up, he said he slept in the front bedroom. Maybe he's popped out for a paper.'

'Or he's done a runner.' Edris nodded to himself. 'Yeah, for all we know he could have buried that kid in the garden and now he's spooked. He probably snatched Ella as well, he did have a key.'

'You think George snatched a baby, jumped over the garden fence, dug a hole, then laid a patio? Still, you never know.' Meadows smiled. 'We'll call back later.'

Raised voices could be heard coming from the sitting room when Brianna opened the door.

'They've been at each other's throats for the past half an hour,' Brianna said.

Meadows entered the sitting room and saw Nia sat in the armchair, her face was flushed and her lips set in a hard line. Natalie was sat on the sofa puffing on a roll-up.

'There have been no new developments overnight,' Meadows said as he took a seat in the remaining chair.

Edris walked a little further into the room but remained standing. Brianna took a seat next to Natalie.

'See, there's no point me sitting around here, it's driving me mad.' Natalie glared at Nia.

'Nat wants to go back to work. I told her it's a ridiculous idea, what will people think?'

'I don't give a shit what people think,' Natalie seethed. 'I need the money, we don't all have a husband and savings in the bank.'

'I go out to work,' Nia retorted. 'I've taken leave to support you. If one of my girls was missing the last thing I would think of is work or bloody money.'

She's got a point.

Meadows leaned forward. 'I understand your frustration, Natalie, but I don't think it's a good idea at the moment. I'm sure your workplace will give you paid compassionate leave. Besides, we are going to need you to be available for further questioning. I have to inform you that we're still treating Ryan as a person of interest and we still can't rule out the possibility that you went into the woods on Sunday night.' He glanced across at Nia.

Maybe she can knock some sense into her sister. Let's see what she makes of Natalie's blackout.

'By your own admission you can't remember what happened that night.'

'What do you mean?' Nia looked at Meadows then turned to glare at Natalie. 'Were you that pissed, or did you take something else?'

'I... what does it matter? I can't remember what happened Sunday night.'

'You stupid bitch!' Nia fumed. 'Well, you can forget going back to work, you can focus on remembering what happened. I'll drag you to a bloody hypnotist if I have to.'

That's a good idea, let's hope she carries out her threat.

Meadows looked at Natalie, her fists were clenched, and eyes narrowed.

'Why don't you just piss off,' Natalie said. 'I'm fed up with you and Leanne telling me what I should do and who I can see. I'm surprised she isn't here sticking her nose in.'

'I told her there was no point in coming over until there was any news. You can't expect her to drag Eli along and sit around waiting.'

'You've no right to decide, maybe I want Leanne to come over.'

'Fine.' Nia threw her hands up in the air. 'Give her a call and ask her.'

'I'm not asking her for anything, I can manage on my own.'

Nia shook her head in frustration. 'Whatever. Maybe she should come, perhaps she can talk some sense into you.'

I wonder how she would react if she knew Nia and Leanne had reported her to social services.

Meadows could sense that Nia was close to losing her temper and walking out. He wanted to see Nia's reaction when asked about Serenity, but thought it best to calm things down a bit first.

'Why did you start pulling up the patio slabs in the garden?' Meadows looked at Natalie.

'What?' Confusion creased her face.

'Most of the patio slabs had been pulled up before the officers searched the garden,' Edris said.

Natalie scowled. 'So now you think I buried that child in the garden.'

'Don't be so bloody ridiculous,' Nia snapped.

'We just need to know if there was any particular reason,' Edris said.

Natalie's face relaxed. 'It was Nia's idea.'

'The old slabs were crumbling and dangerous for Ella, so I thought I would give Nat a hand to clear the garden and organise a new patio to be laid. Not that she took much interest.'

'Yeah, well if you worked as hard as I do then you wouldn't feel like messing around in the garden on your day off.'

'How many hours do you work at the factory?' Meadows asked.

'It depends. I work the two till ten shifts but take overtime when I can. I work on a Saturday and have Monday off.'

Meadows looked at Edris and nodded.

'What about Serenity?' Edris asked.

'What's that?' Colour rose in Natalie's cheeks.

'The place you work part-time,' Edris said.

'No.' Natalie opened her tobacco tin and plucked out a paper. 'I only work in the factory.'

Meadows looked at Nia who had a puzzled expression on her face.

She doesn't know.

'You receive regular payments from them,' Edris said.

'No, I don't.' Natalie rolled the tobacco keeping her eyes down cast.

'Look, Natalie.' Meadows sat forward in the chair. 'We've been through your bank statements and an officer is visiting Serenity to talk to the staff, so there is no point in lying to us.'

'I work there on weekends.' Natalie lit the cigarette and inhaled deeply. 'I needed the extra money.'

'What exactly is it that you do?' Meadows asked.

'I'm a receptionist.'

Nia laughed. 'You can barely spell your own name, let alone anyone else's. What is this place?'

'It appears to be a massage parlour,' Edris said.

'A massage parlour? Are you trying to tell me it's a… it's a whore house?'

'There are rumours that it's not a reputable establishment,' Edris said.

'You're a prostitute!' Nia turned on Natalie.

'No, I'm not.' Natalie leapt up from the sofa. 'Just leave me alone!' She ran from the room and her footsteps could be heard thumping up the stairs.

'I'll go and talk to her in a minute,' Brianna said.

'I wouldn't bother, she won't speak to you for the rest of the day. She'll be sulking, always the same when she's been caught out lying,' Nia said. She ran her hands through her hair. 'I don't believe this. Do you think that she's done something to Ella?'

'We don't know,' Meadows said, 'but if I'm honest it doesn't look good.'

'I can't stay here.' Nia stood up.

'It might help if you spoke to her calmly, we really need her to remember what happened on Sunday night,' Meadows said.

'I'll try, but you have no idea what she's like.'

I think I'm beginning to see.

'Just try your best.' He turned to Brianna. 'Have you seen the next-door neighbour, George, this morning?'

'No, his dog has been outside all night yapping.'

'Okay, if you see him give us a call, we need to speak to him.'

'I will do.'

'I noticed you didn't mention the sex tape,' Edris said as they got into the car.

'No, I think Nia has had enough of a shock for one day. Natalie would probably deny it anyway.'

'Yeah, like Andy said, you can't believe that one's radio.' Edris laughed.

'Let's see what Valentine gets from Serenity. We'll also need to know the types of clients they entertain and if Natalie spent more time with a particular one.' He started the engine. 'We'll try Daisy next, see if she has anything more to tell us.'

'That should cheer you up,' Edris said with a grin.

'Shut up.' Meadows turned on the stereo and the car filled with music.

Chapter Seventeen

Meadows could hear laughter as he approached Daisy's office. The door was ajar, and he could see Daisy with her head turned towards a man perched on the edge of the desk. He had a mop of dark brown hair and steel rimmed glasses. Meadows guessed him to be in his thirties. He sat with an easy manner, his smile flirtatious. He stood when he saw Meadows and Edris approach.

Daisy turned her head. 'Hi, you just caught us taking a break.' She smiled. 'This is Theo, he's a forensic anthropologist. He came down last night to take a look at our little miss.'

Meadows introduced himself as he stepped forward and shook hands with Theo. 'Thank you for coming so quickly.'

'No problem,' Theo said. 'I know Daisy from years back, we studied together.'

Meadows was horrified to feel a sudden stab of jealousy.

'Come on, I'll show you what we've discovered so far, it's not a lot I'm afraid.' Daisy led them out of the office.

They entered the morgue and Meadows felt the temperature drop. Bright strip lights illuminated the sterile, stainless steel worktops and a faint chemical smell hung in the air. They gathered around a trolley where the pitifully small remains were laid out.

'We can now confirm that it is a little girl.' Daisy snapped on latex gloves.

'How do you know?' Edris asked.

'While there are some sexually distinctive traits in the mandible, this alone is not enough to reliably allocate a sex,' Theo said. 'So, we took samples of bone and ran DNA tests. Nuclear DNA–'

Daisy laughed. 'I think you're in danger of losing Edris.'

'Yeah, I think we'll stop at the DNA testing,' Edris agreed.

'We found a fracture to her skull which we couldn't see until we got her out of the ground.' Daisy turned the small skull and pointed to the injury.

'Is that how she died?' Meadows asked.

'I can't say with certainty, it may have been enough to cause a bleed to the brain. Then again, it could have been done post-mortem. My best guess is that it's likely that the head injury was contributory to her death. There are no other signs of trauma to the bones.'

'Any idea how long she's been in the ground?'

Daisy looked at Theo. 'You go ahead but keep it simple.'

'We tested the soil and took into consideration how she was wrapped. That, together with the tests we ran on the bones, gives us an estimate of about twenty-five, thirty years. That's our best guess. It could be more, or less. We have to run some more tests but I'm afraid it's difficult to give an accurate timeframe.'

'You guys must have been working all night,' Edris said.

'We did work quite late,' Daisy said. 'But she deserves no less attention than if she'd only been in the ground a few days.'

'I couldn't agree more,' Meadows said. 'We'll do all we can to find her identity.'

'Theo, do you want to take them through to the lab and show them what else we found? I'll just scrub up.' Daisy peeled off her gloves.

'Yeah.' Theo beamed. 'Come on.' He led the way.

'Winter.'

Meadows stopped and turned, the intimate use of his first name made his skin tingle.

'I should tell you... well, explain my behaviour yesterday.' Daisy took a paper towel and started drying her hands.

'I did get the impression that you weren't yourself,' Meadows said.

'No, I wasn't. When I was–'

'Are you coming?' Edris poked his head around the door.

Great timing, Edris.

'In a minute,' Meadows said, he turned back to Daisy.

'You go ahead, it can wait.' Daisy smiled.

Meadows reluctantly followed Edris to the lab, where Theo stood holding a small tray.

'What are we looking at?' Edris asked.

'These are some of the things we took out of the ground.' Theo pointed to a cluster of small round objects. 'Metal poppers, I suspect from a baby grow.'

'So, she was fully clothed?' Meadows asked.

'Yes, with the remains of a disposable nappy. There's also this.'

He clicked the mouse on his computer and the screen came to life.

'This is an enlargement of a remnant of material, possibly from the edging of a baby blanket. The material is polyester which doesn't break down like natural substances such as wool and cotton. There were more scraps that we need to look at and piece together.'

'You think she was wrapped in a blanket?'

'And plastic – a heavy duty bin bag,' Daisy said as she rejoined the group.

'Poor thing,' Edris said. 'What type of person puts a baby in a bin bag?'

'Well it does look like some care was taken when she was buried,' Daisy said. 'Her arms were folded across her chest and, I guess, wrapped in the blanket.'

'Maybe they thought the plastic would protect her,' Theo added.

'Looks like it's more likely to be a woman, perhaps even the mother,' Meadows said.

'Well, someone who had a bond with the child – she wasn't just thrown into the ground. Not that that's much consolation for her family,' Daisy said.

'No,' Meadows agreed. 'But maybe we can give them some closure and maybe some answers.'

'We'll let you know if we find anything else, like a make for the blanket, but I think it's unlikely,' Theo said.

'You've been a great help, thank you both for moving things along so quickly. Let's hope we can find an identity for her soon.'

Meadows wanted to say more, he wanted to tell Daisy that she could call him anytime she wanted, but it was not appropriate with Theo and Edris in the room. Instead he said goodbye and left the lab.

* * *

'Did I interrupt something back there?' Edris asked as they exited the building into a heavy shower of rain.

'No.' Meadows ran across the car park.

'Looks like you were having a moment,' Edris shouted above the pattering rain.

Meadows jumped in the car and shook the rain from his head.

'I think she wanted to tell me something but didn't want to talk in front of you.'

'Probably wants to ravish your body and is fed up of waiting for you to make a move.' Edris laughed.

'Seriously, I think something is troubling her and it's got to do with the little miss we found.'

'Well, now is your opportune moment to call her up and ask if she wants to meet for a chat.'

'No, I'm not making an idiot of myself, besides, she has her friend there. I'm sure she can confide in him.' Meadows started the engine and turned on the stereo.

Edris turned the volume down. 'Do I detect a hint of jealousy for the geeky Theo?'

Yes.

'No, anyway he's more her age.'

'You're not that much older than her. I reckon Theo is just a friend, she definitely wants a piece of the Winter Man.'

Meadows groaned. 'Only Kevin is allowed to call me that. If you're not careful I'll give you back to Blackwell. I'm sure Valentine won't mind swapping.'

'Okay, I won't say any more, but if you want I can set the two of you up.'

'I'll pass, thanks.'

Meadows turned up the volume and Black Sabbath filled the car. He let the music relax his mind then mapped out the next steps in the investigation as he kept a watchful eye on the road.

'Just in time for lunch,' Edris said as they pulled into the station car park. 'Well, lunch according to your timetable, more like teatime.'

'Go and grab something to eat and meet me upstairs. You can grab me a cheese sandwich while you're at it,' Meadows said.

* * *

The rest of the team were busy on the phone, or typing away at the computer, when Meadows entered the office. He walked through to the small kitchen off the side of the office and made two cups of tea. By the time he returned to his desk, Edris was already seated and munching on a sandwich.

'How did you get on with the staff at Serenity, Valentine?' Meadows asked.

'They were a little cagey to start with, but Hanes used his charm and a couple of the girls agreed to talk to us off the record. They told me that they do offer extras and Natalie works there on Friday and Saturday nights. Their busiest time.'

We need to find out if Natalie favoured any particular client, or if she took her work home,' Meadows said.

'I'll look into it,' Valentine said. 'But it's not going to be easy.'

'We can always threaten to sit outside and watch.' Blackwell sauntered over from his desk. 'I'm sure it will be good for business.'

'Whatever it takes,' Meadows said. 'Have a chat with Natalie's neighbours, see if they've noticed any male visitors. I tried to talk to George, who lives in the adjoining house, this morning but he was out. See if you can track him down. I bet he notices all the visitors to the house. How's it going with the missing babies list, Paskin?'

Paskin lifted her head from the computer. 'Only three in the last thirty years, but I can extend the search to the whole of the UK.'

'No, let's start with the three you've got.'

'Well, it's more like two. First one is a two-year-old boy.'

'Too old, and we now have confirmation that it's a little girl we're looking for.'

'Right, well, that narrows it down.' Paskin grabbed a couple of sheets of paper and joined the group. 'Cerys Lane, newborn baby, taken from hospital in Cardiff, April 1993; and Poppy Moore, four months old, taken from her home in Port Talbot, 1992. Both girls are still listed as missing.'

'First one is a bit young,' Edris said.

'Yes, but whoever took her may have kept her for three months,' Paskin said.

'Have you got the contact details of the parents?' Meadows asked.

'Yes, Cerys' parents are still together and now live in Bridgend. I only managed to trace Poppy's father, he lives at the same address in Port Talbot.'

'Can you contact them please and explain the situation, no doubt they have already heard the news. What about the previous occupants of the house?'

'I've started the list,' Blackwell said. 'Now Valentine's back she can give me a hand to trace them.'

'Good, I think whoever laid that patio is the one who put that little girl in the ground.'

'What sort of person abducts a baby and buries it in the garden?' Paskin said. 'We have to be looking for some sort of weirdo.'

'Yeah, and one that could have abducted and killed again. Poor little Ella could already be in another garden,' Blackwell said. 'So do we search the gardens of all the previous occupants?'

'I think we're going to have to tread a little more carefully than that,' Meadows said. 'According to Daisy, she was buried with some care. Look at the families that have lived in the house, see which ones had children, or maybe lost a child. It could've been a grieving mother.'

'Or someone who couldn't have children,' Valentine said.

'Good point,' Meadows agreed. 'There's also the slim possibility that it's not a missing child but a concealed child. It has been known for young mothers to have babies and hide them. Maybe the mother was mentally unstable, got pregnant and didn't seek medical help.'

'Yes, but surely someone would've noticed that she had a child after three months,' Paskin said.

'I agree, I'm just trying to look at all the possibilities. Right, Blackwell, I'll leave you to talk to George, it may save some time if he has a good memory of his previous neighbours. He's lived there for thirty years so he should remember one of them laying a patio, and there isn't much of a fence between the two properties. Also talk to him about male visitors to Natalie's house. I'll talk to the families of the missing children in the morning, I don't want to keep them waiting any longer, I'm sure they are anxious enough as it is.'

Chapter Eighteen

The front door was opened as soon as Meadows and Edris stepped out of the car. The couple stood side by side, both with a nervous smile. The man was slim, average height with steel grey hair and was dressed in jeans and a navy jumper. His wife was about a foot shorter, plump with copper coloured hair which hung in a straight bob.

'Mr and Mrs Lane?' Edris asked.

'Steven and Jenny.' The man smiled. 'Please come in.'

They were led into the sitting room which, although tidy, looked well used. An overflowing toy box stood next to the television and family photographs festooned the walls. The scent of lavender permeated the air, reminding Meadows of his childhood bedroom, where his mother used to put fresh lavender under the pillows and in the clothes drawers. The lavender in this room however came from an oil burner that was placed in the centre of the coffee table.

'Have a seat,' Jenny said as she perched on the sofa and was joined by Steven.

'Thank you.' Meadows sat in the armchair. 'Did the officer that phoned you explain the situation?'

'Yes,' Jenny said. 'We do understand that it may not be Cerys that you found, and that you need to take a swab for a DNA test.'

'We haven't eaten nor drunk anything for over an hour,' Steven said.

'Okay, that's good. Edris will take a swab from you both. I understand how difficult this must be for the two of you and we will get the results back to you as soon as we can.'

'It's the not knowing,' Jenny said. She opened her mouth and Edris ran a swab around her cheek. He checked the label and repeated the process with Steven before taking a seat in the recliner.

'Thank you both,' Meadows said.

'Would you like a cup of tea?' Jenny asked.

While Meadows didn't much feel like another tea, he found that it helped soothe the atmosphere when interviewing people.

'That would be great, black, no sugar and white with two for Edris. Lovely photos,' he said to Steven who looked a little lost once Jenny had left the room.

'Our other three children,' Steven said. 'All grown up now, we've got a grandchild and another one on the way.'

'That explains the toy box.' Meadows smiled.

'Yes, love having him over but it's great to hand him back. He wears me out.' Steven laughed. 'Would you like to see a picture of Cerys?'

'Please,' Meadows said.

Steven stood and took a silver frame from the mantle. He handed the photo to Meadows.

'That was taken a few hours after she was born. She's our third child.'

The photo showed Jenny with curly hair looking tired but happy cradling the infant.

A happy moment before their lives were changed forever.

Meadows chased away the image of the skeleton as he handed the photo back to Steven.

'It's a lovely photo.'

Steven talked some more about his other children until Jenny came back into the room carrying a tray. She set it down on the table and handed a cup to Meadows and Edris before taking a cup herself and sitting down.

'We only have a few pictures of Cerys,' Jenny said as her eyes fell on the photograph that Steven had laid on the table.

'We haven't had a chance to read the case file,' Meadows said. 'Would you mind talking us through what happened that day? If it is too painful don't worry.'

'It's fine.' Jenny sipped her tea. 'Cerys was born on the fourth of April 1993 at two in the morning, she weighed seven pounds and two ounces. You never forget those things.'

Steven took hold of Jenny's hand.

'Jen had a bit of a rough time and needed an emergency C-section. She had general anaesthetic, so I got to hold Cerys for a little while Jen recovered. I'll always be thankful for having that time.'

Jenny took another sip of her tea and laid the cup on the table.

'That afternoon a nurse came in and said she was going to take her to the nursery for a bath. I slept for a while and when I woke, I asked another nurse if she could get Cerys from the nursery. She said she would when she had finished checking the other mothers. She never came back. She said later that she thought another nurse had fetched the baby for me.'

She paused for a moment and then continued.

'Steven came in a while later with the kids. I asked again for Cerys. It was then that they discovered she was missing. There was a lot of confusion as the hospital was searched and all the babies' identity bracelets checked. There was no trace of the nurse who took Cerys for her bath. The rest, you can imagine. Appeals, days of waiting for news that turned into weeks and months, but even as the years passed we still hoped.'

'I take it the nurse was never identified,' Edris said.

'No.' Steven sighed. 'No nurse of that description worked at the hospital. I doubt she was even a nurse. Probably got the uniform from somewhere and waited for her opportunity.'

'I would imagine that was the case,' Meadows said. 'Could you tell us what she looked like?'

'I'll never forget her face,' Jenny said. 'Every time I went out shopping, or on my way to work, I would scan the crowds or people passing on the bus and in cars hoping to see her face. She was in her mid-thirties, perhaps nearing forty. She was a little overweight, curly short blond hair. She spoke well and wore light make up. I guess she could probably walk by in the street and I wouldn't know her now.'

'It's unbelievable to think that someone could pose as a nurse, walk into a hospital, and take a baby without anyone noticing,' Steven said. 'Of course, they have all sorts of security now.'

'Did Cerys have any health problems when she was born?' Meadows asked.

'No, well none identified from all the initial tests they give a newborn. There were no breathing problems or heart defects if that's what you mean,' Jenny said. 'Is that what you think happened to the child you found, that she was sick?'

'Honestly, we don't know,' Meadows said. 'But it's one possibility we have to look at. Do you have any connection to Coopers Wood estate or the surrounding area?'

'No. Oh, I did have an aunt that lived in Bryn Coed. She's dead now, but I used to visit her.'

'Okay, well thank you for talking to us. I'm sorry that you've had all this brought up again.'

Meadows drained the last of his tea from the cup and stood.

'That's okay.' Jenny smiled. 'It never really goes away, you just learn to live with it. You will call us as soon as you have the result? There's no need to come out to see us.'

'I'll call the minute I know. We'll move it along as quickly as we can.'

'Thank you,' Steven said. 'Maybe after all this time we can have some answers.'

* * *

'It takes some balls to walk into a hospital and steal a baby,' Edris said.

'Or a house. If Natalie and her friends are telling the truth, then someone watched the house and waited for an opportunity to take Ella.'

'If they lived in the house previously then they would know the layout,' Edris said as he slipped on his seat belt. 'I hope the kid turns out to be Cerys. It must be hell not knowing what happened to your child.'

'Yes,' Meadows said, 'but there's another family to see with probably an equally heart-breaking story.'

He pulled on to the main road as Edris fed the postcode of the next address into the sat nav.

'Yeah, and this next one is closer to the age of the child found in the garden, so the odds are in their favour.' Edris leaned back in the seat.

'Not necessarily, whoever took Cerys could've cared for her for three months, even convinced themselves that the child was theirs. Then the child got sick or had an accident and they couldn't risk going to the hospital.'

An image of Ella lying limp in Natalie's arms came to Meadows' mind.

No, she could've called for help, even if she knew she would get in trouble for having Ryan there or taking drugs. If it was some sort of accident, then it's more likely that it was too late to help. Natalie doesn't act like a mother who has lost her child, she wouldn't be able to hide her grief.

150

Edris' voice chased away the thoughts and brought Meadows' mind back to Cerys Lane and the child found in the garden.

'If she cared that much for the child she would've got help even if it meant going to prison. Not just bury her in the garden,' Edris said.

'I guess, but maybe it was too late to call for help. We won't know what happened until we track down the person who took the child, even then they may not tell us. First, we need an identity for our little miss, it should make it easier to find the person responsible for taking her. This person or maybe a couple, at some time, lived in Natalie's house.'

'We still have to track them down though,' Edris said. 'Once they've seen the news they're likely to go into hiding.'

'Or they could think they're safe after all this time. They're probably confident that they won't get caught. It's not going to be easy to prove. I'm assuming there was no DNA or fingerprints from where Cerys was taken. Too many people in the hospital. I've asked Valentine to get hold of the original case files. We've still got Poppy Moore to check out. Maybe there were forensic traces found where she was taken.'

They lapsed into silence and Meadows mulled over the case as he drove down the motorway.

So sad how people's lives can be ruined in a matter of moments. Worse still that Cerys was taken at random. Could've been any of the babies at the hospital that day. His thoughts turned to Ella again. *She definitely wasn't taken at random, and still we can't find her.*

* * *

Port Talbot steel works came into view, stretching over a mile, its structure bellowed clouds of smoke into the sky and left a faint smell of sulphur in the air.

'Wouldn't like to live here,' Edris said as Meadows took the slip road.

'I expect you become immune to the smell and it does have a nice beach.'

'Yeah, I used to come here for days out when I was a kid.'

The road led them past the beach, and two turnings later, the sat nav announced that they had arrived at their destination. Meadows parked the car and looked around the quiet back road. There were pairs of semi-detached houses running the length of the road, with trees dotted along the pavement. Each house had a long front garden with a low fence separating the properties.

Meadows got out of the car, stretched and inhaled the salty air.

'Certainly not the type of place you expect a child to be abducted. Quiet road, probably close watchful neighbours. It's a big risk,' Meadows said as he opened the gate and stepped through.

'Maybe someone who knew the family, or maybe someone could've been stalking them for a while and waited for an opportunity,' Edris said.

'It's a long way to come from Coopers Wood estate.'

Meadows looked at the garden as he walked. There were wide borders filled with rose bushes and in the centre stood a large hydrangea, its leaves poised to unfurl.

'You would need a car, it's unlikely they abducted the child and took public transport.'

Edris nodded his agreement as they approached the door. It wasn't opened on the first knock even though Meadows knew that Tom Moore had been informed that they would be calling. He knocked again and heard footsteps approaching. The man that opened the door looked to be in his late fifties. He had fair, thinning hair that had turned white at the sides. His moustache and sideburns were darker but speckled with grey.

'You must be Detective Meadows,' Tom said.

'Yes, and this is DC Edris.' Meadows smiled.

'You better come in.' Tom turned and led them into the sitting room.

Meadows looked around. There were no family photos displayed, apart from one that sat in a white frame on the mantle. It was of a young woman with long black wavy hair, her face looked familiar, but Meadows couldn't recall where he may have seen her.

'Have a seat,' Tom said.

Edris sat down in an armchair. 'It must be nice living so close to the sea, especially in the summer.'

'Yes, I suppose, I don't go to the beach very often.' Tom turned to look out of the window.

He looks uncomfortable. Can't be easy having the past dragged up.

Meadows took a seat in the other armchair and surveyed Tom. He wore jeans and a T-shirt, no jumper even though the temperature inside was no warmer than outdoors. His arms were muscular and looked like they were regularly exposed to the outdoor elements.

Builder, or a gardener perhaps.

'My daughter should be here soon.' Tom turned around and looked at Meadows. 'I would rather we wait until she gets here.'

'That's okay,' Meadows said.

'It's just the two of us. She rang to say she was running late.' He turned back to look out of the window. 'Ah, here she is.' His shoulders relaxed and he turned and smiled.

I wonder how long it's just been the two of them. Did his wife leave? Or is that photo a reminder of a lost loved one?

Meadows heard the front door open and stood to greet Tom's daughter.

'In here, love,' Tom called.

The door to the sitting room opened and Daisy rushed in. 'Sorry, Dad, I got held up.' She gave Tom a hug and a kiss on the cheek before turning to Meadows. 'I'm glad it's you two.' She smiled nervously.

'Well this is a surprise.' Edris had vacated his chair and now the four of them stood.

It took Meadows a moment to process what he was seeing.

It's no wonder the photo looks familiar. Daisy looks like her mother.

'I didn't make the connection with the surname.' Meadows gave her a smile which he hoped would put her at ease. 'I guess this is what you wanted to talk to me about.'

'Yes, I'm sorry, I should've come out with it as soon as we found her. I guess I needed time to think about it and what it could mean. Then I wanted to be sure, to run the test to see if it was a girl before I spoke to Dad. I didn't want to get his hopes up. I… I didn't know where to start when I saw you at the lab.'

'It's fine,' Meadows said. 'I understand that this must be very difficult for you and especially hard given what you were faced with yesterday.'

'Oh, Daisy love, don't tell me that you–'

'It's okay, Dad.' Daisy cut him off. 'It's my job and I was glad it was me who took care of her, especially if it is Poppy. Come on, let's sit down.'

She sat on the sofa and patted the seat next to her. Tom sat close to his daughter and Meadows and Edris took up their seats in the armchairs.

'Have you already run a DNA test?' Edris asked.

'No, to be honest I was tempted but it's better to have Dad's as well as mine for comparison. I thought it wouldn't be very professional of me to run the tests without telling you, and I guess there are others. I called Dad this morning to prepare him and let him know to expect a call. I knew you would find Poppy on the missing list.'

'It came as a bit of a shock,' Tom said. 'After all this time, I tried to put it to the back of my mind. I thought we

154

would never get answers. It can't bring her back but at least we can put things to rest.'

'It may not be Poppy,' Meadows said gently. 'At the moment, we are testing all the parents of children that went missing over the last thirty years. I'm sorry that we have to put you through this but there is no other way of identifying the child.'

'I understand,' Tom said, 'but you can't help getting your hopes up, even though it could mean that Poppy has been dead all this time.'

Daisy took hold of her father's hand and gave it a squeeze.

'Have you read through the case file?'

'No,' Meadows said. 'We have requested the files, so only have names and dates at the moment.'

'Well, we can tell you as much as we can, obviously we don't know anything about how the investigation was handled. You start, Dad.'

Tom rubbed his hand over his chin.

'My wife Annie went into premature labour on the 1st of March 1992, Poppy wasn't due until April. Poppy was a difficult baby. She didn't sleep well in the night and poor Annie was exhausted most of the time. My mother came around to help when she could and Annie seemed to be coping. We had a good summer that year. It was only just over two weeks to go for school to break up, and we were going to have a family holiday. Poppy was four months old and still not settling at night. Annie used to spend her time out the front garden hoping the fresh air would help Poppy sleep. I remember every minute of the Saturday it happened, I've been over it so many times wishing I had done things differently.' Tom sighed.

'I had to go into work that morning, it was a warm day and Annie wasn't happy with me working on a Saturday. She wanted me to stay so we could take the kids out for the day. I wish I had stayed. Biggest regret of my life.'

'You weren't to know,' Daisy said.

'From what Annie told me later, she sat out in the garden reading, with Poppy sleeping in the pram and Daisy playing on the grass. She developed a headache so went indoors to get out of the sun. She didn't want to disturb Poppy, so she left her in the shade and asked Daisy to call her if Poppy woke up.'

'I was supposed to watch the baby,' Daisy said.

'How old were you?' Meadows asked.

'Six, nearly seven. Old enough to do a simple task like call my mother if the baby woke.'

'No, Daisy,' Tom said. 'You weren't old enough to take responsibility for what happened.'

Meadows could see the years of guilt on Tom and Daisy's faces.

I bet they hardly talk about it, each one carrying the blame for something they didn't have any control over.

Daisy sighed. 'I know, but it doesn't stop the *what-ifs* creeping in over the years. Not all the time. It sneaks up on you when you least expect it. My memory is a bit hazy, but I had to go over the story so many times with the police that I guess the details stuck. I was playing with my dolls when this woman stopped at the garden gate. She said something about it being very warm and asked where my mother was, then she came through the gate and looked at Poppy. She said she was a pretty baby. I don't remember how long she talked to me but she asked for a glass of water. I ran inside, Mum was sleeping on the sofa, so I crept into the kitchen. I didn't want to wake her. When I took the water outside the woman was gone so I just carried on playing. I didn't even check the pram to see if Poppy was okay.'

'What was the woman like?' Meadows asked.

'There's probably a good description in the case file. To me she became an old haggard witch that stole my sister. I guess that's how my young mind dealt with what happened.'

'The police were really good with Daisy, but the description didn't give them a lot to go on. The woman was young, they thought no more than twenty, maybe even younger. She wore a hat and sunglasses.' Tom shook his head. 'Even an adult would have difficulty giving a good description.'

'Did anyone else see her?' Edris asked.

'No, the neighbours were out,' Tom said. 'Annie couldn't be sure of the exact time it happened. She said she must've been asleep for about an hour, maybe an hour and a half. She went outside to check on the girls and the pram was empty. You can imagine the panic. It was a horrible time. The days lasted an eternity and just ran in to each other. Each morning I would wake with my stomach in knots but still hoped that the woman would give herself up and Poppy would be returned to us. There was nothing from the appeal, the newspapers ran a follow-up but with nothing to report, the story dried up and Poppy became yesterday's news.

'Annie blamed herself for leaving the girls outside alone. We tried to move on with our lives and get back to some sort of normality for Daisy's sake. I went back to work, and Daisy returned to school at the end of the summer. Annie was left at home with nothing but her thoughts to torment her. She took her life a year later.'

'I'm so sorry,' Meadows said. It occurred to him how little he knew of Daisy's life outside work.

'Thank you.' Daisy gave Meadows a weak smile. 'That woman not only took my sister, she killed my mother and left me and Dad heartbroken. I can't help wondering, why us? But I guess all the other families you have to visit will say the same thing.'

'Yes, and I wish I had the answers. Were there any visitors to the house in the time leading up to Poppy's abduction? Or anyone that showed an interest in the children when you were out?'

'No,' Tom said. 'We went through the days before over and over to see if there was anything unusual. We'd been to the beach the weekend before. My mother had visited on the Thursday and taken Poppy out for a walk with Annie, but they didn't talk to anyone. Maybe it just was random chance that she walked by the garden and saw the pram.'

'Shall we do the swabs?' Daisy asked. 'The sooner it's done, the sooner we can get the results. I don't want Dad to have to wait any longer than he has to.'

'It's okay, love,' Tom said. 'A few more days won't make a difference.'

'I hope it won't take that long,' Meadows said.

Edris stood and took a swab from Daisy's cheek and was collecting Tom's sample when Daisy's phone rang. Seconds later Meadows felt his own phone vibrate in his pocket. He excused himself and stepped outside the room. Blackwell's name flashed across the screen.

'What have you got?' Meadows asked.

'Another body for you,' Blackwell said. 'Coopers Wood estate.'

Chapter Nineteen

Meadows sat in the passenger seat as Daisy drove towards Coopers Wood Estate. He was happy to spend this time alone with her having sent Edris to deliver the swabs to the lab.

'It must have been hard for you losing your mother and sister,' Meadows said.

'Dad did his best and my Gran stepped in to help when she could. I suppose it did leave a cloud over my childhood.'

'I bet you also had a very protective dad.'

'Yeah.' Daisy laughed. 'No boy stood a chance. I gave up bringing home boyfriends. After the interrogations they didn't last long. Poor Dad, I think I was the teenager from hell. Then I went off to university and had a good time before feeling guilty for leaving him on his own. So I got a job where I would be close to him.'

'I can relate to that, but I stayed away for too long.'

'Is that why you came back? To be close to your parents?' Daisy glanced across at him before returning her attention to the road.

'That was part of the reason. It's just my Mum now, or it has been for a long time.'

'Did you lose your dad?'

'No, he left.' Meadows didn't want to talk about his father. The last memory he had of his father had been a beating and his brother wielding a kitchen knife trying to protect him and his mother. 'I was also a teenager from hell.'

'Really?' Daisy smiled. 'I thought life would have been all about the love.'

'You mean the commune?'

'Yeah, sorry I didn't mean to be disrespectful. I guess I'm just curious.'

It didn't surprise him that Daisy knew his background. It was difficult to have any secrets in the valleys.

'It's fine. I don't mind. It was a different life. We were not bound by the usual rules of society. Everything you do is for the good of the community, and we were fairly self-sufficient. It could be hard work and there were long difficult winters. A yurt can withstand a severe storm but I've seen high winds snap a tepee pole and the land get flooded. We always pulled together like one big family. I don't remember any big disagreements. There was never a leader as such. Everything would be discussed and agreed on without any fuss.'

'What about education?' Daisy pulled out onto the roundabout and Coopers Wood could be seen in the distance.

'I was home schooled. Among the adults there was a wide variety of skill sets, so I didn't miss out. We left when I was fifteen. My brother was ill and he needed a more stable environment.'

'That must have been difficult.'

'It took me a while to adjust.' Meadows smiled.

'Do you ever go for a visit?'

'Yeah, every summer.'

'That's nice.'

'I think that's enough about me. Your turn.'

160

'There isn't much more to say. I think I studied to become a pathologist to help people get answers.'

'To make up for the ones you never got?'

'Yes, I guess so.'

Daisy pulled up outside Natalie's house and Meadows looked at the small crowd that was gathered, their attention on the activity in George's house.

'Thanks for the lift.' Meadows unclipped his seat belt but felt reluctant to get out of the car and leave Daisy's company. 'I guess we better see what Blackwell has for us.'

He climbed out of the car under the watchful gaze of those gathered on the pavement. They became silent as if waiting to hear some snippet of information that would tell them what was going on inside.

Meadows waited for Daisy to collect her bag from the boot before walking through the gate where PC Matt Hanes directed them around the back of the house. Blackwell was talking to Valentine who was sat on a worn plastic garden chair looking shaken. George's dog sat at her feet, his head between his paws.

'Are you okay, Valentine?' Meadows asked.

'She's fine,' Blackwell said. 'Just came out for a bit of fresh air.'

'It was a little warm in there,' Valentine said.

'Two bodies and a missing child and it's only Wednesday. Hell of a way to start your first week, eh?' Blackwell gave Valentine a wink.

A rare glimpse of Blackwell's heart. Maybe Valentine can bring out the best in him.

'What happened?' Meadows asked as he put protective covering over his shoes.

'We got no answer when we called, we came around the back and saw the dog. As you hadn't got an answer earlier, I thought we better check it out. We spoke to the neighbours who said that he usually went to the post office in the mornings to pick up his paper, but no one saw him this morning. They all said the dog is always with him. We

161

called in with Brianna who said the dog had been outside all night. Natalie said she had a spare key to the back door in case of emergency. I figured we had enough cause for concern to go in. Valentine found him in the bedroom. No sign of a break in.'

Probably her first body, no wonder she looks a bit pale.

'You can get off home now, Valentine,' Meadows said. 'We'll finish up here.'

'I don't mind staying or going back to the station to help Paskin.' Valentine stood up and the dog fussed at her feet.

'It's getting late, I'll see you for the briefing tomorrow.'

'Okay, I'll just wait until this little fella gets picked up.' She patted the dog. 'Someone is coming from the dog shelter. Poor little fellow.'

* * *

'Right, let's take a look. After you.' Meadows stood back to allow Daisy to enter first; he followed behind with Blackwell.

They followed the pathway set out by forensics, walking single file through the sitting room and up the stairs. They found Mike and his team collecting samples in George's bedroom and taking photographs of the body.

Meadows' eyes fell upon George who was naked and spread-eagled on the bed. His wrists and ankles were bound to each bed post, his lips pulled back into a grimace.

Oh George, what have you got yourself into?

'Hi Mike.' Daisy approached the bed and opened her bag.

'I'll give you some space,' Mike said. He called out his team and they left the room.

Meadows stepped closer to the bed and looked at George's ankle which was tied with dark yellow twine. The skin was bruised and torn, he moved to check the other

162

ankle and found the same. The twine was wrapped around several times and knotted.

'Looks like a sex game gone wrong,' Blackwell said. 'Poor old sod probably had a heart attack, or he was into erotic asphyxiation and couldn't say the safe word.'

'Well I don't know what you are into, but I don't think George here was a willing participant,' Daisy said, grinning.

'I'm not into anything,' Blackwell snapped. 'I'm just saying what it looks like. I've read it somewhere.'

'Read it?' Daisy raised her eyebrow.

'A case, I'm not a pervert.' Blackwell reddened.

Meadows was trying not to laugh at Blackwell's discomfort.

'So not a, erm, sexual game then?' he said to Daisy.

'Not a heart attack. Asphyxiation. My best guess is with a pillow. He's been dead about thirty hours. I think he was bound so he would be helpless. If you look at the twine it's knotted tightly and cut into the flesh. I don't reckon they intended to free him, it would have to be cut off and that wouldn't be easy with swollen flesh, but who knows, maybe Blackwell is right and it's a sex game gone wrong. I'll know more when I get him back and run some tests.'

'So, she lured him to the bed with a promise of some fun, tied him up and killed him,' Blackwell said.

'Or he,' Daisy said. 'It depends on his tastes.'

'From his porn collection, I reckon we are looking at a female,' Blackwell said.

'You noticed that too?' Meadows asked.

'Yeah, there's a drawer full of them.' Blackwell pointed to a chest of drawers with a TV and DVD player sat on top. 'Guess he didn't know about the online availability of free porn. No computer anywhere.'

'Could've been stolen… then again, he has a collection downstairs. Maybe he wasn't very technical. The question is, was this a regular arrangement? I can't see it being a first-time thing.' Meadows said. 'If he's been dead for thirty hours then it would be at the time forensics were working in the garden next door. It takes some confidence to walk in, kill him, then casually leave.'

'Or it was somebody who was sure they wouldn't be recognised, or maybe someone that wouldn't look out of place,' Blackwell said. 'Either way it doesn't look good on us. The press is going to make us look like right dicks.'

Meadows looked at George's wrists again.

'It looks like he put up a struggle but didn't get a chance to cry out. If it was a pillow then it would've muffled his cries, no chance of anyone hearing from outside.'

'Just goes to show that too much porn can be bad for you,' Edris stated as he appeared at the door. 'Maybe he was one of Natalie's regulars and wanted a freebee to keep quiet.'

'That would be a brilliant theory if it wasn't for the fact that Natalie was at the station when George was killed and Brianna has been with her the whole time. You may be onto something, though. He knew something about Ella's abduction or the child in the garden, so had to be silenced,' Meadows said.

'If he knew something about Ella then he would've been silenced before now,' Blackwell said.

'Unless he was blackmailing them and they decided not to pay up. Claire could've done it,' Edris said. 'Yeah, she wouldn't look out of place on the estate. She could have dressed up in some kinky outfit and lured George up here and persuaded him to play some games.'

A hint of a smile played on Blackwell's lips. 'You must have some interesting images in your mind.'

'I have now.' Edris grimaced. 'I'm going to be scarred for life.'

'George already told us he saw Natalie go out in the car. He would've held onto that snippet of information if he had wanted to blackmail them. Maybe whoever killed him thought he knew more than he did,' Meadows said.

'It's worth checking where Claire and Jamie were yesterday afternoon and early evening.'

'Then there's the child in the garden,' Blackwell said.

'Makes more sense,' Meadows said. 'He would know who laid the patio, who had a child that had disappeared, or a child that appeared from nowhere. Maybe this was his payment for keeping quiet.'

'So why kill him now?' Edris said.

'Because the child has been discovered, there is no secret to keep, idiot,' Blackwell snapped.

'Mind you, if he's been dead for thirty hours then the killer wouldn't have known the child had been found. It wasn't released to the media until this morning,' Meadows said.

'Unless George had told the person in question that the garden was being searched,' Blackwell said.

'Or they could've been watching the house,' Edris added.

'We'll need to check his phone records, see if you can find a mobile phone anywhere,' Meadows said.

'I'm just about finished here,' Daisy said. 'He can be moved now. I can tell you more after the post-mortem, like if he managed to have his fun before he went.'

'Thank you.' Meadows smiled. 'There's no rush. You should get yourself some rest, you've had a tough day.'

'I'll have something for you by morning. To be honest, I don't want to go home and watch the clock drag its arms while I wait for the DNA results.'

I'd be happy to keep you company.

Meadows became aware that Edris and Blackwell were stood watching the exchange. 'Okay.'

'I'll see you in the morning.' Daisy picked up her bag and smiled at Meadows before leaving the room.

'One of the families we went to see today was Daisy's. Her sister was abducted as a baby,' Meadows explained to Blackwell. 'That reminds me, George mentioned that he

165

had a daughter. She lives in London. We need to get hold of her before news spreads.'

'I'm happy to do that,' Blackwell said.

'Good, you can take the lead on this one.'

'Great, but I'll let you get the post-mortem results. Don't want to deprive the lovely Daisy of your company.' Blackwell grinned.

That's the second time I've seen him smile today.

'I don't think she'll mind who turns up.'

'Oh, come off it, I'm drowning in sexual tension here,' Blackwell said.

'I don't know what you're talking about.' Meadows felt the heat creep up his neck.

It's bad enough having Edris tease me, but Blackwell. I'll have to watch how I behave around Daisy.

'If it's okay with you I'll contact George's daughter then call it a day,' Blackwell said.

'Got a date, have you?' Edris teased.

Meadows waited for Blackwell's snarling retort, but none came.

'I've got plans.' Blackwell shrugged.

So that's the source of his happiness. Good for him, the man's worked like a machine this week.

'Yeah, that's no problem, Edris and I can finish up here, and you get off.'

* * *

After Blackwell left the room, Meadows and Edris searched George's bedroom, looking through drawers and under the bed. Meadows took another look at George's wrists.

'Odd thing to use to tie him up. Looks like garden twine. Isn't it usually silk scarves?'

Edris smirked. 'If you say so.'

'I'm just thinking, if the killer planned this or it was some regular arrangement, then they would have brought something more enticing.' He opened the wardrobe and searched through the contents. 'George wasn't a tie man, which would've been a better choice. Looks more spur of the moment and they grabbed the nearest thing to hand. Why else would he allow himself to be bound by twine?'

'Or the killer just wanted it to look like a sex game gone wrong. Maybe it was a man,' Edris said.

'There is no sign of a struggle. Nothing knocked over or defence wounds,' Meadows said.

'Killer could have drugged him, then taken him upstairs when he was groggy and tied him up.'

'It's possible but still means he would've known the killer to let them in and maybe drink or eat with them. We'll have to wait to see what Daisy finds. Come on, let's see if we can find a mobile phone, see who he's been in contact with.'

'You can finish up in here now, Mike,' Meadows called out as he walked downstairs.

'I'm thinking of camping out here,' Mike said. 'I'm spending more time on this estate than I do at home lately.'

'I know the feeling,' Meadows said.

There was a large storage cupboard under the stairs and Meadows rummaged around in the boxes while Edris searched for the phone. One of the boxes was filled with gardening tools. At the bottom Meadows found a pair of secateurs and off cuts of the same twine that bound George.

'George was a gardener,' Meadows said over his shoulder. 'Bits of the same twine here, which means there must be a roll, unless the killer took it with them.'

'Got his phone,' Edris said.

'Great, check the log.' Meadows joined Edris in the sitting room.

'Only one number called in the last few days, his daughter. No incoming calls logged.'

'Then it's someone he met up with yesterday or they called at the house.' Meadows moved to the kitchen and looked around. A single mug and cereal bowl stood on the draining board. 'Doesn't look like they had a drink before they went upstairs. Unless the killer washed up.'

'Poor old George,' Edris said. 'Should have stuck to watching his films for entertainment. Let's hope no one else knows the secrets of this estate.'

'Oh, somebody knows, and we need to find them before someone else dies.'

Chapter Twenty

Meadows' phone rang as he was driving toward the hospital to see the post-mortem results for George. Edris turned the music down and hit the answer button. The lab technician introduced herself before giving the results of the DNA tests.

'Neither sample?' Meadows repeated.

'No, there were no similarities between the DNA samples you sent in yesterday and the DNA of the child. I've given Daisy the results, she asked to be called as soon as they came in.'

'That's fine,' Meadows said. 'Thank you.'

'Now what?' Edris asked. 'I was sure that it would be one of them.'

'So was I.' Meadows sighed. 'I guess we have to look further afield or hope that Paskin turns up something from the previous residents. We better call Jenny Lane, I promised to call as soon as we had any news.'

Meadows felt his stomach tighten at the thought of delivering the bad news. *Poor woman probably hasn't slept all night and is sitting by the phone.*

The phone was answered on the first ring. 'It's DI Meadows.'

'Tell me,' Jenny said.

'I'm sorry, the results were negative. It's not Cerys.'

There was silence on the end of the line.

'Jenny, are you okay?' Meadows asked.

Stupid question of course she's not okay.

'Yeah, I will be. Well at least I can go back to hoping that she's still alive and could one day turn up.'

'I really hope that's the case. I'm sorry we had to put you through this,' Meadows said.

'It's okay, thank you for letting me know so quickly,' Jenny said and quickly hung up.

'I feel bad,' Meadows said. 'It's not fair to get people's hopes up.'

'We didn't really have much of a choice,' Edris said.

'No, I guess not but it would be different if one of them had come back positive. It wouldn't feel like we had turned lives upside down for no reason.'

'Well, cheer up, you'll see Daisy in a minute. That will put a smile back on your face.'

Daisy was sat at her desk alone when they arrived, and Meadows was secretly pleased to find that Theo had gone. She smiled at Meadows even though she looked tired.

'I'm sorry about the results,' Meadows said.

'That's okay. It was a long shot anyway. Maybe next time.'

I hope there isn't a next time. I don't want to see another child in the ground.

'I'm happy to look into the case for you when things quieten down,' Meadows said.

'Thank you, but I can't see that there would be anything new after all this time. I appreciate the offer. Come on, I'll take you through to see George.'

'Lovely, can't wait,' Edris said.

'Nothing like a dead body to wake you up in the morning and make you feel alive,' Daisy said. 'Makes you realise you've got a lot to be thankful for.'

'I think I'd rather have a coffee,' Edris said, laughing.

George looked peaceful, his face muscles now relaxed. He was laid out on a trolley, his body covered by a sheet.

'There's not much more to tell you than what we saw yesterday. Cause of death, asphyxiation; his tox screen was clear, no drugs or alcohol. He had a heart attack at some time in the past and there was warfarin in his system. His ankles and wrists show signs that he struggled against his bonds, as you saw. No signs of sexual activity.'

'Poor old sod,' Edris said. 'They could've at least let him have his fun before croaking him.'

'I don't think George would've seen it as any consolation,' Meadows said.

'Well, whoever killed him wasn't bothered about leaving traces,' Daisy said. 'They didn't wear gloves when tying him. I spoke to Mike earlier, they have plenty of samples from the twine and the pillow used to kill him as well as fingerprints at the scene.'

'Just have to find the person to match them,' Meadows said.

Daisy pulled back George's blanket and pointed to two symmetrical bruises on his chest.

'The bruises are consistent with being straddled. I guess your killer sat on his chest with knees either side and held the pillow over his face. He would've bruised easily given the warfarin he was taking.'

'Okay, thank you.' Meadows smiled. 'His daughter is coming down from London today to see him.'

'Not to worry, George, I'll smarten you up and send you to the chapel.' She replaced the sheet. 'Much nicer for her to see him there.'

'I've just got to step out to make a call, excuse me a moment.' Edris hurried out of the room.

What's got into him?

Meadows turned his attention to Daisy.

'I'll leave you get back to work. If you change your mind about having me look into your sister's case, or you just want someone to talk to…' Meadows could feel the heat rising in his neck '…you can call me anytime.'

'So that's all it takes! A missing sister to get your number. If I'd known, I would've told you sooner.' Daisy's eyes twinkled.

Meadows felt his skin tingle. 'You already have my number.'

'Yeah but not an excuse to call it.' Daisy gave him a coy smile.

'You don't need an excuse.' Meadows felt a sudden urge to reach out and touch her. 'Like I said, call me anytime.'

'You better get going or Edris will wonder what you're up to,' Daisy said with a grin.

I better go before a make a complete fool of myself.

'See you soon.' Meadows left the building and could still feel the smile on his face when he reached the car where Edris was waiting.

'So, did you ask her out?' Edris asked.

'Not exactly, but I think you were right. She was waiting for me to make the first move.'

'Yeah, and if you had listened to me months ago you could've been shacked up in lovers' bliss by now.'

'I don't know about that–' Meadows laughed '–but I will call her when we've solved this case. Anyway, who did you have to rush out to call?'

'No one, just thought you needed a moment alone.'

'Anyone would think you were trying to hitch me up. Not a word about this to the team. Or to my mother for that matter. She'll have Daisy around discussing grandchildren before I've got a first date.'

Edris smiled. 'My lips are sealed.'

* * *

As they entered the office, the whir of the helicopter vibrated through the windows as it passed low, heading for the mountain in the continued search for Ella. Lester

172

joined the team for the briefing and they all gathered around as Meadows took off his jacket and approached the incident board.

The first thing he noticed was that a picture of George had been added, which left the board crammed with information.

'Firstly, we need to act quickly to find out who killed George. For one, we have no more room on the incident board, secondly, it is too much of a coincidence that he lived next door to the abducted child and the child that was buried in the garden. He knew something about one of the children, or both. He most certainly knew the killer well enough to let them in, be persuaded to go to the bedroom, and allow himself to be bound. No break in, no drugs in his system. We are working on the assumption that it's a woman. She's killed once and there may be others who know her secret,' he said.

'George was killed late Wednesday afternoon,' Meadows continued. 'There was plenty of activity next door. Forensics were working out the garden as well as conducting a thorough search inside. The killer was confident enough to walk in the house, maybe she was well known in the neighbourhood or a regular visitor to George. She didn't wear gloves so there is plenty of forensic evidence.'

'I talked to the forensic team,' Blackwell said. 'They didn't notice anyone hanging around but the dog was out the garden yapping most of the afternoon. They couldn't give an exact time that the dog was put outside and they didn't see or hear George. Uniform are conducting house to house enquiries to see if anyone saw who went into George's house, or if anyone was hanging around that afternoon.'

'This isn't going to look good for us,' Lester said. 'A murder next door to a house full of officers. I've already had calls from the residents of Coopers Wood estate concerned for their safety and that of their children.'

'I don't think anyone on the estate is in immediate danger unless they are withholding information,' Blackwell said.

'I've set up a press conference. I'll tell them we believe that George's murder is connected to the disappearance of Ella Beynon.' Lester nodded to himself. 'That should reassure the residents and prompt anyone with information to come forward.'

'Then people are going to assume that George had something to do with Ella's disappearance,' Blackwell said. 'That's not fair on his daughter.'

'I'm sure I can manage to phrase it in such a way that that won't be the case.' Lester gave Blackwell a stern look.

'I think George's murder has more to do with the child found in the garden than Ella Beynon,' Blackwell said.

'Fine, I'll go with that,' Lester said.

'Or we could be looking at the same person for all three crimes,' Meadows said. 'Our priority is to find Ella but it's also important to find the identity of the child. The two possible missing children, Cerys Lane and Poppy Moore, were not a match. Did your search show up any other possibilities, Paskin?'

'Not for a child that age. I'm looking at cases where a child is believed to have been taken by the father and possibly out of the country. I found one where the baby was one month old. The mother went out shopping and when she returned both child and father were missing. The father was Iranian. I think it's worth following up to see if there's evidence that the child and father are in Iran. Or if he had any connection with this area.'

'That's definitely worth following up. In the meantime, I think the answer lies with the previous residents of the house. It's not beyond the realms of possibility that one of them buried the child in the garden. Who would miss the child if that was the case? They could've moved around a lot. There's even the possibility that for some reason the pregnancy was kept secret and the mother couldn't cope.

Perhaps mental health issues. Might even be a whole family covering it up?'

Meadows could see the discomfort on Lester's face.

I bet he's imagining holding a press conference where he has to explain how the death of a child went unnoticed.

'Anyone have a better theory?' he said.

'It seems a bit, well, incredible that a three-month-old baby could disappear and no one notice. There's neighbours, grandparents, and health visitors,' Valentine said.

'Well that's the point, George may have noticed but for whatever reason kept quiet. Or he could've just suspected and only when the body was found knew for certain. There may not have been grandparents involved, could've lived too far away, or the family was estranged. As for a health visitor, I wouldn't think it difficult for one child to get lost among the workload. If the family moved away shortly after, then the child would easily be lost in the system, no one would be looking. It's the only thing we've got to go on at the moment. I don't think it's possible that someone could've chosen that garden randomly and sneaked in to bury a child. The only access is around the side of the house and overlooked by the bedroom windows as well as the neighbours. One of the previous occupants has to be involved at some level.'

'How many families are we looking at?' Lester asked.

'Six,' Paskin said. 'If you include Natalie and go back to 1973.'

'I think that's far enough back and covers the timeframe we were given, even allows for a bit extra. Any of the families have children? Girls specifically.'

'Yes.' Paskin tucked a strand of hair behind her ear. '1973 to 1980, John and Mary Evans; two children, Andrew and Vanessa. 1980 to 1991, Raymond and Susan Davis; three children, Rachel, Robert, and Rhian. 1991 to 1993, Sally Matthews, single parent; one child, Jade. 1993 to 2001, Helen and James Morris; four children, Owen,

Rhys, Rhodri, and Shannon. 2001 to 2014, Michelle and Jason Stanley; three children, Preston, Abigail, and Keira. Then there's Natalie.'

'Was the house unoccupied for any length of time?' Meadows asked.

'No.'

'Okay, we need speak to the families and check out all the girls.'

'Valentine and I have been working on tracing the families, well, the parents. It's going to take longer to check if all the children are still alive. We'll start with school records,' Paskin said.

'We only need to check the girls. I think we can discount the last family before Natalie, if they only moved into the house in 2001 it doesn't work into our time frame, unless the child hasn't been buried as long as the initial tests show. But it's still worth talking to them, see what they can tell us about George. Maybe we should just DNA test the lot of them, quickest way to get our answers.'

'I think forensics are already stretched,' Lester said.

'Yes, but I don't see what choice we have. It's the only sure way of knowing,' Meadows said.

'Talk to the families first, see what reaction you get and if all the girls are accounted for. If you have reason to believe one of the families is involved, get a DNA test. As it is, I don't think it's reasonable to ask for a sample from all these families and they don't have to co-operate.' Lester looked around the team.

'And what reaction are we looking for exactly,' Blackwell said. 'Just ask these families if anyone has buried a child in the garden, and flipped and taken Ella Beynon?'

'There's no need for sarcasm,' Lester said. 'I just don't think we have enough grounds to ask all of them for a DNA test.'

'Keep the enquiry simple. We want to establish the whereabouts of their children, well, their daughters, and their relationship with George. It would be useful to know when the patio was laid,' Meadows said.

'Couldn't they have dug up the slabs to bury the child?' Paskin asked.

'Yes, but it's unlikely they'd go to that much trouble. They would've picked an easier spot in the garden. It could be that the patio was laid at a much later date but I think it's possible that the person that laid the patio did so to make sure the child remained concealed.'

'I think that's a fair assumption,' Lester said.

'Okay, so let's make a start. Paskin, could you print out copies of all the information you have so far on the families? We'll split the interviews between us. Edris, give Martin Hughes a call, see if social services have had any dealings with the families.'

'I'm seeing George's daughter,' Blackwell said.

'That's fine, you can take the last family on the list, and the rest of us will interview the others.' Meadows turned to Lester. 'Any development on the search for Ella?'

'No, it's been five nights so it's not looking good. No new reported sightings and the search team is still working around the clock. There's talk of scaling down the search. Without a suspect...' Lester let the sentence hang in the air.

Meadows turned and looked at the incident board where Ella's photograph smiled sweetly. All his earlier euphoria had dispersed and was replaced by a heavy, sinking feeling.

I'm not giving up on you yet.

'Did you manage to get a list of Natalie's clients from Serenity, Valentine?'

'Not so easy. They don't keep records as such and they assured me that the workers' real names are not given out. To be honest I can't see that she would have invited anyone home. She managed to keep her work a secret.'

'Well it was a long shot,' Meadows said. 'What about Clare and Jamie?'

'Both have alibis for when George was killed, volunteering with the search,' Blackwell said.

'I caught up with Brianna earlier. She said tensions are running high between Natalie and Nia,' Paskin said. 'The other sister, Leanne, has arrived and is staying with Nia. Brianna thinks that the two of them are going to put a lot of pressure on Natalie.'

'Could be a good thing,' Meadows said. 'Maybe they'll have better luck than us getting information out of her. Come on, Edris, I think we need to pay a visit to the sisters, see if they have anything new to tell us.'

Chapter Twenty-one

Nia looked flustered when she answered the door.

'Is there any news?'

'No, I'm afraid not,' Meadows said. 'We heard that Leanne is staying with you.'

'Yes, she arrived late last night.' Nia made no offer to invite them in.

'We'd like to talk to her,' Edris said.

'She's just about to put Eli down for a nap. He had a long journey yesterday so is a little bit fractious.'

'We won't keep her long,' Meadows said.

'Fine.' Nia huffed. 'Police are here and want a chat with you,' she called out as she led them into the sitting room. 'I did tell them you were about to put Eli down for a nap.'

'It's okay,' Leanne said.

'We won't keep you long,' Meadows said. He immediately saw the resemblance between the sisters. Leanne had the same strawberry blond hair which was braided in a long plait that swung as she jiggled the toddler on her hip. The little boy had the same blue eyes as his mother but his wispy short hair was brown. He looked at the strangers then buried his head in Leanne's chest.

'I'll take him for you.' Nia held out her arms.

Leanne handed over the child who clung tightly to Nia as she left the room.

'Have a seat.' Leanne pulled her green jumper down over her jeans and plonked down in the armchair.

'Nia said you arrived yesterday. Did you fly into Cardiff?'

'No, I took the ferry crossing to Heysham. It's cheaper.'

'Quite a drive.' Meadows smiled.

Leanne shrugged her shoulders. 'It's not that bad. I've done it a few times.'

'Have you seen Natalie?'

'No, I went to see Mum this morning. Once Eli settles, I'll leave him with Nia and go and see Nat. I'm not looking forward to it.'

'I can imagine,' Meadows said. 'It must be difficult for you all, having your niece missing and trying to comfort your sister.'

'Comfort?' Leanne scoffed. 'That's the last thing she'll be getting from me. Nia has filled me in on everything. Working as a... as a whore.' Leanne shook her head. 'And now she claims that she can't remember what happened the night Ella went missing because she was off her face. What sort of mother is she?'

'I understand that you made a report to social services,' Meadows said.

'Yes, last time I was here, Christmas holidays. The house was a state, I don't mean untidy but filthy. That Ryan creature was hanging around. Nat only seemed interest in enjoying herself, she hadn't even bothered putting up decorations. I tried to talk to her, get her to take some interest in Ella. Even took them shopping for presents. At first, she didn't want to go but I made an excuse that I needed her to drive me to town so she came. I shopped for new clothes and toys for Ella. Nat spent the whole time looking at her phone and texting. I tidied up Ella's room. Put clean sheets on the bed. The next evening, I called around, she had her friends over. The house stank of weed and Ella was screaming in her cot.'

'Did you talk to Natalie about your concerns?' Meadows asked.

'That night there was no point. I told her Ella was crying but she didn't go upstairs. She said Ella would settle and that I should stop fussing. I changed Ella's nappy, she was soaking, then settled her down. I went to see Nat the next morning. She was hungover, lying on the sofa while Ella played on that filthy carpet. I told her she was a selfish bitch. Well, I said a lot more than that.'

'I can imagine,' Meadows said.

'I couldn't even take Eli to visit, I had to leave him with Nia. There's no way I would expose him to a house stinking of weed. It broke my heart to see Ella playing quietly while Nat ignored her. I had no choice but to report her to social services. Not that it did any good. If they had taken my concerns seriously then Ella would be…' Leanne bit her lip.

She thinks Ella's dead.

Meadows waited for Leanne to continue but she folded her arms and sat back in the chair.

'Do you think Natalie would harm Ella?'

Leanne shifted in her seat. 'I don't think she would hurt her deliberately, but she did neglect her. Then there's Ryan. Nat seemed to care more about him than her own daughter. I don't trust him and I think he's capable of anything.'

'Do you really think that Natalie would protect Ryan if he had done something to Ella?' Edris asked.

'Yeah, I think she would.'

'Do you think Natalie will confide in you, if that's the case?' Meadows asked.

'No, she'll just continue to lie, but if I have to shake it out of her I will. Nia has arranged an appointment with a hypnotist. I'll drag Nat by the hair if that's what it takes.'

'I guess a hypnotist is worth a try,' Meadows said. 'If Natalie really can't remember what happened that night. At the moment, we have no sightings of Ella and not enough evidence that Natalie or any of the others are involved.'

'I wouldn't trust any of them,' Nia said as she walked into the room. 'Eli is out for count.'

'Thank you for being so frank with us.' Meadows smiled at Leanne as he stood. 'We'll see ourselves out.'

* * *

'No family loyalty there,' Edris commented as he put on his seatbelt.

'I think they are more concerned about their niece than protecting Natalie.' Meadows ran his hand over his chin. 'Were they concerned enough to take matters into their own hands?'

'I don't see how,' Edris said. 'Nia has been over at Natalie's house most of the time and we searched her house. Leanne wasn't here when Ella went missing.'

'Unless someone is helping them.'

'You think they would arrange to have their own niece kidnapped by some stranger?'

'No. I doubt they'd put Ella through the trauma. Right, we better get a move on and interview the previous residents of Natalie's house.'

Meadows started the engine.

'Okay we've got Helen and James Morris who lived in the house until 2001 and Sally Matthews until 1993.' Edris read from the list. 'Where first?'

'The Morrises live closer, in Bryn Coed, so we'll visit them.'

Meadows pulled out of the car park.

'Paskin and Valentine got quite a bit of information. According to this, James Morris is on disability and his wife claims caring allowance.'

'Well at least there is a good chance we will catch them home,' Meadows said.

'Yeah and they'll confess to the murder of George and burying their child in the back garden, oh and then tell us where we can find Ella.'

Meadows glanced sideways. 'What's up with you?'

'Nothing, I guess I don't see how we are going to achieve anything this way. Lester should've just let us get DNA samples from the lot.'

'Yeah, well I guess he has to keep to the budget. We've probably blown six months' worth this week alone.' Meadows smiled. 'He also has a point about getting the samples without good cause. At least we get to meet some of the families, see how they react to the visit, maybe something will stand out.'

'I'll leave it up to you to feel the vibes,' Edris said. 'You're good at that.'

The Morrises' house was a mid-terrace set off the main road. The door was opened by a harassed-looking woman. She was short with a full figure and dark hair cropped short.

'DI Meadows and this is DC Edris we–'

'Oh God, what's happened?' Her hand flew to her chest as her eyes widened in panic.

'There's nothing to worry about,' Meadows reassured her. 'We're talking to all the previous occupants of 109, Coopers Wood estate. Are you Helen Morris?'

'Yes, is this about George? I heard it on the news.'

'Yes, and about the child that was found in the garden,' Edris said.

Meadows watched Helen's reaction. She showed no signs of alarm or guilt.

'Come in,' she said. 'Such a shame about George, I was shocked to hear the news.'

She led them into a sitting room where a man sat in an armchair and a toddler sat on the floor watching the television.

'Take a seat, excuse the mess.' She turned to the man in the chair. 'Police, Jim. They want to talk about when we lived on Coopers Wood estate.'

The man nodded but his face remained expressionless. Meadows moved some toys and sat on the sofa next to Edris.

'Glad we don't live there anymore,' Jim said. 'With all that's been going on, you wouldn't feel safe in your bed.'

Meadows noticed that Jim spoke softly and deliberately, there was also a tremor in his hands.

'We believe there's a connection between at least two of the incidents on Coopers Wood estate. There really is no need for the residents to be concerned.'

'Would you like a cup of tea?' Helen asked. 'I've just boiled the kettle as we were about to have one.'

'Please,' Edris said.

As Helen left the room the programme on the TV came to an end and the toddler ran to Jim and climbed on his lap. Wary eyes looked at the visitors sat on the sofa.

'Grandson?' Meadows asked.

'Granddaughter,' Jim said. 'Can't really tell the difference with her hair cut. Shannon always had long hair as a child.'

Something about the comment struck Meadows but he couldn't grasp the importance. 'Shannon is your daughter?'

'Yes, she works at the DVLA so we look after this little tyke three days a week, saves a bit on childcare.'

Well that answers the question of the daughter still being alive. Could they have had another?

'Just the one daughter you have?'

'No, we have three boys, they're all grown up now. Youngest is in university.'

'Did you have Shannon when you lived in Coopers Wood estate?'

'Yes, we moved there just after she was born.'

'She's in her twenties now?' Edris asked.

'Twenty-five. They grow up so quickly.'

Helen came back into the room carrying a tray, she placed it on the table before removing the child from Jim's lap.

'Come on, I'll put something on for you to watch.'

She put the child down and pressed a button on the remote control. The screen came to life with brightly coloured singing animals. She turned to the tray and took a beaker and biscuit and handed it to the child.

'Help yourself to sugar,' she said before taking a mug and handing it to Jim. The mug shook violently in Jim's hands.

'Parkinson's,' he explained.

'How long?' Meadows asked.

'Seems like forever. I was diagnosed ten years ago.'

'Can't be easy,' Meadows said.

'We manage,' Helen replied.

Meadows studied Helen as she sipped her tea.

She's not that old and things must get on top of her looking after Jim. Maybe she sought some affection from George, an escape for a couple of hours. They were neighbours for eight years so could've known each other well. He would've let her in. Maybe brought up the child found in the garden and his suspicions.

'So, you lived in the house until 2001?' Edris' questions snapped Meadows out of his thoughts.

'Yes, we moved in when Shannon was born, we'd been living with Jim's parents in Carmarthen and not really getting on. We were on the waiting list so when the house became free we jumped at the chance. I don't think we would've cared what area we moved to as long as we had our own place.'

'Did you meet the previous occupant?' Edris asked picking up a mug of tea.

'No,' Helen said. 'She'd already gone, left the place in a hell of a state. Didn't take much with her, all the furniture was still there. Single parent from what George told us.'

'How did you get on with George?' Meadows asked.

'He was a good neighbour. We didn't have any problems, did we, Jim?'

'No, he was tidy. Used to go out together for a pint now and then. I think he found it hard with no work. He'd been down the pits since he left school, then they closed and he worked for a private mine for a while. I guess the poor sod didn't have a chance when he left there. He wasn't trained to do anything else. Spent a lot of time in the garden. Always giving us fresh veg.'

'Did he have a girlfriend?' Edris asked.

'Not that I saw,' Helen said. 'He told us that he was divorced.'

'You said George was a keen gardener. What about you?' Meadows looked at Jim.

'No, the time I came home from work I didn't feel like doing much else. There's not a lot you can do with a garden when there's four kids,' Jim said.

'It was enough to get him to cut the lawn,' Helen said. 'Oh, do you think that poor child was buried in the garden the whole time we lived there? It doesn't bear thinking about.' Her eyes shifted to the little girl sitting on the floor.

'We're not sure,' Meadows said. 'Was there a patio when you moved in?'

'If you can call it that,' Helen said. 'A few slabs, not laid very well. I did nag Jim to pull it up and lay a new one but we never got around to it. Why? Is that where you found the skeleton?'

'We're just looking at any changes that were made to the garden,' Meadows said.

'Was the house empty for any length of time?' Edris picked up a biscuit from the plate. 'Did you go on regular holidays?'

'No,' Jim said. 'We couldn't afford a holiday.'

'Any visitors? Or someone showing an unusual interest in the house?' Meadows asked.

'No, not that I can remember,' Helen said.

'When was the last time you saw George?'

'We haven't seen him for years, have we, Jim?'

Jim shook his head. 'We haven't had reason to go down that way.'

'Okay, well that's about all for now.' Meadows stood. 'We may have to come back to ask some more questions.'

'That's fine, we're usually in,' Helen said.

'One more thing I have to ask. Where were you yesterday?'

'That's easy. I was here, like most days,' Jim said.

'I went shopping in the morning and I was here with Jim after that.' Helen looked at Jim as she spoke. 'Not sure what time I came back.'

* * *

'She could've done it,' Edris said as soon as they were back in the car. 'She wouldn't be noticed on the estate. Probably has a few friends there. George would've let her in – she did say she was out yesterday. Quick bit of shopping then over to George's. Kill him and home in time to give Jim his tea.'

'And the motive? Sounds like her daughter is still alive. Easy to check out with the DVLA.'

'That daughter may still be alive but she could've had another one. Child could've died at three months. She must find it very difficult looking after her husband. Maybe turned to her old neighbour for comfort, she sees Ella, hears about the neglect and parties and flips.'

'And what would she do with Ella?'

Edris shrugged his shoulders.

'If they had a child that died, they would've had to move away before anyone noticed and when they did move, they didn't go far. I can't see how they'd pull it off,' Meadows said.

'I suppose. So we cross them off our list?'

'Not yet, we need to check out the daughter. There's still another four families to check out and Paskin has to check out the other missing baby. We don't want them all

187

to be suspects, otherwise I'll have to persuade Lester to DNA test them all.'

'Maybe we'll have some luck with Sally Matthews,' Edris said. He looked at the notes. 'Actually, it's Sally Anderson, married to a Doctor Anderson. She works as a nurse in the special care baby unit. She doesn't sound like a baby killer.'

'Who does?' Meadows said. 'She could've changed her life around. You better call ahead, see if she's in work or at home. I don't want to be driving around Cardiff.'

'Okay, but we need to stop off for food. I'm wasting away,' Edris said, laughing.

Sally Anderson arranged to meet them at home so Meadows drove along Cyncoed Road while Edris tried to make out the numbers.

'Look at the size of some of these places,' Edris said. 'Her old man must be minted, or maybe he was born into money.'

'A different world from Coopers Wood estate,' Meadows said.

'I think it's the next house.' Edris pointed.

Meadows pulled into the circular drive. In the centre, a stone fountain stood among white pebbles. The house was impressive, with bay windows and a double garage to the side. A silver BMW was parked in front of the garage door.

'Nice place,' Edris said.

Sally Anderson appeared at the door as Meadows climbed out of the car. She was smartly dressed in a pale blue woollen dress, her cardigan draped on her shoulders. Her dark blond hair hung over her shoulders, with the fringe cut and straightened to a perfect line at her eyebrows.

Has she changed to meet us? Or does she always dress like this?

'I'm DC Edris, we spoke on the phone, and this is DI Meadows.'

'You better come in although I don't know what help I can be, it must be nearly twenty-five years since I lived on Coopers Wood estate.'

She turned and led them inside.

They entered a hallway where a table stood against the wall, holding a large floral arrangement. On the opposite wall, an oval gilded mirror reflected the flowers. A wide staircase ran up the centre. There wasn't a coat or pair of shoes in sight. Sally led them to a formal sitting room where Meadows felt an urge to remove his shoes before stepping onto the thick pile cream carpet. The ceiling was high, with ornate coving; a large oil painting hung above the fireplace. There were no ornaments, family photos, or even a television.

'Please take a seat.'

Meadows sat on one of the two leather sofas next to Edris and watched Sally take a seat. She crossed her legs at the ankles and placed her hands folded on her lap. Meadows noticed that she had short nails.

Could she have bound George to the bed?

'It's a lovely home,' Edris said.

'Thank you. How can I help you?'

'You were a resident of 109, Coopers Wood estate from 1991 to 1993,' Meadows said.

'That's correct.'

'And our records show that you lived there with your daughter, Jade. Was it just the two of you?'

Sally's shoulders stiffened. 'Yes, and if that's your way of asking if I was shacked up with some man, then the answer is no. I was a single parent. Jade's father wasn't around and I really didn't have any interest in men at that time.'

'Is Jade your only child?'

'No, I have a son, he's five years younger than Jade.'

'So, Jade would be about twenty-four now?' Meadows asked.

'Yes.'

189

'Is she still living at home?'

'No, but I don't see how that's relevant. She was only a baby when we lived on Coopers Wood estate.' Sally hands clenched on her lap.

Meadows got the sense that Sally was uncomfortable talking about the past. *Is she ashamed of where she came from or is it something else?*

'I expect you've seen on the news that a child was found buried in the garden and your old neighbour, George, was found dead in his home yesterday. We are treating his death as suspicious,' Edris said.

'Yes, I did hear something about it on the radio.'

'Did you know George well?' Meadows asked.

'Not really, I haven't seen him or anyone else from that area since I moved away.'

'Did you get along with him when you lived there? We understand from previous occupants that he was very friendly and helpful.'

'I only saw him occasionally, going in and out of the house. Just to say hello. Sometimes I would see him out the garden. I didn't live there that long.'

'When you lived in the house was there a patio in the garden?' Edris asked.

Sally looked down at her hands and pursed her lips, seemingly thinking about the question.

'No, I don't think so. It was just a grassy area from what I remember. Why?'

'We're just looking into any changes that were made to the garden and when these changes took place,' Edris explained.

'Well, that's about all, for now,' Meadows said. 'We just need to ask about your movements yesterday.'

Sally bristled. 'Surely you don't think that I have anything to with this.'

'We have to ask so we can eliminate you from our enquires.' Meadows smiled. 'We are asking all the previous occupants.'

'I worked in the morning then spent the afternoon on the phone. Jade is getting married next week so there are a lot of arrangements that need checking.'

'Where is she getting married?'

'Cardiff Castle,' Sally said.

'How lovely, well I hope you have a wonderful day,' Meadows said as he stood.

'We may need to speak with you again,' Edris said. 'We'll be in touch if that's the case.'

'I've told you everything I can and it's a very busy time for me at the moment. Jade will be arriving Sunday afternoon with the bridesmaids. We have rehearsals and relatives coming to stay. So, if you do need to talk to me again, I would appreciate it if you would leave it until after the wedding.' Sally stood up. 'I'll see you out.'

'We just need an address for Jade before we go,' Edris said.

Sally's eyes narrowed. 'Why would you need Jade's address?'

'We just need to establish the whereabouts of all the children that occupied the house during that time period.'

'Fine.' Sally left them in the hallway, then returned with a piece of paper. 'I can assure you that she's very much alive, but if you can't take my word for it.' She handed Meadows the paper. 'Jade is obviously busy, so I would be grateful if you didn't bother her.'

* * *

'I can't see her in leather boots, tying up George and brandishing a whip,' Edris said as they drove towards Bryn Mawr.

'Who said anything about a whip?' Meadows laughed. 'You really need to keep your imagination under control.'

'Nothing wrong with my imagination. I still think we can cross her off our list. The daughter is alive and she wouldn't have had time yesterday to get to Coopers Wood estate, kill George and get back unnoticed.'

'It's not impossible, it's only just over an hour's drive. She could've left work and driven straight to George's house. Nothing stopping her from making the phone calls as she drove.'

'Yeah, I suppose, but she's a bit of a snob, can't imagine what she would be doing with George.' Edris put the chair back and stretched out his legs.

'I guess she would do anything if she was desperate to keep her secret. Tired, are you?' Meadows teased.

'Just chilling. I can't see that she'd make up all that stuff about a wedding. Easy for us to check out that it is Jade getting married.'

'Yes, but she could've had another child, she didn't stay in the house that long. Maybe she needed to get away fast so no one would notice. I don't know.' Meadows sighed. 'Perhaps Paskin and Valentine will have had better luck or, you never know, Martin Hughes might be waiting with the answers.'

'Or we just DNA the lot and tell Lester later,' Edris suggested.

'Sounds like a plan to me,' Meadows said with a smile.

They drove along in silence and Meadows let his mind turn over the conversations they'd had with Sally and the Morrises.

Was there something about the way they acted, their reactions to the questions? Helen talked a lot, that could be nerves or maybe, because of her situation, she didn't get out to socialise very much. Sally was definitely uncomfortable. Maybe her family and friends didn't know about her past. Perhaps she was getting away from Jade's father. *What was it Jim said? I thought it was important at the time but couldn't think why.* Meadows turned on the music hoping it would relax his mind and something would surface. *It will come back to me.*

Chapter Twenty-two

Meadows and Edris walked into the deserted social services office. All the staff had gone home for the evening, apart from Martin Hughes, who they found waiting for them in his usual chaotic room.

'Good to see you, Martin.' Meadows smiled. 'How are things?'

'Snowed under as usual. The number of cases just keeps rising each week and we're so short of foster carers. On top of that, I feel responsible for Ella Beynon. Sorry, rant over,' Martin said.

'Sounds like you're having a shit week,' Edris said.

'No worse than yours, I expect.' Martin moved some files from the chairs to make room for them all to sit.

'Sounds like you need a holiday,' Meadows said.

'Or some loving,' Edris suggested.

'Edris is on a matchmaking mission this week.' Meadows laughed as he took a seat.

'Well don't bother with me. One failed marriage is enough and I doubt you'd find any woman to put up with me,' Martin said. 'So, can you tell me anything about how the case is going with Ella?'

'Yes,' Meadows said, 'but there isn't much to tell. No leads, apart from Ryan. His footprint was found next to the buried clothes, but we don't have enough to charge him with abduction. He's on remand for drug charges so at least he's not going anywhere.'

'I had heard,' Martin said. 'What about Natalie, do you think she's involved?'

'It's possible, she was seen going out in the early hours of the morning but claims she can't remember anything from that night. Our only witness is now dead.'

'You can't charge her?'

'Not until we have some evidence and know what's happened to Ella, all we have is her clothes,' Meadows said.

'Basically, you're saying you need a body before you can do anything.' Martin shook his head sadly.

'I'm still hoping for a better outcome but we're running out of options.'

'Yes, and questions are already being asked about how a child supposedly under our care is missing. If Natalie is responsible then we failed another child. Anyway, you came about the previous occupants of the house and we've digressed,' Martin said. 'Another poor little mite.'

'Yes,' Meadows said. 'We're looking into the background of each family and also if there is any possible link to Ella Beynon's disappearance.'

'We're hoping you've got something for us,' Edris said.

'I've searched through all our records but there isn't anything major on any of the families that I can see. There were some concerns raised with Ray and Susan Davies who lived in the house during the eighties. Their son Robert had a number of visits to casualty. Stitches, broken arm, among the injuries. We were notified by the hospital and a thorough investigation was made but there was no evidence to suggest that the injuries were not accidental. It seems Robert was a very active and fearless child.'

'And the other children?' Meadows asked.

'Two girls, a lot quieter than their brother by all accounts. The school was happy with all three children, no concerns of neglect,' Martin said.

'What about the other families?' Edris asked.

Martin shuffled through the papers on his desk.

'Sally Matthews, young single parent, lived in the house in the nineties. She suffered with postnatal depression, the father of the child wasn't around and there was no family support. There were no concerns over the child's wellbeing, the baby was thriving, clean clothes, and no health issues apart from colic. It was a case of just offering support and advice. She moved out of the area, but the last visit recorded that she was doing well and was considering going back to education.'

'If she suffered from postnatal depression, is it possible that she had other mental health issues? Something that could have returned years later?' Meadows asked.

'There are women who suffer from postpartum psychosis, but it is a rare and a very serious condition. I see nothing in the file that would suggest this. You would have to examine her medical records to establish if she had any other illness.'

'We saw her today and she seemed well and to have done very well for herself,' Meadows said.

'All airs and graces now,' Edris said.

'Well, I'm pleased to hear that she's doing well, even if that is the case,' Martin said. 'That's it, apart from Helen and James Morris, but that doesn't have anything to do with the children. They needed help to get modifications to their home and benefits to make their life a little easier. We still continue to support them, it's not easy for Helen to be a full-time carer and the situation is likely to worsen.'

'Nothing else at all?' Meadows asked.

'No, but that's not to say there weren't any problems with the other families, it just may not have been brought to our attention.'

Meadows ran his hand through his hair.

I was hoping for something more.

'Do you think it's possible for a child to lay buried in a garden for twenty-five to thirty years and no one to notice that child is missing?'

'Is that your line of enquiry, you think that the child's parents are on this list?'

'We haven't found a DNA match to any of the families we know about. It has to be a child that wasn't reported missing.'

Martin leaned back in his chair and rubbed his hand over his chin.

'I suppose it's possible given the right circumstance. You would need the mother, or both parents, to be isolated from their families. Maybe not have any close friends. They could've moved away from the area. A health visitor or doctor is unlikely to be chasing up a child on the list if the family is the responsibility of another county. The child could get lost in the system. I guess it's possible, but then you would find that one of the families has a child missing.'

Jim Morris's comments came back to Meadows.

What was it he said about children looking the same? No he didn't say that but maybe... An idea came to him.

'What about if they swapped the child?'

'What? You mean bury their own child in the garden and nick another one to replace it,' Edris said. 'Someone would be bound to notice that.'

'Not really,' Martin said. 'Less noticeable than the complete absence of a baby. Think about how many children a health visitor sees each month. Yes, there may be a difference in the weight and height but if the child hasn't been seen by a health professional for a month, I doubt they'd notice. I guess they see so many babies that one looks about the same as another.'

'And if the parents had no close family or friends, who would notice the baby looked different?' Meadows said.

'Bloody hell,' Edris said. 'That means that one of the missing children could be alive and living under a completely different identity. That's going to be a real mess to sort out.'

'Let's see what the others have come up with and take it from there.' Meadows stood up. 'Thank you, Martin, you've been a great help as always.'

'You're welcome, if you need anything else give me a shout.'

* * *

Back at the station Meadows felt the adrenalin pumping through his body and sharpening his thoughts.

We're close to finding the identity of the child and George's killer, I can feel it.

Paskin and Valentine were in the office, eyes fixed to their computers and fingers flying over the keys.

'I think we're getting somewhere,' Meadows said. 'Have the files on Cerys Lane and Poppy Moore come in yet?'

'On your desk,' Paskin said.

'Thanks.' Meadows sat at the desk and picked up a file. 'Edris, can you give the DVLA a call and make sure they have Shannon Morris working there.'

'Yeah, no problem, then I'll make a cuppa. Want one?'

'Yes please,' Paskin and Valentine chorused.

'Thanks.'

Meadows returned his attention to the files. He read through each case which gave the same information he had got from Jenny Lane and Daisy. He made some notes then dragged another incident board next to the first one and wrote down the names of the previous occupants of Coopers Wood estate along with the daughters' names. Below he wrote the birth dates of the missing children and date of abduction. He looked at the information and satisfied returned to his desk where Edris had placed a cup of tea.

'Where is Blackwell?' Meadows took a sip of his tea.

'Not back yet, he was visiting Michelle and John Stanley. Probably stuffing his face with tea and cake,' Valentine said.

'What's that about tea and cake? I wouldn't say no,' Blackwell called out as he sauntered into the office.

'Sorry we just had one,' Paskin said.

'Fine, I'll make my own,' Blackwell growled.

When Blackwell returned with his tea Meadows gathered the team around the incident board.

'Right, we've interviewed all the previous occupants of 109 Coopers Wood estate. Let's see what we've got. Paskin?'

'The Evans' daughter is grown up with children of her own. They were happy to show me the photos of Vanessa growing up, getting married and the grandchildren. There was no patio in the garden when they lived there, and they moved out before George took up residence next door.'

'Okay, so looks like we can rule them out.' Meadows put a line through their name on the board. 'Valentine?'

Valentine flipped open her notebook. 'Ray and Sue Davies. They seemed genuinely sorry about the untimely death of George. They said he was a friendly man and a good neighbour. Their oldest daughter Rhian was killed in a car crash shortly after her eighteenth birthday. I checked it out. The death is registered and there was an enquiry into the crash. The older daughter, Rachel, turned up for a visit while we were there. Again, there was no patio and the only work they did in the garden was to plant some bulbs.'

Meadows put another line through the name on the board.

'Okay, next is Sally Matthews, now Anderson.' Meadows nodded at Edris.

'Daughter Jade is getting married on Saturday, we have an address but still need to check it out.'

'I can help out there,' Paskin said. 'When I was running my checks on all the children I came across an adoption for Jade Matthews. Dr Laurence Anderson formally adopted Jade when she was three years old. She became Jade Anderson.'

'Well that puts Jade out of the picture,' Edris said. 'Also Sally claims there was no patio when she lived at the house.'

Meadows didn't put a line through Sally and Jade's name, instead he pointed to the next.

'Helen and James Morris were the next occupants. Their daughter Shannon works in the DVLA.'

'Checks out,' Edris said.

'They claim there was a patio when they moved in. That leaves the Stanleys.' Meadows nodded at Blackwell.

'All the children accounted for and still in school. I checked it out. Only good things to say about George. Never saw him with a woman and there was a patio. So that stuffs up your theory that one of the previous occupants buried their child in the garden,' Blackwell said.

'Not necessarily,' Meadows said. 'Paskin, did you check out the details on the other missing baby we thought may have been taken to Iran by the father?'

'Yes, I spoke to the mother. Apparently, the father sends pictures of the child on each birthday. I guess he must've used a false passport to get out of the country. The mother is still campaigning for the government to get involved in getting the child back.'

'So that just leaves us with Cerys Lane and Poppy Moore,' Meadows said.

'Which we already know are not a match to the child in the garden,' Blackwell huffed.

'But they could be a match to Shannon Morris or Jade Anderson.' Meadows looked at the confusion on the team's faces. All except Edris who was nodding. 'Bear with me on this. Sally Anderson said there was no patio in the garden, yet Jim and Helen Morris said there was a patio when they moved in. One of them is lying.'

'Yeah but that doesn't mean Jack,' Blackwell said.

'Not on its own,' Meadows said, 'but look at the dates. Sally moved into the house in 1991, her daughter Jade was born on the 2nd of April 1992 and would have been three months old when Poppy Moore was abducted on the 2nd of June 1992. The same age as the baby we found in the garden. There is only a month difference in age between the two children. If Sally didn't have any close family or friends it would be easy to pass off Poppy as Jade. Especially if the babies had the same hair colouring. A health visitor wouldn't have picked it up, they see too many babies. That's if Sally even bothered to see a health visitor. She moved out of the area in 1993 and wanted a new life where no one knew her.'

'Yes, but Poppy Moore's abduction would've been on every news channel and newspaper. Her face would be well known. Surely someone would notice,' Valentine said.

'Not really.' Paskin tucked her hair behind her ear. 'Sally would've already been seen with a baby long before Poppy Moore was abducted. Why would anyone suspect her? It's not like someone is going to stop her on the street and say "your baby looks like the missing child. Did you abduct her?".'

'I guess,' Valentine agreed.

'Only someone close to her would be able to scrutinise the child and maybe George was the one to suspect,' Meadows said.

'Okay, I buy it,' Blackwell said. 'Let's bring her in and get a DNA test on Sally and the daughter.'

'It's not as straightforward as that,' Meadows said. 'I wish that was the only possibility. After Sally moved out the Morrises moved in with their baby daughter, Shannon. She was born on the 31st of January and would have been three months old when Cerys Lane was abducted from hospital. There is a three-month difference in age.'

'You couldn't pass off a newborn for a three-month-old,' Valentine said.

'No, but again the Morrises were new to the area so unlikely to have made any close friends. There wouldn't be any visitors to the house. Helen indicated that she didn't get on with the in-laws. You would see a difference with a newborn but not as the child got older. If they were careful for a few months, didn't go out anywhere where they'd meet people that knew them. The news of the abduction would've died down and by the time the child was, say, six months old no one would notice. You certainly wouldn't pick up a three-month age difference by the time the child went to school. It's a possibility that Shannon Morris is Cerys Lane. The Morrises stayed in the house for eight years. I reckon they had to move when Jim got ill, to a house where they would have room for a downstairs bedroom. They probably thought it would be safe by then.'

'But the child would look different from their other children,' Valentine said.

'Sally has a son by a different father and the Morrises have three boys so I guess you wouldn't notice a difference,' Edris said. 'I think it makes sense that one of the girls was snatched to replace the dead child.'

'There are no other missing babies,' Meadows said.

'One of them could've had another child,' Valentine suggested.

'There would've been a record of the birth,' Paskin said.

'Shannon is the right age to be Cerys and Jade is the right age to be Poppy,' Meadows said. 'It's the only logical explanation.' He looked around the team for their agreement.

'I agree,' Paskin said. 'But it's a hell of a mess to sort out and think of the poor girl.'

'What if we've got it wrong?' Blackwell said.

'We upset a few people, we've got nothing to lose,' Meadows said.

'Okay, let's get them all in,' Blackwell stood.

'I think we'll have to be more subtle than that,' Meadows said. 'We'll ask Sally Anderson and Jim and Helen Morris for a voluntary DNA test. If they have nothing to hide, then they should cooperate.'

'And if they don't?' Blackwell asked.

'Then we bring them in for questioning.'

'Are we going to ask Shannon Morris and Jade Anderson for a DNA sample?' Paskin asked.

Meadows thought for a moment.

'That would certainly get the Morrises or Sally Anderson worried if they're guilty. Yes, I think we are going to have to if we are to be sure. I'll go with Edris in the morning to get samples from Sally and the Morrises. Paskin, see if you can persuade Shannon Morris to give a sample. Blackwell and Valentine, you can take Jade Anderson. If she's anything like her mother she may be difficult.'

'What do we tell them?' Paskin asked. 'We don't really want to give them the idea that they may be an abducted child.'

'No, not at this stage,' Meadows agreed. 'Just say that it's for elimination purposes and we are testing all children that were living in the house. That should do. Hopefully by this time tomorrow we can give that little girl in the morgue a name, but we must also bear in mind that we could tear apart a family, so some sensitivity is needed.'

'So where does Ella Beynon fit into this?' Blackwell asked.

'Well, one of these two' – Meadows pointed to the board – 'either walked into a hospital or into a garden to abduct a baby. They may have done it again. If we establish the identity of the child, we'll have good grounds to get a search warrant for the house.'

'I hope you're right,' Blackwell said.

So do I, Meadows thought.

Chapter Twenty-three

The police came today. It was a bit of a shock at first but I don't think they suspected anything. Maybe this will all go away and you'll never have to read this. It's my prayer every night before I sleep and in the morning as soon as I awake. I beg and plead with God, even make deals. I'd do anything for you not to be hurt.

I amazed myself at how calm I felt when the police talked to me, the lies rolled off my tongue with ease. I guess if you pretend for long enough it's not that difficult. I'm not sorry about George. He knew all along, even though he didn't say it out right. He even helped to lay the patio. Maybe he wasn't certain about what lay underneath the slabs but he dropped little hints. Always when I was alone. He would come to the house with some excuse to see me. It didn't take him long to let me know what he wanted from me.

I always went to his house, I couldn't bear the thought of having him in my bed. Afterwards I would come home and run a bath so hot I could barely stand it, I would scrub my skin until it was raw, but I never felt clean. That's another thing you can add to my crimes. I prostituted myself – a common whore. It seemed to go on forever, he got greedy wanting more and more. I was afraid we would get caught and the truth would come out. There seemed no way out of the hell but that was the price I had to pay.

I got to the point where I wanted to end it all. I guess by now you think that I deserve to die – you're right, I should have ended it then. I stockpiled paracetamols and bought a bottle of whisky. I sat on the patio and drank to work up the courage. I thought of my beautiful girl beneath my feet and how I had failed her and the child asleep in the cot. Then I had a sudden moment of clarity. Death wasn't punishment enough. I had to live and try and atone for my crime. I made a plan to better myself, be the best mother I could. I could endure George, maybe I could even get away from this place, but I couldn't bear to leave the garden.

The police say they may come back. Maybe George told someone what he knew. I may not have much time, so I need to tell you what happened that day…

Chapter Twenty-four

'I'm sorry to call so early,' Meadows said as he stood on the Morrises' doorstep, 'but it's important that we talk to you again.'

'Okay, you better come in.' Helen Morris was wearing a faded pink dressing gown, her hair stuck up on one side, and her eyes were sleepy. 'Jim is just getting up, he had a bad night.' She led them into the sitting room. 'Take a seat for a minute, I won't be long.'

Edris sat while Meadows took the opportunity to have a closer look at the photographs that were positioned around the room. The photos showed the Morris children at various ages. Meadows peered at a school photo which showed three mischievous boys, one with his front teeth missing. Behind them sat a girl with her hair in braids, one hand on the shoulder of her brother.

Could you be Cerys Lane?

Muffled voices came from the room next door. Meadows moved on to the next photo, this one showing Shannon holding a baby. He tried to pick out any features that would resemble the Lanes. The muffled voices grew clearer, so he moved away from the photo and took a seat.

Jim came into the room first, his gait unsteady, and a tremor in both arms. He was dressed in a stripy robe with slippers on his feet. Helen hovered behind him and looked relieved when he finally managed to plonk himself down in the armchair.

'I'm a bit slow in the morning, have to wait for the meds to kick in.'

'I'm sorry to have disturbed you,' Meadows said. 'We won't keep you long. Following our enquires yesterday we have reason to believe that the child we found in the garden was put there somewhere between 1991 and 1993.'

'Oh, but surely you don't think we had anything to do with it,' Helen said. 'We have four children of our own, we would never have kept quiet if we knew someone had buried a child in our garden.'

Yes, but you would keep quiet if it was you that buried the child.

'There are things regarding the case that we cannot discuss, but it would be really helpful if the two of you would provide us with a DNA sample.' Meadows eyes moved from Jim to Helen watching closely for a reaction.

'What does it involve?' Helen asked. 'Jim has had a bad night and I don't think it's a good idea to take him out and have him pulled around.'

'It's just a swab of the inside of your cheek,' Edris explained. 'I have a kit with me, so we can do it here. You don't even have to leave your chair, Jim.'

'Fine by me,' Jim said.

'Okay, if it helps,' Helen said.

They don't look very concerned. Meadows watched Edris take the samples and check each label.

'Thank you,' Meadows said. 'We really appreciate your cooperation. We won't need to trouble you further, one of our officers will call with Shannon to see if she is happy to give a sample.'

'Shannon?' Helen's eyes widened. 'Why do you need a sample from Shannon?'

That got a reaction. Interesting. 'We have to test all the girls that lived in the house. It's just for elimination purposes. Nothing to worry about,' Meadows said.

'Right, I see,' Helen said.

'We'll see ourselves out.' Meadows said. 'Thanks again for your help.'

* * *

'She looked worried when I mentioned we would be testing Shannon,' Meadows said as they drove towards Cardiff.

'Maybe she thought that the test was only to eliminate them from George's murder and not to test for a match against the child we found,' Edris said.

'But that doesn't make sense, there was plenty of DNA left in George's bedroom.'

'Yeah but they don't appear to be sharp tools, probably don't really understand how the tests work. Whoever killed George took the remainder of the twine, obviously thinking that would help, yet didn't wear gloves or wipe down the bedposts. You'd have to be a bit thick to think you could get away with it.'

'Or it was just a spur of the moment act,' Meadows said.

'Well, Jim didn't look a bit bothered. You'd think that he would notice if his wife buried their child in the garden and swapped it for another. He didn't react at all when we mentioned we would be testing Shannon.'

'No, but then Parkinson's can cause a loss of facial expressions. So even if he was panicked we might not be able to tell. We're just going to have to wait for the test results.'

'Can't wait to see Sally Anderson's reaction when we turn up again and interrupt her busy life,' Edris said grinning.

* * *

This time it wasn't Sally that stood on the doorstep but a portly man with receding grey hair. He wore rimless glasses and held himself with an air of authority.

'Mr Anderson?' Meadows asked.

'Doctor Anderson.' He pulled his shoulders back.

Oh, so he wants to use titles, well I can play along with that.

'Detective Inspector Meadows, and this is Detective Constable Edris.' He showed his ID. 'We would like to speak to your wife if she is in.'

'My wife is very busy, as am I. Perhaps it would be better for you to call back. If you leave your contact details, I'll ask my wife to contact you with a convenient time. I would imagine that it won't be until after next week.'

He's obviously someone who is used to getting his own way.

'I'm afraid that won't be possible. It's important that we speak with your wife now. If it's not convenient to do so here, then I'm happy to conduct an interview at the station.' Meadows gave what he hoped was a tight smile.

Dr Anderson's eyes narrowed, and he looked like he was about to protest before a look of curiosity flashed briefly across his face.

'What is the nature of your call?'

'I'm afraid we can only discuss that with your wife. We spoke with her yesterday.'

By the expression on Dr Anderson's face it was clear that Sally hadn't mentioned their call. 'I suppose you better come in, but I would appreciate it if you kept the visit brief.'

They were led into the hallway where the floral arrangement had been changed and ivy interspaced with flowers decorated the stair banister. Meadows imagined that it was set up for the bride's grand entrance.

'Sally!' Dr Anderson's voice echoed through the hallway. 'You have visitors.' He turned to Edris and Meadows. 'You can wait in here.'

He showed then into the same room that they had been in yesterday. The scent of lilies tickled Meadows nose as he entered the room. Two large floral arrangements stood either side of the fireplace and a table had been set out with upturned champagne glasses.

Sally walked into the room and stopped when she saw the visitors. Her shoulders stiffened and her jaw clenched.

'These detectives said that they spoke with you yesterday.' Dr Anderson raised his eyebrows.

'Yes.' Sally smoothed down her dress although it was not creased. 'With everything going on, I forgot to mention it.' She forced a smile. 'They just wanted some information about a neighbour from years ago. You go ahead and carry on, I can deal with this.'

'What neighbour?'

'Coopers Wood estate,' Edris said. 'You may have heard of the recent events on the news.'

'You never said you lived there.' Dr Anderson glared at his wife. 'I think we better sit down.'

'It was years ago, well before we met.' Sally perched on the edge of the armchair. 'I didn't live there very long.'

What else hasn't she told her husband?

Meadows took a seat. The atmosphere in the room was tense.

I imagine there is going to be a few chosen words said when we leave.

'Some information has come to light since we spoke yesterday, and we'd like you to provide us with a voluntary DNA sample.'

'What?' Dr Anderson's eyes widened. 'Are you saying my wife is a suspect in, well, whatever it is you are investigating? From what I've heard on the news there was an abduction and a suspicious death. I can't imagine why you'd think my wife has any involvement in either of these cases.'

'We are investigating both, as well as the discovery of a three-month-old baby found in the garden of 109,

Coopers Wood estate, where your wife lived from 1991 to 1993,' Edris said.

'We believe that there's a connection between the discovery of the child and the death of George Williams who lived next door,' Meadows said.

'Did you know this man?' Dr Anderson glared at his wife.

'Not really, like I explained yesterday to the detectives, we were only neighbours for a short time, I knew him to say hello to, but that's about all.'

'Then I don't see what this has to do with my wife,' Dr Anderson said.

'The DNA sample is just for elimination purposes,' Meadows explained.

'We're collecting a number of samples,' Edris said. 'So far all the previous occupants have been kind enough to provide a sample.'

'Unfortunately, this is the only way we can isolate the person responsible. Once we have the sample results we can eliminate you from our enquiries and we won't need to bother you again.' Meadows smiled at Sally.

'This is ridiculous,' Dr Anderson said. 'Just give them the sample so we can put an end to this nonsense.'

'Fine,' Sally said.

Edris stood up, snapped on latex gloves and took a swab from the inside of Sally's cheek. 'Thank you,' he said. 'We appreciate your co-operation.'

'Is that it?' Sally asked.

'Yes, we only have a couple of more samples to collect then they can be sent off for analysis. One of our officers is calling on your daughter so we won't need to trouble you again today,' Meadows said.

'My daughter! No, you can't,' Sally stiffened. 'You can call your officers and tell them they're not to bother Jade. It's bad enough you come here harassing me.'

'I don't see what this has to do with my daughter,' Dr Anderson said.

Same reaction as Helen had to her daughter being tested.

'There are certain aspects of the case that we cannot disclose but I assure you that it is necessary to request a sample from Jade. She is an adult in her own right and therefore has the right to decide to take or refuse the test.'

'Please.' Sally's eyes pleaded. 'It's her wedding day soon. I don't want anything to ruin her day. Can't it wait until after she comes back from her honeymoon?'

'Mrs Anderson, I'm sorry but this cannot wait. I am a little confused as to why you'd think a simple DNA test would cause distress to your daughter,' Meadows said.

Sally looked at her husband then back to Meadows.

'She doesn't know anything of my past. I mean about her biological father. Laurence is the only father she has known, and we have never told her the truth.'

'I see, but surely she would've found out at some time. What about her passport application? She would need her birth certificate for that.'

'Her father's name was not put on the birth certificate. We told her that we weren't married when she was born so Laurence had to go through a formal adoption so she could change her name to Anderson. She accepted the explanation.'

'Well, I can assure you that the request will be handled with sensitivity. As Jade's biological father has no bearing on the case, as far as we know, then there's no reason that she hears this, erm, revelation from us.'

Dr Anderson looked at his wife, the resentment evident on his face.

'We'll have to tell her that we stayed in that house while we were waiting for the sale of our property to go through. I don't like to lie to her but it seems you have put me in an awkward situation. She has more important things to think about, so I doubt she will question it. We can put this behind us and get on with the preparation.' He looked at Meadows. 'If that's all, we have things to attend to.'

211

Meadows could sense that Edris was itching to say something, but he remained silent until they were back in the car.

'That Dr Anderson is a control freak. I think he was pissed that you didn't take any shit from him,' Edris said.

'Yes, I got the impression that he's used to getting his own way. His only concern seemed to be that Jade would find out that he is not her real father. And Sally doesn't want the embarrassment of anyone knowing that she once lived on a council estate and had a child by, well, who knows.'

'Can you imagine Dr Anderson's reaction if he found out his wife is a murderer? He'd probably drop dead from shock.' Edris laughed.

'He seemed fairly confident that she had nothing to do with it,' Meadows said, 'but it looks like she has kept her past life from him. Still, I would've expected more resistance from her if she was guilty. She gave the sample without much fuss.'

'Yeah because he told her to do so.'

'We'll find out soon enough.'

* * *

They dropped the samples off at the lab and went back to the station where the rest of the team were working at their desks.

'All samples are in,' Blackwell said. 'Who's your money on?'

'I don't think I would bet on either of them,' Edris said. 'They're all acting weird if you ask me. Especially when we mentioned the DNA test on their daughters. That certainly caused a reaction.'

'Maybe they're all guilty,' Paskin said. 'We could hit the jackpot and find Cerys and Poppy in one go.'

'Yeah and find Ella alive and well in one of their houses,' Blackwell snapped.

'Well it's going to be a long wait for the results, lucky if we get anything back for a week,' Valentine said. 'Not a lot we can do in the meantime.'

'Not with Mike's new toy,' Meadows said. 'He will have the results in sometime tonight.'

'What new toy?' Valentine asked.

'His Rapid Hit machine, he's trialling it. Apparently, it can process the results in two hours,' Blackwell said. 'If the trials go well, we could end up having one at the station. No need to wait for forensics. Couple of weeks training and anyone can use it.'

'Yeah and we'd probably be the last to get one,' Edris said. 'I wonder how Mike managed to wriggle in on the trial.'

'Obviously got connections,' Paskin said.

'Yeah but how reliable is it?' Valentine asked.

'Mike's impressed with it, although it could end up doing him out of a job in the future,' Meadows said.

He sat at his desk and saw that Brianna had phoned in and asked to be called back.

'Well, it's going to be a long wait this evening and a busy day tomorrow so maybe you all better get off home and get some rest.'

'I'm staying until the results are in,' Blackwell said.

'Me too,' Paskin said.

Valentine nodded.

Meadows looked around at his team and admired their determination and commitment. It had been a long week and not one of them was willing to take up the offer to go home.

'Okay, while we're all here we may as well make ourselves useful. I want to go over everything we have so far on Ella. Sightings, statements, DNA results, Natalie's finances and anything we have on Ryan. I want to make sure we haven't missed anything. If it turns out there is no connection between the child in the garden and Ella's abduction then Natalie and Ryan are still our only suspects.

Edris, call Brianna and see what's happening with Natalie. If it's not urgent it can wait.'

* * *

They divided the files among themselves and the office fell silent as they combed through details. Meadows was looking through Natalie's bank statements when he came across a payment to Bradbury farm dated a month before Ella's disappearance.

'Anyone got a reference to a Bradbury farm?' Meadows looked around the office and was met with a shake of heads. He checked the reference then googled the name. It appeared to be a holiday cottage rental in Lancaster. He felt a flicker of excitement as he dialled the number. A man answered and confirmed that he had received payment from a Natalie Beynon for a booking of one of the cottages. His wife had also called the incident line to report this after seeing the appeal. Meadows thanked him and hung up.

'How was this missed?' Meadows said. 'This cottage was booked over the weekend that Ella went missing, and is paid up to today. A woman and a child, the owner thinks. He said he would check with his wife as she was the one to hand over keys.'

'The sub team checked the finances,' Blackwell said. 'We would've done a better job even if we were up all night.'

'Who's checking the reported sightings?' Meadows asked.

'Me,' Valentine said.

'Anything from Lancaster?'

'Yes,' Valentine bit her lip. 'I remember this call coming in.' She looked at Paskin.

'Yeah, I did mention it at the time but I think we dismissed it as being too far away,' Paskin said.

'The lady who called in claimed that Natalie stayed at one of her cottages with a child. Requested a cot,' Valentine said.

'Edris, get hold of Lancaster police. Ask them to check it out. See if the cottage has any neighbours and if anyone saw who was staying there.'

'But Natalie couldn't have been at the cottage on Sunday night and got back in time to report Ella missing,' Blackwell said.

'Let's see.' Meadows pulled up a map on the computer and keyed in a route planner. Four hours and sixteen minutes. 'If she stuck to the speed limit and she left after Nia saw her at ten then she could have been in Lancaster at just after two in the morning.'

'But George saw her leave at two,' Paskin said.

'Okay, she leaves at two and gets there at half six. What time did she call in to report Ella missing?'

'Eleven,' Blackwell said.

'She could've got back by eleven.'

'Pushing it a bit,' Blackwell said. 'And why drive there and straight back again?'

'Because she had arranged to drop Ella off,' Valentine said.

'Yeah, but there's been no payment,' Paskin said.

'Unless she has another account, or she could've hidden the cash somewhere,' Valentine said.

'Or she just wanted rid of the child,' Blackwell said.

'Check out traffic cameras for all the routes to Lancaster. See if you can pick up her car on Sunday night,' Meadows said.

'But George saw her come back in half an hour,' Edris said.

'He could've been mistaken, let's see what Natalie has to say. What did Brianna say when you called her?'

'Something about a hypnotist,' Edris said.

'Great, well you never know, it may have jogged her memory. I'm beginning to wonder if I mistook Natalie's hangover on Monday for tiredness. She would look rough if she had driven all night. I think it's time we got tough with her.'

Chapter Twenty-five

Natalie was laying on the sofa in a thick haze of smoke, her eyes fixed to the television screen.

'Sorry to call on you so late,' Meadows said, 'but we have a few questions and I understand that you wanted to see me.'

'Yeah.' Natalie hit the mute on the control. 'Nia and Leanne took me to see some guy about remembering Sunday night.'

'A hypnotist?' Edris asked.

'Yeah, if you can call him that; bloody weirdo, if you ask me, but it worked. I didn't go out Sunday night and neither did Ryan, so you can get off my case about it.'

'Natalie, just because you've seen a hypnotist and you claim to remember Sunday night doesn't prove anything.' Meadows sat down. 'A witness saw you get into your car in the early hours of the morning. Was this session taped?'

'No, but she came with us.' Natalie looked at Brianna.

'Nia asked me to go along,' Brianna said. 'Natalie did appear to be under hypnosis and I did take notes.'

'Okay, let's hear it,' Meadows said. 'I want to know everything you remembered from Sunday night and not an edited version.'

'You already know most of it.' Natalie huffed. 'Fine, I put Ella to bed about seven. Ryan was down here watching TV. She was still awake when I put her in the cot, I turned off the light and shut the door. Claire and Jamie came with Dan, they had some cans and a couple of flagons of cider. We sat in here and had a few drinks and a smoke.'

'A spliff?' Edris asked.

Natalie glanced at Brianna. 'Yeah.'

'How much?'

'I dunno.'

'Did you share one?' Edris asked.

'What does it matter how much we smoked?' Natalie glared at Edris. 'We had a few okay. Then after Nia left we made a brew.'

'Who brought the mushrooms?' Meadows asked.

Natalie shrugged.

'You said that Ryan had some mushrooms and suggested a brew when you were with the hypnotist,' Brianna said.

Natalie's eyes narrowed. 'Whatever, we all took them. Then everything changed. It was like seeing the world for the first time. The sofa was like liquid, it made waves of different colours. I just kept wanting to touch it but at the same time I wanted to leave the room to see more. We went out into the garden. The rain was like silver ribbons, twirling and dancing. I could feel it on my face; soft. It made me sparkle, made me beautiful.' Natalie smiled. 'The grass became tiny fingers, I fell to my knees, and I wanted to be part of the earth. I dug with my hands, made shapes that changed on their own.'

'How long did you stay out the garden?' Meadows asked.

'I dunno, it could've been minutes or hours.' Natalie shrugged. 'Time didn't seem to matter. When we came back inside we were wet and dirty and laughing. We came in here and stripped off, then I heard Ella crying. Well it was like singing, a beautiful song.'

Meadows looked at Brianna who shrugged and raised her eyebrows.

She was probably still tripping. We're never going to get any sense out of her.

'So, Ella was crying, what did you do?'

'I went to go upstairs but Ryan came after me. He grabbed me around the waist and said to leave her, so we came back in here and we…'

'Had a sex orgy?' Edris asked.

'None of your business,' Natalie snapped.

'Did you know Ryan filmed the whole thing and uploaded it to his computer?' Edris said.

Natalie looked down at her hands. 'He took some pictures, that's all. Nothing wrong with that.'

'He filmed you,' Meadows said. 'I bet he never told you that. It wasn't the only time. Did he go upstairs after?'

'No.'

'Why do you keep protecting him? We know he was in the woods the night Ella went missing. His footprints were found next to where Ella's clothes were buried. We also suspect that he is responsible for Ella's so-called accidents over the past six months. Surely your daughter means more to you.'

'He didn't go upstairs and he didn't go into the woods that night. He didn't take Ella. Why would I let him do that?'

Meadows shook his head. 'I really don't know. Maybe you're only remembering what you choose.'

'No, I've told you everything that happened. We all stayed here in the room. Claire, Jamie, and Dan fell asleep first, then Ryan. I was cold so I lay next to Ryan on the sofa and put a blanket over us. That was it until I woke up.'

'Not quite,' Brianna said.

'Oh yeah, something woke me up. I thought I heard someone on the stairs, but I was too tired to go and look so I just went back to sleep.'

Sally Anderson or Helen Morris creeping through the house?

'You mean someone walking up or down the stairs?' Meadows asked.

Natalie shrugged her shoulders.

'The hypnotist thought that Natalie could benefit from a few more sessions,' Brianna said.

'See, so I couldn't have gone out, I would've remembered. I was asleep the whole time. I just want to get back to normal.'

Normal? Her child has been missing for six days and she thinks she can just move on as if it was a lost purse. She probably faked being under hypnosis. I wouldn't put it past her.

Meadows sat forward in the chair. 'Natalie, we are doing everything we can to find Ella, but you haven't exactly been honest with us from the start. You could've saved us a lot of time if you had told the truth about Ryan and your extra job which involves contact with all sorts of men. Can't you see how difficult it is for us to believe what you are saying now?'

'I'm telling you the truth, I didn't go out.'

'Tell me about Bradbury farm holiday cottage.'

'I don't know anything about a holiday cottage.'

'It's in Lancaster.' Meadows could feel his patience slipping.

Natalie frowned. 'I've never been to Lancaster.'

'Yet you booked a cottage for last weekend. The payment is dated a month previously and taken from your account.' Meadows took out a sheet of paper and handed it to Natalie.

Natalie's eyes scanned the entries. 'But I didn't book a cottage, it must be a mistake. The bank has made a mistake.'

'I spoke to the woman who took the booking, it was booked in your name,' Meadows said. 'When was the last time you used your card?'

Natalie shrugged her shoulders. 'I think I took out money last Saturday.'

'You did, there is an entry on the statement. Can you see another entry on the statement that's out of place? Another payment you didn't make?'

Natalie looked at the statement again. 'No, the rest looks okay to me.'

'Well, don't you think that's a bit odd? The card hasn't been stolen and if someone had got hold of your card details, I think they would've done a bit more than book a cottage in your name. Do you see our problem? It looks like you made that booking and payment. Someone stayed at the cottage last weekend.'

'Well it wasn't me.' Natalie scowled. 'You know it wasn't me, I was here all night. Nia saw me.'

'Nia saw you at ten, you were seen getting into your car at around two in the morning. That leaves enough time for you to drive to Lancaster. What were you doing there? Did you arrange to meet someone to hand over Ella?'

'No! I didn't go anywhere. Ella was in her cot asleep Sunday night.'

'We are checking all the traffic cameras, if you drove to Lancaster Sunday night we will pick up your car.'

'Look all you fucking want, you won't find anything because I was here all night.' Natalie stood up, her fist clenched and her face contorted with rage. 'I want you all to go, get out of my house and leave me alone. I've had it with your questions and accusations. I've had Nia and Leanne on my case all day, I told them to piss off. I don't want to see them.' She turned to Brianna. 'You can fuck off as well. I don't need you here pretending to be my friend and spying on me.'

'Brianna is here for your benefit,' Meadows said. 'She's giving up time with her family to be here to help you in any way she can.'

'Yeah, well there is no point in her staying. I'm going back to work on Monday, no one can stop me.'

221

Edris' phone rang and the room fell silent. 'Excuse me a moment.' Edris stepped out of the room and closed the door.

Meadows looked at Natalie who looked close to tears. She stood rigid, with her left leg shaking.

Maybe I've pushed her too far but she's either lying or someone is playing a wicked game.

'Natalie, you're right, no one can stop you from going back to work, if that's what you want to do. At least let Brianna stay for the weekend. It's not good to be on your own at a time like this and she will be able to keep you updated on any developments.'

'There haven't been any developments, sitting around here is driving me crazy.'

'The cottage is a breakthrough and we are checking it out. Someone booked it and someone stayed there. That person is likely to be involved in Ella's abduction,' Meadows said, although doubts were starting to creep in.

Edris walked back into the room and caught Meadows' attention. 'The results are in.'

Chapter Twenty-six

Meadows felt the adrenalin fizzle through his veins as he rushed to the lab with Edris close behind. He pushed away the niggle of doubt that the results could all come back negative. Mike was waiting in his office, a small room positioned outside the laboratory.

'What have you got for us?' Meadows asked.

'Eager for the results, are you?' Mike teased. 'Okay I'll put you out of your misery. Helen and Jim Morris were not a match to the child found in the garden. Helen Morris was a match to Shannon Morris, but Jim Morris was not.'

'You're saying Jim is not Shannon's father,' Edris said. 'No wonder Helen was cagey about the DNA test.'

'Sally Anderson on the other hand is a match to our garden child.'

Meadows felt his stomach harden in anticipation of the next result.

'And Jade Anderson?'

'Jade Anderson is a match to Tom and Daisy Moore,' Mike said.

'So Jade Anderson is Poppy Moore,' Edris said.

'Yes, I will check all the results, but I'm fairly certain of the accuracy. I haven't spoken to Daisy, it's going to come as a bit of a shock.'

'I'll talk to her tonight,' Meadows said. 'I don't want her finding out through station gossip. The news will soon spread when we make the arrest. All we need now is to match Sally Anderson's DNA to the samples taken from George's bedroom, but I think that's just going to be a formality.'

'That's my next job,' Mike said as he stifled a yawn.

'Leave it until tomorrow,' Meadows suggested. 'Go home and get some rest, we have enough to arrest Sally Anderson.'

'No, I'd rather stay and get it finished. That way I can have Sunday at home and I don't intend to come back until Monday, so don't go finding any more crime scenes. I'm going to switch off my phone,' Mike said with a smile.

'I don't blame you,' Meadows said. 'Have a good time with the family and thanks for all your help. I appreciate all the extra hours you've put in.'

'Yeah, well the little one in the garden deserved some answers and everyone here is fond of Daisy. At least this will put an end to years of not knowing what happened to her sister.'

'I'm not sure her sister is going to be happy to hear the news. At the moment, she is in blissful ignorance,' Meadows said.

'Sad thing is it's the children that suffer, the baby in the garden, Daisy and her sister, and poor Ella Beynon who is Lord knows where. Some people shouldn't be parents. Good luck tomorrow, I have a feeling you're going to have a bitch of a day.'

'Yeah,' Edris agreed. 'Perfect end to the week.'

Meadows sent a quick text message to Daisy and by the time he had driven to the station car park she had replied and given her home address.

'I'll leave you to fill the team in on the latest developments. I have something I need to do.' Meadows turned to face Edris.

'Daisy?'

'Yes, I don't want to leave it until the morning. Better tell Blackwell to give Lester a call and fill him in. Then you all better get off home. I want to make an early start in the morning.'

'Tell Daisy I'm thinking of her, it's not going to be easy news to deal with,' Edris said before climbing out of the car.

Meadows' mind raced as he pulled up outside the address Daisy had given him. It was a block of four flats and Daisy lived on the first floor. He had kept his message brief, giving no indication of why he needed to talk with her and now he wondered what reaction he would get.

She could be angry that I didn't tell her we were running the DNA test again. She has every right to be, I could've let her know but she's already been on a roller coaster of emotions this week and I didn't want to put her through another wait if it turned out negative. I've probably blown any chance of a date now.

He turned off the engine and checked his reflection in the rear-view mirror. Dark stubble covered his chin and his hair looked in need of a cut. *Oh, what does it matter what you look like, you're not here to impress her.*

Daisy was stood outside her flat door when Meadows reached the top of the stairs. Her long dark hair was loose and cascaded in waves over her shoulders. Her creamy complexion was accentuated by the red jumper she wore.

'I'm sorry to call on you so late.'

'I take it this is not a social call.' Daisy returned his smile. 'Come in.'

The flat was lightly scented with vanilla, the source of which came from a candle that burned in a glass jar on the coffee table. The room was cosy with a large brown suede sofa. Landscape pictures of mountains, sea, and forests were hung against cream painted walls.

'Lovely place you have,' Meadows said.

'Thank you. You better sit down and tell me what's on your mind.' Daisy sat on the end of the sofa.

As there didn't appear to be any other seating Meadows took a seat on the opposite side of the sofa and sat at an angle facing her. He wasn't sure how to start.

Better get straight to the point.

'When we didn't get a match for our little miss in the garden we started interviewing the previous occupants of the house. We looked into their backgrounds hoping to find some discrepancy with the children that were living there, perhaps one of them missed by the authorities. Or maybe a child was born and not registered for whatever reason. We ran DNA tests on some of the parents to compare them to the child we found.'

'And you found a match?' Interest sparked in Daisy's eyes. 'I knew I could count on you to get our little miss an ID.'

'Well, now we know the identity of the mother of the child, a child she claimed to be still alive. So, we ran another test, this time against two of the grown-up children of the previous occupants and compared them with the parents of missing children. We got a match – to you and your father. We found Poppy, she is alive but living under a different identity.'

Daisy stared blankly at Meadows. It seemed to take a few moments for the information to sink in.

'Are you telling me that some woman killed her child and took Poppy to replace her?' Her voice trembled.

'Yes, it looks that way, I don't have all of the facts yet. I'm sorry, this must be quite a shock for you. I didn't tell you that we were running the tests because to be honest I had no evidence that this would be the case. It was just a slight possibility.'

Meadows tried to pick his words carefully, he didn't want to give away Poppy's identity until he had made an arrest.

'There was more than one family that we suspected of being responsible for concealing the child in the garden and more than one family that had a child abducted during that time. It was a little complicated. I didn't want to put you, your father, and the other parents involved through the wait and disappointment of another test.'

'It's okay, I understand, it's just a lot to take in now. I do appreciate that you came to tell me.'

Meadows felt his body relax. 'Can I do anything for you? Make a cup of tea?'

Daisy smiled. 'The answer to all problems, a cup of tea.'

'If you rather I left so you can be on your own, I won't be offended.'

'I'd very much like you to stay.'

Meadows felt his skin tingle. 'Then I'll make you that cup of tea.' He walked into the kitchen which was small and neat. There were a few dishes on the draining board and a solitary cactus on the windowsill. Meadows flicked the switch on the kettle and took two mugs from the mismatched set hanging on the mug tree.

'There are some biscuits in the cupboard if you're hungry,' Daisy called from the sitting room.

'I'll bring some in,' Meadows called back as he opened the cupboard door and rummaged around.

When the tea was made, he carried it through to the sitting room and handed Daisy a cup before placing his on the table. He quickly grabbed the biscuits from the kitchen then took up a seat on the sofa. He was pleased to see that Daisy looked a little more composed although he was certain that she would be bursting with questions.

'Have you seen her?' Daisy took a biscuit from the packet and dunked it in her tea.

'No, Blackwell and Paskin took her sample. I'm going to arrest the mother in the morning. I guess then we will learn the whole story.'

'I know you can't give me any specific details, but does it look like she had a nice family?'

'Yes, well, a nice home at least, and both parents seem to be protective of her.'

'That's something, I suppose.' Daisy sipped her tea. 'Her whole life has been a lie. I can't imagine what that's going to do to her. She's not going to know me or Dad, she was too young to have any memories of us. She has her own family.'

'I think you're going to have to be patient and give it a little time. I'm sure she will be eager to meet you and your dad once the initial shock has worn off. Would you like someone with you when you talk to your dad?'

'No, I think it will be better if it is just the two of us. I'll do it in the morning.'

'As soon as I can, I will give you all the details. There will obviously be some press interest so take what help you need.'

'Thank you, and thanks for staying.' She reached across the sofa and placed her hand on his.

Meadows felt the tingle run up his arm. He leaned back against the sofa, at this moment in time he was happy to stay all night if that was what Daisy wanted.

Chapter Twenty-seven

The rain hammered down on the windscreen as Meadows pulled the car into the Andersons' driveway. He looked in the rear-view mirror and could just about see Blackwell and Paskin pull up behind.

'Lot of cars here, I guess they have visitors ready for the wedding,' Edris said.

'I don't like what we are about to do to that poor girl, but I guess we don't have a choice.' Meadows yawned.

'Tired? Late night, was it?' Edris grinned.

'Yes, because I was still working when you were tucked up in bed.'

Well, keeping Daisy company most of the night but he doesn't need to know that.

'Working?' Edris laughed. 'If that's what you call it.'

'Come on, let's get this over with.' Meadows opened the door and stepped out into the rain.

They ran for the cover of the porch and Meadows rang the bell as Edris shook the rain from his hair. Blackwell and Paskin stayed in the car keeping a watchful eye.

The door opened and Dr Anderson immediately pulled back his shoulders. 'What are you doing here again? This is harassment.' His eyes narrowed.

'Is your wife home?' Meadows asked.

'It matters not if she's home. You're not coming in.' Colour rose in Dr Anderson's cheeks. 'We have a house full of guests, so you'll have to come back some other time.'

'We have a warrant for your wife's arrest so if you'll step aside, sir.' Meadows stepped forward.

'I'll do no such thing. Just because you imbeciles can't do your job properly doesn't mean I'll let you in to ruin our day.' Dr Anderson stepped back and started to close the door.

Meadows quickly slung his arm out and the door bounced back. He turned his head and nodded at Blackwell. 'Step aside or I'll have you arrested for obstruction,' Meadows said.

Blackwell and Paskin appeared at Meadows' side.

'What's it going to be? I can cuff you and take you to the station or you can let us inside to do our job,' Blackwell said.

Dr Anderson puffed out his chest and his face took on a purple hue.

'Let them in.' Sally appeared behind her husband.

Dr Anderson stood back and all four officers entered the hallway. Sally stood with an envelope clutched in her hand, she was dressed in a pair of jeans and a soft pink jumper. Her hair was coiled and pinned on top of her head.

'I thought you would take longer.' She looked at Meadows.

'What are you talking about?' Dr Anderson's voice boomed around the hallway.

'What's going on?' A young woman appeared at the top of the stairs with two young girls.

Meadows looked up and immediately saw the resemblance to Daisy. She was a little taller but had the same heart shaped face and creamy complexion.

'Stay upstairs, Jade, and look after the girls.' Dr Anderson waved his hand. 'It's nothing for you to worry about.'

Jade ignored her father and shooed the two girls away before coming down the stairs. 'Mum, what do these people want?'

'I'm so sorry, love.' Sally turned to Meadows. 'Why couldn't you have waited? It's not fair, she doesn't deserve this.'

She would have let the wedding go ahead even though she knew she'd been found out. Let her daughter get married under a false name.

'Sally Anderson, I'm arresting you on the suspicion of the murder of George Williams, for the murder of Jade Matthews in June 1992, and the abduction of Poppy Moore on the second of July 1992. You have the right to remain silent—'

The rest of Meadows caution was drowned out by Jade's and Dr Anderson's protests.

'Mum, say something,' Jade pleaded. 'Say it isn't true.' She turned on Meadows, her fists clenched and face drained of colour. 'You've made a mistake. You said she murdered Jade Matthews in 1992. I'm Jade Matthews, or I was before Dad adopted me. I can show you my birth certificate.'

'Jade, maybe we should find somewhere quiet for you to sit down.' Paskin put her hand on Jade's arm.

'No, I don't want to sit down.' Jade shrugged off Paskin's hand. 'Mum, will you please tell them they have made a mistake.'

'Is any of this true?' Dr Anderson asked.

Sally handed the envelope she was clutching to Jade.

'I'm so sorry, I have explained everything in the letter. Your real name is Poppy, but you'll always be my Jade.' She turned to Meadows. 'I'd like to go now please.'

'No.' Jade threw her arms around her mother.

231

Meadows looked at Dr Anderson who had a bewildered expression on his face.

'DS Blackwell and DS Paskins will stay with you to explain what will happen next and answer any questions you may have.'

'Come on, love.' Dr Anderson pulled Jade away from Sally.

'Jade, I'm sorry you had to find out this way,' Meadows said.

Tears ran down Sally's face and mixed with the rain as she was led to the car. She kept silent on the journey, the only sound was the occasional sniff. When they arrived at the station she answered the custody sergeant's questions with her eyes downcast and hands clutched tight.

'Would you like to contact your solicitor now?' Meadows asked. 'As soon as your legal representative arrives, we can start the interview.'

'I doubt Laurence will pay up for a solicitor. It doesn't matter anyway, I don't want one. What's the point? They can't do anything for me. Let's just get this over with.'

'That's fine by me, but we can provide a duty solicitor for you,' Meadows said.

'No, I don't want one.'

While they waited for Sally to be processed through custody, Meadows and Edris headed to the canteen.

'She seems very calm,' Edris said as he stirred sugar into his tea. 'I expected a little more protest.'

'She's had enough time to prepare.' Meadows sat down at a table. 'She knew we'd be coming after we uncovered the baby in the garden. She must've been living for years with the guilt, and the fear of being found out hanging over her head. All it would've taken is a simple blood test for Jade, well Poppy, to find out the truth. Maybe in some ways it's a relief. I suppose if Ella hadn't gone missing the truth may never have surfaced.'

'Yeah and that poor girl would've lived her whole life as someone else.'

'I expect she's wishing now that she didn't know. The look of shock on her face said it all.' Meadows shook his head sadly. 'It's going to take a long time to adjust.'

'Imagine finding out you have a different identity and a family you knew nothing about,' Edris said.

'A family that's going to be desperate to see her after all these years.' Meadows drank down his tea. 'Come on, let's go and see why Sally chose to destroy a family and murder George.'

Sally didn't look up when Meadows and Edris entered the interview room. She sat with the sleeves of her jumper pulled over her hands and her shoulders hunched as if trying to keep a chill out. She kept her eyes downcast as Meadows read out the time, date, and those present for the recording device.

Meadows pulled the chair forward. 'Sally, I have to remind you again that you are entitled to legal representation, either one of your choice or we can provide a solicitor for you.'

Sally looked up. 'No, I'm happy to proceed without a solicitor.'

'Okay, but you can change your mind at any time,' Meadows said.

'We would've been having fun now.' Sally sighed. 'I arranged for a professional hair and make-up artist to come to the house for a practice. It was going to be a wonderful day. I guess I won't get to see how beautiful she looks in her wedding dress.'

'But it's not Jade that's getting married, not Jade that's in your house. Jade died twenty-four years ago, didn't she?'

'Yes.' Sally nodded. 'That Jade died.'

'Would you like to tell us about that?'

Sally shrugged her shoulders and looked down.

I hope she is not going to clam up, Daisy and her father deserve an explanation.

'We know you were on your own at the time with no support from your family. What about Jade's father? Did he support you and Jade? Was he a part of your lives?'

Sally looked up. 'No. Why do you think his name was never put on the birth certificate? I met Mark when I was sixteen, he was twenty-three. I didn't know at the time that he had a girlfriend. He said we needed to keep our relationship a secret because he was worried that my father would object to the age difference. It made sense at the time. When I got pregnant, I had just started my driving lessons and was taking my A-levels. I had my whole life planned and suddenly my life was turned upside down. I was afraid of what was going to happen, how I would cope, and tell my parents. They were very strict and my father had a temper. I was sure Mark would look after me.'

'I got all dressed up and did my hair and make-up to perfection. I arranged to meet Mark by the river, it's where we always met. I remember the day clearly, the sun was shining, it lifted my spirits and I thought everything would work out okay. When I told Mark he was furious, even accused me of sleeping around to try and trap him. Then he told me about his girlfriend and that they had just got engaged. I only saw him twice after that. Once when he came to see me to say he was happy to carry on our relationship as long as no one found out. I told him I didn't want anything to do with him, and the baby and me would manage without him. It hurt me but I couldn't bear the thought of being with him and knowing he would go home to his fiancé,' she continued.

Meadows tried to imagine what it must have been like for Sally. He wanted to understand what would drive her to kill her child.

Pregnant and alone with a broken heart. She must have ended up hating Mark. Did Jade remind her of the hurt? A constant reminder?

'I guess you had to tell your parents.'

'Yes, they wanted to send me off to stay with my auntie and have an abortion, but I couldn't. Part of me hated Mark but a part of me loved him and I couldn't take it out on the baby. Maybe if it had been my decision, I would've considered my options. Maybe it would've been for the best. My father gave me an ultimatum, have the abortion or leave. So, I left.'

'You moved to Coopers Wood estate,' Meadows said.

'Yes, I was lucky to get the house so quickly. I'd been sleeping at a friend's house, but I could tell she was getting fed up with me, didn't want to hear my problems every day. I knew I had to leave school, so I confided in one of the teachers. She was very good to me. Helped me get the house, wrote to the council.'

'Was George living next door when you moved in?' Edris asked.

'Yes, he was okay at first. Went out of his way to help. He brought around vegetables he'd grown in his garden, helped me get furniture. When I moved in I had nothing, just my clothes. George managed to get hold of some second-hand furniture from a mate, even helped to move it. I had no money or job, so I had to take what I could. Even the cot and pram were freebies. Jade's clothes I picked up from jumbles sales.' A bitter laugh escaped Sally's mouth. 'Hard to think I once lived like that.'

'So, you were worried about money, no boyfriend or family, and a baby on the way. You must've been feeling pretty low,' Meadows said.

'Not at that point. I was excited and scared at the same time. I was going to be a mother but I didn't have a clue about looking after a baby. George drove me to the hospital the night I went into labour. There was no one else to ask.'

'What about your friends? Couldn't one of them have gone with you?' Edris asked.

'No, they were all still at school, going out and enjoying themselves. They would've found the idea of sitting

235

through a birth appalling. It was just the midwives and me, they were very nice but it was a horrible experience. The labour went on for hours and it was an unpleasant delivery. They kept me in for a few days but then I was on my own. I had visits from the health visitor and George popped in but that was it. I felt so lonely.

'It was an effort to go out anywhere, I was so tired, and Jade never seemed to sleep. She had colic which went on forever, then she was teething. I felt useless and ugly. My life was just looking after a screaming child. Some days I didn't even bother to wash or dress. I did try to get help. The doctor said it was only natural that I should feel down with a new baby and being a single parent. I got a few visits from social services. All well-meaning advice but it didn't make me feel any better. I'm not trying to excuse what I did but I'm not that person anymore.'

Meadows now had a clear picture of Sally's life. *Not a unique story, there are lots of single parents struggling with money and feeling isolated. She was clearly depressed and tried to get help. I guess everyone has a breaking point. What drives a mother to kill her child?*

'What happened to Jade?'

'She'd been up most of the night. She had a bit of a temperature so I gave her paracetamol and rubbed some gel on her gums, but nothing seemed to work. I was going to take her to the doctor that morning but I was so tired. She slept on and off during the day but by the evening she was yelling again. The noise seemed to magnify in my head. I walked around the house carrying her, trying to soothe her. When she fell asleep, I put her in the cot and I climbed into bed. I must've only been asleep for about half an hour and she started screaming again.' Sally bit her bottom lip then let out a shaky breath.

'I just lost it for a moment. I leaned into the cot and grabbed her. I shook her, screamed at her to shut up. I think I knocked the back of her head against the cot bars because she let out this piercing wail. I let her go and ran from the room. I shut myself in the kitchen and sat there smoking and drinking tea. I don't know how long I sat there for but the house was silent when I went back to bed. I thought Jade was asleep, so I just crept into bed.'

'When did you realise something was wrong?' Meadows asked.

'I woke up about three. I think I was so used to being woken up during the night that it became second nature. I checked on Jade, she was still, and so cold. Fear gripped my body so I couldn't move for a moment. I could feel my heart thudding in my chest. I wanted to scream but I couldn't make a sound. I took her out of the cot and held her tight. She wasn't breathing, her lips were blue. Pain tore through my chest like nothing I've felt before.'

'Why didn't you call for help?' Edris asked.

'Because I'd killed her. I was alone and scared. A baby killer who everyone was going to hate.'

Tears tracked down Sally's face and she wiped them away with the back of her hand.

'So, you buried her in the garden,' Meadows said. He could almost understand how Sally had lost control for a moment. Almost felt sorry for her if it wasn't for what he knew she did next.

'I wrapped her in a blanket and covered her in plastic. I couldn't bear the thought of bugs crawling over her. I dug a hole as near to the house as I could. I didn't want her to be too far away. I cried the whole time, my body shaking. It was like some bizarre nightmare and I couldn't wake up.' She took a tissue from her sleeve and blew her nose.

'Did you bury her alone?' Meadows asked.

'Yes, it was still dark. No one saw me. I left the kitchen light on so I could see but I didn't use a torch. After, I just sat in the kitchen in a daze. When the sun came up I realized that I couldn't just leave that little patch of earth. What if an animal got into the garden and dug her up? What if George asked why I had been digging the garden?'

Sally rubbed at her arms as though the memory brought a chill to her skin.

'I went to see Mark; it was early and I knew I would catch him before he went to work. He was angry that I called at his home and I guess I must've looked a state. I told him that Jade was very ill in hospital and I needed a car for a few days. He refused so I threatened to tell his fiancé about Jade, he gave in. I didn't have a full licence then, but I'd had a few lessons and I didn't care if I was caught.'

'Didn't Mark ask to see Jade?' Edris asked. 'If you managed to convince him the child was so ill, surely he would've wanted to see for himself.'

'No, Mark only cared about himself. As long as I kept his secret he was happy. I drove to the builder's yard and bought some slabs and cement. I had to make a few trips. George came over when he saw me working in the garden. I told him that my mother had taken Jade for a few days to give me a break and that I wanted to use the time to make the garden nice so she would have somewhere to play. He helped me lay the patio and tidy the borders.'

'Did he give any indication that he knew what lay under the slabs?' Meadows asked.

'Not then. He seemed happy with my explanation, although I knew he would ask questions when Jade didn't come home. I thought I could tell him that my mother had decided it was best to raise Jade as her own, that I was too young to have a child. It seemed like a good idea but then what would I tell the health visitor and social services if they checked up on me? They would follow up my story and soon find out the lie. I tried to think of all ways to cover up, even thought of running away but there was nowhere I could go.'

'So, you decided to replace Jade,' Edris said.

Sally's eyes narrow. 'It wasn't like that. It's okay for you to sit and judge me but you've no idea what it was like for me then. I was out of my mind with grief. I've already told you I wasn't myself. I wasn't thinking straight.'

'Yet you could come up with a plan to abduct a child,' Meadows said.

'I didn't plan, well not like you think. I drove around for a couple of days, visiting parks and shopping centres. Just watching. I must've looked in countless prams and complimented mothers on their beautiful babies, while all the time I was looking for a baby girl, looking for Jade.

'I was walking along the seafront when I first saw her. She was being pushed along by her grandmother. A little girl with dark hair in pigtails skipped alongside the pram. I stopped to talk to them and when I saw her, I knew I had been given a second chance. My Jade had been given back to me. I followed them home, then went back the next day. The mother sat outside in a chair reading while the baby slept in the pram and the little girl played with a doll. Then the mother went indoors, just left them outside. When she didn't come back out I went through the garden gate and asked the little girl for a glass of water. I took Jade from the pram, put her on the floor on the passenger side and drove back to Mark's house. She only woke a few times on the way home. I left the keys in the car and carried her home.'

'Didn't you worry that the car would be identified and traced back to Mark?' Edris asked.

'No, he wouldn't say anything because it would mean that he'd have to explain about Jade. There was no chance he would risk being found out, even if he did have suspicions.'

'Didn't anyone comment on Jade's appearance?' Meadows asked. 'Poppy Moore's abduction would've been on every news channel and in every newspaper. Her face would have been well known.'

'There wasn't anyone around to notice. I didn't go out much and it was over a month before I saw the health visitor. It was a huge relief when she didn't notice any difference, I felt safe and knew then that I had done the right thing in taking my child back.'

My child back?

Meadows let the comment go. 'But George knew the difference, didn't he?'

'He never said it outright but yes, I'm sure he knew. He would drop little hints. Bring around paper clippings of the abduction and always talked about the family of the missing child, like he knew them personally. He soon let me know what he wanted in return for keeping the secret.' Sally wrapped her arms around her body. 'I hated myself for getting into his bed. He liked to play games to prolong his pleasure, I played along to keep him happy. In the end, I saw it as my punishment. The longer it went on, the more worthless and dirtier I felt. I got to a point where I wanted to end it all. I even bought the pills. Then I realised that I owed it to Jade to give her the best life I could.

'I managed to get a transfer to a council house in Cardiff. I said I needed to be near my family. I went back to college, then trained as a nurse. That's how I met Laurence.'

'So why kill George now? Did he contact you when we found Jade?'

'No, he had no idea where I was and I had changed my surname. I'd put the past behind me. It was just some distant nightmare at times. I believed I had dreamt the whole thing.'

'So what happened to make you go back and take Ella Beynon?' Meadows asked.

'Ella Beynon?' Confusion creased Sally's face. 'I didn't take her. Why would I do such a thing?'

Meadows felt his hope of finding Ella draining away.

'We are searching your house.'

'Search all you want. You won't find anything. What sort of monster do you think I am?'

'Then why go back?'

'The little girl went missing. I saw it on the news, saw the house and it all came back to me, the guilt and fear. I had to come and look, I couldn't help myself. When I walked past the house, I saw them searching the garden. I couldn't move for a while. I knew if they found the body then questions would be asked. George might say something. I realised how stupid I had been to come, but as long as George didn't see me, I'd be safe. Maybe he would keep quiet. How would he explain that he knew all those years ago but didn't report it? I hurried back towards my car but I ran into George. He recognised me straight away. Asked me back to his house for a cup of tea. I could see the excitement in his eyes and knew what he wanted. I was never going to escape, he would never leave me alone. All he had to do was to tell the police that I laid the patio, that he had no idea what was under there. I told him not to bother with the tea and went up to the bedroom.'

There was a look of pure disgust on Sally's face as she twisted her hands.

'I told him I had learned some new tricks but needed something to tie him up, told him it would heighten the pleasure. He told me where to find the garden twine and he happily let me tie his legs as he groped my body. Every touch made my skin crawl but I kept smiling, kept teasing until I had tied his hands. I had to put an end to it, he would've ruined Jade's life. I took a pillow and held it over his face. He struggled but couldn't get free. It seemed to take forever for him to die but when it was over all I felt was relief. I got dressed and went home. I knew you would come for me, but I so wanted to see my little girl get married.'

Sally hung her head as sobs wracked her body.

Chapter Twenty-eight

Meadows felt drained when he walked into the office on Monday morning. It had been late when the paperwork for Sally Anderson had been completed and he had finally gone home. He felt no satisfaction from solving the case. Too many lives had been turned upside-down and he doubted Jade would be running into the welcoming arms of her lost family. He had been tempted to call Daisy but figured she needed the space. He'd cooked himself a meal, tried to read and listen to music but couldn't relax. His mind was full of images of Ella, keeping him awake then invading his dreams. He felt like the answer was lurking in the back of his mind, just out of his grasp.

He sighed as he approached the incident board. Edris had removed all the information relating to the murder of George and the discovery of Jade Matthews. Now the names and pictures had been removed, it left a clear picture of the investigation into the disappearance of Ella.

George and Little Jade Matthews certainly clouded the search for Ella, maybe now we can find some answers.

As Meadows updated the board with the information on the cottage in Lancashire he heard the rest of the team come in with the usual chatter.

He turned and looked at Blackwell. 'How were the Andersons when you left them?'

'The Doc spent most of the afternoon slugging one whiskey after another. He was pretty wasted by the time we left. Can't say I blame him,' Blackwell said.

'Poor bugger was in shock,' Paskin said. 'He had no idea. Jade, or should I say Poppy, went from sobbing to hysterics to silence. The guests were dispatched and the fiancé turned up with a load of questions. In the end, they decided they wanted some time alone.'

'Can't blame them,' Meadows said. 'They're not going to get a lot of peace when the media sniff out the story.'

'I liaised with the local station so they're aware of the situation,' Blackwell said. He sat down in his chair and put his hands behind his head. 'Still, not a bad weekend's work. Cleared up two cases. I just wish that we had found Ella in the process.'

'So do I,' Meadows said. 'We've still got the cottage in Lancaster as the best lead we've had all week. Did the police up there come back with anything, Valentine?'

'Yeah, I put the report on your desk. They interviewed the owner of the cottage and then the neighbours on either side. There was a woman staying there with a young boy, the neighbour thought him to be about two years old. The description isn't a match for Natalie and the child is the wrong sex.'

'What? So Natalie was telling the truth. If she wasn't using the cottage, who was? We need to find this woman, and see if she has any connection with Natalie. Anything from traffic?'

'No.' Valentine shook her head.

'I'll chase them up,' Blackwell said.

'We need to check if Natalie or any of these lot' – he pointed to the names on the board – 'have any connection to Lancaster. Check the phone records, look who they've been talking to in the last month.'

'It could've just been a meeting point,' Edris said. 'Could be halfway to wherever they were taking Ella. Maybe this woman was just there to take Ella and hand her over to someone else.'

'Maybe,' Meadows agreed. 'Then that would mean she was taken to somewhere in Scotland. There are some remote places there. Easy to hide a child. But why?'

'If she was there at all,' Paskin said. 'As the neighbour said, it was a woman and a little boy who were seen staying at the cottage, no mention of another child.'

Something niggled at the back of Meadows' mind. He sat down at his desk and picked up the report from Lancaster police. The woman was described as being around five foot five, wearing a pink coat, jeans, and a hat.

Same height as Natalie and a pink coat.

He continued reading. The child. A boy of around two with brown hair.

What was it that Jim said the other day? Cut their hair short and they all look the same.

'When we were interviewing Jim and Helen Morris, I mistook their granddaughter for a boy because she had short hair. What if Ella's hair has been cut? Everyone is on the lookout for a little girl. They wouldn't take any notice of a boy.'

'I suppose it's one way of moving the child around unnoticed. Still a big risk,' Paskin said. 'No money has changed hands from what we can see. If it was some attempt at an illegal adoption there would be all sorts of paperwork to get around. False birth certificate for a start.'

'Yeah, well, people with enough money have a way of getting around these things,' Edris said.

'But there would've had to be some sort of communication,' Valentine said.

'Then we go back and look again,' Meadows said.

'Traffic haven't picked up anything on Natalie's car,' Blackwell said. 'So, we can knock that theory on the head.'

'Why would Natalie book the cottage for that weekend? It was booked until the Friday morning, enough time for an exchange and to lay low,' Meadows said. 'It's the only thing we've got to go on so far.'

'Only Natalie insists she didn't book the cottage,' Edris said. 'Her car would have been picked up on camera and she was home on the Monday morning. Why pay for the cottage for a week? Besides which, she would have to be pretty thick to book the cottage in her own name.'

'She's lied about everything else so far and we've already established she's not the brightest. The only other explanation is that someone else booked that cottage in her name, someone with access to her card details. Then they took Ella and handed her over to whoever was staying in the cottage. Buried the clothes to confuse us.'

'Ryan,' Valentine said. 'He could have arranged to meet a woman in Lancaster, stopped in the woods first. We did find his footprints near the clothes.'

'Could be,' Meadows agreed. 'Only Natalie swears he was on the sofa all night, and Claire, Dan, and Jamie would've noticed his absence for that length of time.'

'Unless they were all in on it,' Blackwell said.

'And they buried the clothes in the woods to make it look like an abduction,' Valentine said.

'Yeah but if they were going to be that clever about it, they wouldn't have used Natalie's name to book a cottage,' Edris said.

'Have we got the forensic report from the house and the car?' Meadows asked.

'I was looking at that on Friday.' Paskin shuffled through some papers on her desk. 'Yeah nothing useful. Only fingerprints found in Ella's bedroom were Natalie's, Ryan's, Nia's, and Claire's, which can all be explained. Lots more in the car. Same as the bedroom but also Dan's, and Jamie's along with a couple of unidentified. They've been run through the database, but no matches were found.'

'Why were Nia's prints in the car? She has her own,' Meadows said.

'Well maybe she had a lift at some time with Natalie, or used the car whilst hers was up the garage. I can ask her but as it's her sister's car, I don't think finding her prints is suspicious,' Paskin said. 'I guess whoever took Ella could have wiped their prints, wore gloves or–'

'–it was one of these four,' Meadows said.

'Three,' Valentine said. 'Ryan, Natalie or Claire, unless you think Nia had something to do with the abduction.'

Meadows ran his hand over his chin and sighed.

'I don't know what to think anymore. Nia puts on an appearance of being worried about Ella and has been supporting Natalie, although she is hard on her at times. She did report Natalie to social services and expressed her concerns about the way Natalie was bringing up Ella. Same with Leanne, she was appalled by Natalie's behaviour. Leanne didn't arrive until Thursday night. She didn't rush over here when she heard her niece was missing.'

'And she didn't stay long, went home yesterday,' Valentine said.

'Okay so we know that Nia was there at ten, enough time to take Ella and drive to Lancaster and home again,' Blackwell said.

'Yeah but Nia cares for the child, she's not going to hand her over to some stranger,' Edris said.

'So maybe we need to look at Nia's contacts, it would have to be someone she trusted to hide Ella. Although, I can't see what she would achieve by doing that,' Meadows said.

'Maybe she would rather see the child brought up by a loving family than with her sister,' Paskin suggested. 'Back to the illegal adoption theory but money wasn't the motive.'

'But Natalie says she heard Ella crying later in the night and George was certain that he saw Natalie go out at two in the morning,' Valentine said.

'Natalie was off her head on shrooms,' Edris said.

'Yes, but George saw two cars. Nia was in work by nine and dropped the children off at school before she left, so wouldn't have had enough time to drive to Lancaster and back,' Meadows said.

'Okay not Nia but what about the other sister, Leanne?' Valentine asked.

'The one who lives on the Isle of Man?' Blackwell smirked. 'I would say that was a fairly tight alibi.'

'Just a thought,' Valentine said.

'Who spoke to her when Ella first went missing?' Meadows asked.

'Me,' Paskin said. 'She seemed genuinely upset and shocked about Ella's abduction.'

'The contact number Nia gave for Leanne was a mobile,' Meadows said.

'Which means she could have taken the call anywhere,' Edris said.

Meadows called a map up on his computer. He zoomed in on Lancaster, then zoomed out; as he did, he saw the blue dotted lines tracking across the sea to the Isle of Man.

'Heysham is not far from the cottage, it's one of the main crossings to the Isle of Man. Leanne said she used that route on Thursday. Bit too much of a coincidence.'

'Nah,' Blackwell said. 'She'd have to get a crossing, drive to Coopers Wood estate, snatch Ella, and drive back to Lancaster without being seen. That's quite a journey alone with a young child. Then she would need to get Ella back to the island with a boat full of people as witnesses.'

'And she would need a passport for the child,' Edris said.

'No, she would just need a passenger ticket. If she came over with her own car she could've driven on the boat with the child in the back seat,' Meadows said.

'All the airports and ports were alerted as soon as we established that Ella had been abducted,' Blackwell said.

'She wouldn't have been able to sneak Ella aboard and even if she did someone would have noticed and reported it later. The child's picture was on every news channel.'

'It's not impossible though,' Meadows said. 'Especially if she had help from Nia. When I saw her at Nia's house she had a little boy with her, what if the child was Ella with her hair cut and dressed as a boy? What better way to hide the child than in plain sight? Ella has been missing for a week so, if Leanne travelled yesterday it's unlikely that anyone would take any notice of what they thought was a little boy.'

'But why do it? Why would they put their sister through that ordeal?' Paskin asked.

'When Sally Anderson was telling us how she lost control for a few moments and killed her baby daughter, all sorts of thoughts went through my mind,' Meadows said. 'I thought how different things may have been if she'd had some support, someone to turn to, or even if social services had been more involved.'

'But Natalie has plenty of family around to help. Are you saying the sisters would take Ella to help?'

'Perhaps they took Ella because they couldn't help. They had tried social services. Nia has her own family to take care of and a sick mother. She can't always be watching Natalie, and Leanne lives too far away,' Meadows said.

'It's a bit extreme,' Blackwell said.

'It's worth checking out – at least see if Leanne was on the passenger list last weekend,' Meadows said.

'I'll get on to it,' Edris said.

'But the woman in the cottage had a little boy when she arrived on Saturday,' Paskin said.

'Leanne has a son, according to Nia. See if you can find out, Paskin. Valentine can you get back onto Lancaster police and ask them to send a team of forensics over to the cottage. If Ella was there maybe we'll be in luck and they'll pick something up.'

'We should just get Nia in here and grill her,' Blackwell said.

'No, if Ella is with Leanne, I don't want her tipped off. Let's see if Nia's car was picked up on the traffic cameras and if she has any contacts in Lancaster,' Meadows said.

'Steam Packet are checking the passenger lists, they'll get back to us,' Edris said.

'I guess we just have to sit around and wait,' Blackwell grumbled.

'Yes,' Meadows said. 'There are plenty of checks to do in the meantime. Finances and call logs from Ryan and Natalie's phones. If you're really desperate for some action you can go and see Claire, Dan and Jamie, see what reaction you get when you question them about the cottage in Lancaster.'

'Yeah, I'll go and see them.' Blackwell grabbed his jacket and sauntered out of the office.

* * *

The rest of the day was spent obtaining information and tracking calls made by Natalie and Ryan. They had already been through them once but now they were looking for any connection with Lancaster. Apart from the occasional phone call, the office was quiet as the team scanned information. Blackwell returned to the office claiming that despite a good grilling he was met with vacant expressions when mentioning the cottage in Lancaster.

'Nothing on social media,' Valentine said. 'It would be the obvious way to make contact if it wasn't by phone call.'

'I asked the tech guys to check Natalie's laptop again. She didn't make the booking from that computer and the booking was made online,' Paskin said.

'So maybe Natalie is telling the truth for a change and she didn't book the cottage,' Edris said.

'What about Ryan's computer?' Meadows asks.

'I got them to check that as well,' Paskin said. 'He didn't make the booking.'

'I still think we should get Nia in, get a warrant to search her house so we can check her computer. At least we can rule her out,' Blackwell said.

'At the moment, we don't have any evidence that Nia is involved,' Meadows said. 'We're not going to get a warrant unless her car is picked up by traffic driving to Lancaster on the night Ella was abducted.'

'Leanne does have a son, a two-year-old. I checked it out,' Valentine said. 'So, it could have been her at the cottage.'

The phone on Edris' desk rang, and the team fell silent as Edris lifted the receiver. Meadows felt a tinge of excitement when he saw the smile on Edris face.

'Well?' Meadows asked as soon as Edris ended the call.

'Leanne Gillis and her son Elijah travelled in their car on the eight o'clock crossing, Saturday twelfth of March. They docked at eleven thirty. They returned to the Isle of Man yesterday.'

'So, she was here when Ella was abducted,' Meadows said, 'and has been hiding out in the cottage in Lancaster.'

'The only problem being is that she travelled with her son. I think they would have noticed at the check-in if she had an extra child going back,' Edris said.

'Unless she didn't bring her son over, and like I said earlier, if she cut Ella's hair and dressed her as a boy no one would notice,' Meadows said.

'Yeah, but Steam Packet is certain that the child was checked in on both journeys,' Edris said.

'And there was a child at the cottage before Ella went missing,' Paskin added.

'It was a good theory,' Edris said.

'I think Leanne is definitely involved somehow.' Meadows sat down at his desk. 'Why else would she lie about coming over on the ferry on Thursday? She could've had both children with her when she stayed at Nia's house.

Nia looked worried when we visited. Or maybe someone already picked up Elijah and took him home. Leanne's husband? Then again, she could have risked taking the two children on the boat, if one was sleeping and covered up at check-in, after that I doubt anyone would take any notice.'

'Can't see that,' Blackwell said. 'I think you are making this up as you go along. We all want to find the child alive but let's face it, she was probably dead before she left the house.'

Meadows sighed. 'You could be right, but no matter how small the possibility is that she is alive, we owe it to her to check it out. Leanne could have pulled it off, even left Ella here with someone. We've already searched all the houses, so it would be easy to hide her now.'

'So, you want us to search all the houses again?' Blackwell said.

'No, I think we should pay a visit to Leanne, it's the only way to be sure. I'll call when I get there and you can visit Nia at the same time. That way the sisters won't have time to come up with a story of why Leanne was here when Ella went missing.'

'I think it's a waste of time.' Blackwell huffed. 'I can't see Lester agreeing to it.'

'I'll tell him when we get back,' Meadows said. 'Come on, what have we got to lose?' Meadows looked around the team.

'I'm with you,' Edris said.

'You would be,' Blackwell snapped.

'I think it's worth a try,' Paskin said.

'Valentine?' Meadows looked at the newest member of the team.

Valentine nodded. 'I agree.'

'Right, Edris, go home and get some rest, we have an early start in the morning,' Meadows said.

Chapter Twenty-nine

Meadows felt the tension leave his shoulders as the plane made its descent into Douglas airport. It was the only time during the flight that his hands hadn't gripped the armrests. He hated flying – being confined to a small space with his legs cramped. Edris, amused by Meadows' discomfort, had gazed out of the window giving a running commentary throughout the flight.

The plane touched down on the runway with a jolt and Meadows let out a breath that he felt he had been holding since take off.

'Feeling better?' Edris said grinning.

'I will when I get my feet on the ground.' Meadows unclipped his belt, stood and joined the queue.

Edris laughed. 'Can't believe you're scared of flying.'

'I'm not frightened, I just don't like someone else being in control of my life. If we had the time, I would've insisted we take the boat.'

'Then you would've been on your own, I get seasick,' Edris said.

A bitter wind ruffled Meadows hair as he descended the steps onto the tarmac. He pulled in a lungful of sea air.

'Lovely, there never feels like there's enough oxygen on the plane.'

'That will be down to your anxiety.' Edris pulled up the collar on his jacket. 'Maybe you should have a few pints before the return flight, you'll feel much better.'

They were met in arrivals by DS Jim Kelly, a greying, thickset man with a broad Irish accent. 'Welcome to the mainland.' Kelly smiled. 'Picked a nice day for it. Wind's a bit choppy but it's blown the clouds away.'

'Thanks for meeting us,' Meadows said.

'No problem, not a lot going on. The car is out front. I'll take you on the coast road, give you a chance to see the scenery.'

Kelly continued to chatter as they drove out of the airport, giving them a description of life and the lack of crime on the island.

'So, you think that Leanne Gillis has some involvement in the abduction of Ella Beynon? I've been following the story, I've got a grandson the same age.'

'We're just following a line of enquiry, need to ask her a few questions,' Meadows said.

'She's the auntie of the missing child?' Kelly asked.

'Yes,' Edris said from the back. 'She took a ferry over the weekend of the abduction.'

'Do you know the family?' Meadows asked.

'Not Leanne, but her in-laws are a well-respected couple. Will Gillis is a paramedic and his wife a teacher. Both born on the island. I can't see that they would knowingly be involved.'

'Like I said, we just need to ask a few questions,' Meadows said.

And hopefully find Ella in her house.

Meadows gazed out of the window and let his eyes trail the lush fields to the cliff edge. As they left Douglas, the road wound higher, and he could see the sea crashing against the rocks below. They travelled past Ballabeg, crossing over the tramline with its wooden station. As they passed through Laxey, Kelly pointed out the enormous wheel that turned slowly against the landscape.

'Cool,' Edris said. 'Can you climb to the top?'

'Yeah, if you've a head for heights,' Kelly said.

* * *

As they drove into Ramsey, the sea came into view again and Kelly took a left hand turn so that they were driving alongside the sea wall. He pulled the car up and pointed out of the window.

'That's the cottage. I'll wait here, no point in us all going in.'

'Okay, thanks.' Meadows climbed out of the car.

'Nice location,' Edris said. 'Imagine coming out of your garden gate, down the steps and onto the beach. Great in the summer.'

'Probably freezing in the winter.'

Meadows stepped through the gate and passed a palm tree that swayed in the wind. There was no answer when they rang the doorbell but voices could be heard coming from the back of the house. They took the side path which led to a large lawn. Towards the back Leanne, dressed in a long skirt and leather boots, was pushing two children strapped in a set of swings. The children squealed in delight as they swung back and forth.

'Leanne,' Meadows called out as he approached.

Leanne turned and froze. She took a few moments to compose herself then gave them a forced smile.

'You took me by surprise, have you come to tell me you found her?'

Meadows tried to look at the faces of the children but Leanne obscured his view. 'Perhaps we could go inside.'

'Erm, okay, let me just get these little rascals out.'

She unstrapped each child and took their hands leading them past Meadows. One child was dressed in a green coat with blue wellington boots, the other in a blue coat with ankle boots. Both wore woolly hats.

They both looked like boys. Meadows followed Leanne towards the house. *Judging by Leanne's nervous demeanour I think one is definitely Ella, just need a closer look.*

'I wanted to stay longer,' Leanne said. 'But it's difficult. I have Eli to look after and Nia thought it best I come home.'

'Which one is your son?' Meadows asked.

'This is Eli.' She touched the head of the taller child. 'The other little fellow is Cory, I look after him for a friend when she's working.'

Leanne opened the door and the children ran inside. The house was warm and the kitchen spotless. Both children were pink in the cheeks from the cold sea air. They sat on the floor and pulled off their shoes, then their woollen hats. Meadows smiled down at the children. Eli with his dark brown hair smiled back. The other child stared at Meadows as if not sure whether to smile or hide. The child's face was the same as the one he had stared at on the incident board all week, although her hair had been cut short and dyed.

'Can I offer you a drink?' Leanne asked.

Meadows knelt so he was level with the child. 'Hello Ella.'

Leanne stiffened. 'That's Cory. I guess he has the same large blue eyes as Ella.'

Meadows stood. 'Do I really need to ask for an examination of the child? Why put her through that and waste both our time.'

'Please, don't do this,' Leanne said. 'She's safe here.'

'Even if that was the case, you can't take the law into your own hands. You abducted a child from her home and sparked a major search operation.'

'You call that a home?' Leanne's voice rose and the children stared at her.

'Perhaps we should sit down,' Meadows suggested. 'Edris will make the tea.'

Leanne nodded. 'Come on, you two, let's go and play in the sitting room.'

Meadows followed Leanne into the light and spacious room. Wall to floor windows gave a view over the sea and the theme continued on the walls with oil paintings of tall ships. In the corner of the room a brightly coloured mini table and chair set was placed next to various toys. Leanne settled the children then took a seat, indicating that Meadows should do the same.

'I'm not a criminal,' Leanne said as she smoothed down her skirt. 'I understand that I have wasted police time, but I didn't have a choice. How many times have you seen reports on the news of neglected children, children beaten, starved, or killed at the hands of their parents or the mother's boyfriend? The question is always asked. Why didn't anyone report it, do something to stop it? It's too late when the child is dead. Asking questions won't bring the child back. Now put yourself in my shoes. Would you wait until it was too late, then shout accusations, attribute blame while all the while knowing you could've done something to stop it? Well, I would rather take what punishment comes than be mourning the death of my niece.'

When you put it that way it makes perfect sense.

Meadows studied Leanne. *She seems bright, has a nice home and family. Why would she risk all this? She must really believe that Ella's life was at risk.*

'But you did act, you reported Natalie to social services. They are fully aware of the situation. You could've spoken to them again or even the police. We have a dedicated child protection unit.'

'And what good would that have done? Social services didn't do much and you've spoken to Natalie, you must realise that lying is second nature to her, I doubt even she knows the truth half the time.'

'Yes, I did get that impression. But I don't understand what you thought you could achieve by doing this. You couldn't have kept this up for much longer. How long could you pretend that Ella is a little boy?'

'We had a plan.'

'You and Nia?'

Leanne nodded.

'And Dylan?'

'No, Dylan wasn't involved. I hated causing him so much distress but it was better that no one else was involved.'

'What about your husband?'

'I told him the same story. That I was looking after a friend's son. I told him it would be for a few weeks as she was very ill.'

'Didn't he get suspicious when Ella was reported missing?'

'No, why would he? Like I said, the less people who knew the better,' Leanne said.

Edris came into the room and placed three mugs on the table before taking a seat.

'We know from social services, Nia, and what you told us that there were concerns about Ryan. Did something happen to make you take such drastic action?'

'We had concerns long before she shacked up with Ryan. I don't think Natalie ever wanted Ella. Well, maybe to start with but she was like a child with a puppy or kitten that gets bored. She went back to work as soon as she could, and Mum looked after Ella most of the time. We suspected that she wasn't working all the hours she claimed. She certainly didn't have the money judging by the debt she was in. Mum paid her rent, bought clothes for Ella and made sure there was food in the house. Things got worse when she got with Ryan. She was more interested in him than her own daughter. Then the bruises started to appear on Ella. There was always some excuse, even for the so-called accidents that put Ella in hospital.'

'We've read the reports,' Edris said.

'Did you talk to Natalie about your concerns for Ella's safety?' Meadows picked up a mug from the table and took a sip.

'Yes, both me and Nia tried. Even Mum had a go at her, but she ignored us. She'd walk out of the room. Every time I visited, things were worse. It was obvious from her appearance that Nat was taking drugs. She lost weight and her face was drawn, dark circles under her eyes. It was Mum that went there every day. Cleaned the house and washed the clothes. Then Mum got ill and it all fell on Nia. Nia couldn't keep up with looking after Mum, her own family and working. Nat's house was stinking. I don't mean untidy, I mean filthy,' Leanne said.

Edris grimaced. 'We've seen.'

'Yeah, I wouldn't want an animal to live there let alone a child. Nia made a call to social services and I made a follow-up call a few weeks later. Social services sent a letter to make an appointment to see her. Nat took a few days off work. Made an effort to clean although I doubt it would have made that much of a difference. She then presented herself as a perfect mother struggling to raise a child on her own,' Leanne continued.

'I know the police raided the house and found drugs. Nat told social services that she had split with Ryan, they believed her. She even left that druggy to look after Ella when she worked on the weekends. I told you what happened when I visited at Christmas. Then Nia found a letter from social services stating that they were satisfied and would no longer need to visit. We were so afraid something would happen to Ella, but no one would take us seriously.'

'So, you decided that your only option was to take her away from your sister,' Meadows said.

'We thought if we could do something that would make social services and the police look properly into Nat's life, they would see that she wasn't a fit mother. Dylan was going to apply for custody and we were going to support his case in any way we could. We didn't involve him because we needed Ella to have a safe home when all of this was over. Better for her to have her dad.'

'We know you travelled on the Saturday evening ferry with your son,' Edris said. 'But we haven't figured out how you managed to get Ella out of the house, back to the cottage, then on the return ferry without being detected. It must have been quite difficult with two children just to make the journey, let alone conceal Ella on the boat. You only had a ticket for one child.'

'I didn't take Eli, he stayed with his father. You can now buy life size replicas of your toddlers from the internet. I suppose some parents want them for memories, a bit like footprints. I bought a doll, strapped it into the car seat and put a blanket over it. It was getting dark when I caught the ferry so it looked like a sleeping child. I held my breath through the check-in but I didn't have any problems. The guy took a quick glance in the back and wished me a pleasant crossing,' Leanne said.

'When I drove on the boat I took the doll from the seat and laid it on the floor under the blanket then joined the other passengers. It was late when I arrived at the cottage, the lady met me at the door and I carried the doll in the blanket straight upstairs to the bedroom. She thought she saw a sleeping child. I slept all day Sunday then I drove to Nia's house. The family was asleep when I arrived and no one noticed Nia slip out of the house,' Leanne continued.

'Nia had a key to Nat's so she let herself in, grabbed the car keys, put on Nat's pink coat then looked in the sitting room. They were all crashed out, naked with clothes strewn across the floor. She grabbed Ryan's trainers then got Ella from her cot. No one woke up.'

'Why go to the trouble of burying the clothes in the woods?' Meadows asked.

'Because we wanted the police to think something had happened to Ella and we needed to implicate Ryan and Nat. It also gave us more time for me to get back to the cottage. Nia was convinced that Ryan had an unhealthy interest in children. We got into Nat's car and drove to the footpath. Nia ran into the woods to throw in Ella's toy, then we drove in through the main track. The woods were deserted at that time of night. I changed Ella and Nia put on Ryan's trainers and we went into the woods to bury the clothes. We dropped the trainers and the keys back at the house and I dropped Nia home before driving back to the cottage. Ella slept all the way back,' Leanne explained.

'I cut Ella's hair then just waited in the cottage until I drove back to see Nat. It was a bit of a risk especially when you turned up to speak to me.' Leanne smiled. 'The return ferry wasn't a problem. No one was looking for a little boy. I had booked a cabin so once we were aboard we went to sleep. Didn't see any other passengers until it was time to go to the car deck.'

'So, what did you plan to do with Ella? You couldn't keep her indefinitely,' Meadows asked.

'No, we were going to wait until things calmed down. We knew Ryan was in custody and hopefully would be given a sentence so at least he would be off the scene. I was to bring Ella back, call Nia from a phone box. She would tell the police that she had received a call telling her where she could collect Ella but was warned not to call the police or she wouldn't get the child back. Ella of course would never have been left alone.' She stopped and looked at both officers in turn. 'What's going to happen now?'

'We are going to have to take you and Ella back with us,' Meadows said.

'But you're not going to give her back to Natalie, are you?'

'I'm sorry, that's not up to me.'

Meadows looked across at the little girl happily playing with a car. *I wish it was.*

Chapter Thirty

'Are you sure you're happy with tea?' Meadows asked. 'I've got a bottle of wine someone gave me.'

'Tea is fine.' Daisy smiled as she took the offered cup, from her position on the sofa.

'I need to get some shopping done.' Meadows sat down on the armchair opposite.

'Lovely place you've got,' Daisy said.

'Thanks. I was hoping to get the decorating finished but haven't found the time. I bought it from my mum so she could get a flat. I was going to do some work on it, then sell but I kinda got used to living here now.'

'I think you should stay, it has a nice feel to it. Perhaps I can give you a hand with the decorating.'

'I might just take you up on that,' Meadows said.

'I'm sorry I haven't called around sooner. Things have been complicated with Poppy coming back into our lives. It's not that I haven't wanted to see you outside of work.' Daisy smiled coyly.

'It's fine, I did expect things to be difficult for a while and you would all need some time to adjust. How are things with Poppy?'

'She still insists on being called Jade. Dad is trying his best, but she still thinks of Laurence as her father and Sally as her mother. She's even been on prison visits. You'd think she would be angry and blame her but I guess it's the only mother she's known. Things have been better since Jade Matthews' funeral and that's down to you.'

'Me?'

'Yes, she told me what she said to you. That the name on the grave should have been Poppy Moore and not Jade Matthews, that Poppy stopped existing the day she was abducted.'

'Yeah she said something like that,' Meadows said. 'I don't think she meant it.'

'Oh, I think she did, but you told her that Poppy existed for me and Dad all these years, that we never forgot her. That's what made a difference. She's even invited me and Dad to the wedding.'

'Well, I'm glad things are improving.'

Daisy reached into her handbag and took out an envelope. 'I got this for you to say thank you.' Daisy stood and handed Meadows the envelope.

'Thank you for what?'

'For everything you've done, reuniting me with Poppy.'

'But that's just my job.' Meadows squirmed with embarrassment.

'It's more than that. The calls you made to me, the visits to my father. Don't think I don't know about the funeral and service you arranged for Jade Matthews. No one else would care enough to give that child a decent burial. The little white coffin and the flowers, organising Sally Andersons' leave to attend, even gathering the team so there was enough people to give our little miss a send-off. Then you spoke at the bail hearing for Nia and Leanne so they could stay with their children until the trial. Shall I go on?'

'No, please, you're embarrassing me and I'm beginning to think you're stalking me.' Meadows laughed.

'You're a good man and I just wanted to show that your kindness is appreciated. Now open the envelope.'

'Okay.' Meadows tore the seal and took out the contents. Excitement fizzled in his stomach when he saw the two tickets to an AC/DC concert.

'It's been my dream since I was a teenager to see them, I never got around to going.'

'It was Edris' suggestion.'

'Are you going to come with me?'

'Wouldn't miss it for the world,' Daisy said.

Meadows stood up and scooped Daisy into his arms. He was about to kiss her when his phone rang.

Oh great, perfect timing. This better not be work.

He took out his phone and saw Folland's name flash across the screen.

'What's up?'

'I thought you would like to know that an ambulance was called out to Coopers Wood estate this evening. Ella Beynon was pronounced dead at the scene,' Folland said.

Meadows felt his stomach twist.

'I'm on my way.'

Ella's smiling face flashed across his mind along with Leanne's words. "It's too late when the child is dead. Asking questions won't bring the child back. Now put yourself in my shoes. Would you wait until it was too late, then shout accusations, attribute blame while all the while knowing you could have done something to stop it?"

'I take it it's not good news.' Daisy touched his arm.

Meadows shook his head.

'Ella Beynon died at home this evening. I should have done more. I should have made sure she was safe. I could've let her stay with her auntie, she was happy and cared for.'

'You know you couldn't have done that. Your job was to find her. You weren't to know that this would happen.'

Daisy rested her hand on his arm.

'My job should have been to protect her. By bringing her back I handed her a death sentence. All the signs were there. I gleaned enough from my observations of Natalie's lifestyle to realise that she wouldn't change her ways and priorities. I failed that little girl.'

'No, you didn't, the system failed her. Social services should have ensured her safety.'

'Me, the system, the child's mother, what does it matter? It's too late now. Sorry I didn't mean to lay this off on you. I better get going.'

'It's fine,' Daisy said. 'I'm here if you need me.'

'Thanks.' He walked her out and watched her drive off before climbing into his own car. He sat for a few moments and let the images of Ella play in his mind.

I'm so sorry.

He shook away his thoughts and locked them deep in his mind with his guilt. *There's work to be done.* He started the engine and drove towards Coopers Wood estate.

List of Characters

Bryn Mawr police station:

Detective Inspector Winter Meadows
DC Tristan Edris
Sergeant Dyfan Folland
DS Rowena Paskin
DS Stefan Blackwell
DC Reena Valentine
PC Matthew Hanes – uniform officer
Chief Inspector Nathaniel Lester
DS Brianna Lloyd – family liaison officer

Others:

Daisy Moore – pathologist
Fern Meadows – Winter's mother
Martin Hughes – social worker
Ella Beynon – missing child
Natalie Beynon – mother of missing child
Nia Taylor – Natalie's sister
Leanne Gillis – Natalie's sister
Mary Beynon – Natalie's mother

Dai Lewis – Ella's father
Ryan Phillips – Natalie's boyfriend
Sally Anderson née Matthews
George Williams – next-door neighbour
Jim Morris
Helen Morris

If you enjoyed this book, please let others know by leaving a quick review on Amazon. Also, if you spot anything untoward in the paperback, get in touch. We strive for the best quality and appreciate reader feedback.

editor@thebookfolks.com

www.thebookfolks.com

Also available in this series:

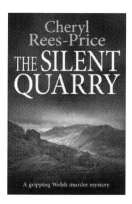

Following a fall and a bang to the head, a woman's memories come flooding back about an incident that occurred twenty years ago in which her friend was murdered. As she pieces together the events and tells the police, she begins to fear repercussions. DI Winter Meadows must work out the identity of the killer before they strike again.

Free with Kindle Unlimited and available in paperback

When the boss of a care home for mentally challenged adults is murdered, the residents are not the most reliable of witnesses. DI Winter Meadows draws on his soft nature to gain the trust of an individual he believes saw the crime. But without unravelling the mystery and finding the evidence, the case will freeze over.

Free with Kindle Unlimited and available in paperback

Printed in Great Britain
by Amazon